FOR THE LOVE OF MARK TWAIN

A COZY ACADEMIA FRIENDS-TO-LOVERS
STORY

KALYN GENSIC

***

To BJ, for unwise investments that could maybe one day pay off, sort of.
And for believing.

— • —

PROLOGUE

FALL, 2007

Perhaps every female college student has nursed a crush on a tweed-clad, leather-elbow-patched professor at some point during her undergraduate education. One might even say it is a rite of passage on the road to womanhood. However, for very few young women does this school-girl crush dictate the course of their career and, well, existence for the following decade.

But that is exactly what transpired for Lucy O'Shields.

It all began ten years ago, on the first day of her senior year at Paducah State University. The small, liberal arts college in Western Kentucky had become a refuge for Lucy over her first three years as an English major.

Lucy was a Southern girl born to a Southern belle. Her mother, petite and feminine and absolutely certain she knew what was best for her only child, had pushed Lucy to attend PSU. What Lucy chose to study was irrelevant. What mattered to her momma was that PSU was close to home, the Alma Mater for the past two generations of the O'Shields family, and, most importantly, rife with gentlemen in need of wives. Lucy had agreed to attend PSU because she had heard their English department, though small, was staffed with an exceptional faculty and provided an intimate, rigorous educational experience.

Lucy knew from a young age that she would one day major in English. Books had been for her what they have been for so many not-perfectly-happy adolescents throughout modern history: an escape. For Lucy, an escape from a world in which she never quite belonged. A world where the dresses felt too ruffly, the tea tasted too sweet, the bless-your-hearts had a few too many syllables, and she herself was a little too (in her mother's words) "cerebral." And when her mother was not feeling so censored, the terms "big-boned" and "unfeminine" had also been mentioned.

Five minutes early to her first class of the fall semester, Lucy sat in the second row of a lecture hall. The second row was Lucy's sweet spot. Not so close she would be noticed overly much. Just close enough she wouldn't miss a single bullet point. Despite how unladylike her mother would probably find it, Lucy loved to learn, and she planned to soak in every kernel of knowledge she could during her final year at PSU.

In a PSU sweatshirt, jeans, and navy Chuck Taylor All Stars, Lucy felt comfortable and at home as a college student. If she were being honest, she dreaded the day she left campus for good. After all, what would she wear? She hadn't shopped for clothes outside of the campus bookstore in years.

"So, what have you heard about the new prof?" Miriam Howatch asked Lucy as she plopped into the seat next to her, shoving her over-full backpack under the desk.

For the past three years, Miriam had been Lucy's closest friend. Lucy valued the memories of sitting by Miriam through their English courses, and she looked forward to this, their final year. They had been inseparable since Freshman Welcome Week. Miriam was from Louisville and had chosen PSU for the same reasons as Lucy. She, too, had wanted the small-school experience. While she was outgoing and extroverted and always full of energy, she was also deeply authentic and caring. Her big personality complimented Lucy's warmth and gentleness, and the pair had become a valued fixture of the PSU English department.

"So...the new prof?"

Lucy shook her head. Clearly, she needed more coffee this morning. "Not much. Obviously, he is an expert in American lit from the 19th century. Hence, why we're currently sitting in American Literature from the 19th century."

"You are a trove of knowledge."

Lucy chuckled and then waited. Miriam always had more information than seemed possible (*or prudent*, Lucy mused). Miriam knew everyone in the department, and everyone in the department liked talking to Miriam. She was the sort of person one spilled the beans to without even realizing one was talking.

It was only a matter of time before her best friend's self-reserve gave way to a greater desire to gossip.

As expected, a mischievous grin broke across her face, and Miriam began aggressively whispering, "So here's what I've heard so far: He is a Western Kentucky boy from a poor town who barreled through undergrad, graduate, and post-grad freakishly fast. At the ripe old age of 27, he's been published in no less than three journals. And, here's the best part..."

Miriam grabbed Lucy's wrist, leaned over, and, in a conspiratorial whisper, said, "He is apparently, so I've been told on good authority, cute. Not hot in a Firehouse Calendar kind of way. Nothing like that. *Better* than that. He is cute, in an adorably nerdy kind of way. You know, the way us English-majors picture Mr. Darcy."

Lucy shook her head and laughed. She responded, "Here's what I want to know: is this cuteness of a caliber to make a seminar course in 19th century American literature feel more exciting than an afternoon of CSPAN? That is the real question."

"Unfortunately, my source was not that specific."

"I'll have to admit, I'm glad I put off this course until Dr. Jones retired."

"Oh my goodness. Can you imagine? The last course we took with him, he actually put *himself* to sleep."

Lucy put her hand to her forehead, shaking her head at the memory. "I'll never forget sitting quietly for fifteen minutes until he woke up and resumed his lecture."

Looking at the clock, Lucy saw that they still had a couple of minutes left before class began. She asked Miriam, "Have you been to the Career Counseling Center yet? Apparently, all seniors are supposed to go this semester to, you know, figure out the rest of our lives."

"Not yet. How about you?"

"No," Lucy sighed. "What's the point. All English majors become secretaries, right?"

Lucy and Miriam were smiling at this little inside joke when a deep voice from over their shoulders said: "I think we can do better than that."

The girls turned around to see a tall, trim, bearded man smiling at them with laughter touching his eyes. He did, indeed, looked like Mr. Darcy. That is, if Mr. Darcy had been American. American and heading West on a horse or some kind of raft. The beard, though perfectly groomed, was definitely a bit Western for Jane Austen's hero. But despite that, Lucy had no doubt she was meeting the new professor.

Her heart made the funniest little tap, and Lucy thought to herself, *Don't even go there, Lucy O'Shields. He is your professor, and you are no Elizabeth Bennett.*

***

Forrest Graham woke up to the white empty walls of the apartment he had moved into only a week prior. The job offer to work at Paducah State University had come in late June, a mere six weeks after he had successfully defended his dissertation. It had only taken a few weeks to make the arrangements to move back to Western Kentucky after spending the past ten years earning his degrees in the Northeast.

Forrest was uncertain if he had made the right decision coming back home. He feared this new adventure would feel like running a marathon in ill-fitted shoes.

For one thing, Forrest no longer sounded like he belonged here. His accent was as neutral as he could achieve through years of consciously training his tongue. Though he had grown up in Kentucky where a Southern drawl was a point of pride, Forrest could not separate those stretched-out vowels from the broken mess of a family he'd sprung from. While the Southern accent might serve well the Southern gentleman, it did not get a poor Southern boy very far.

Despite his misgivings, Forrest was encouraged by his father's joy at his returning. He was thrilled to have his son only a half-hour's drive away, but no amount of joy over Forrest's return was likely to banish his father's affinity for Kentucky bourbon. His father was not a cruel drunk. He was just a chronic drunk, and Forrest could not think of many memories from the past twenty years in which his father's speech was not at least a little slurred.

In truth, the decision to move back had not been all that optional. It was the first job offer Forrest had received, and he knew that it was crucial he not let too much dust settle on his doctorate before beginning his career as a professor. Nascent Ph.D.'s can't afford to be too picky.

During his youth, the world of academia had always been distant and foggy to Forrest. His parents and grandparents had never attended college, and coming home to a father who was wasted and smelled of liquor each night had made the thought of ivory towers as fantastical and seemingly likely as an enchanted castle. When he had started showing academic promise in high school, encouraging teachers began pointing him in the direction of higher education. And when he finally graduated from high school and found himself a student within an English department, Forrest knew he was home.

He sped through his undergraduate and master's degrees within five years, and he immediately dove into his doctoral program to become an English professor. The feverish pace didn't daunt Forrest. He would have walked through fire if it meant a life of study and research and teaching and knowing he was good at something.

Forrest rolled out of bed to prepare for his first day of teaching as Dr. Graham. After a quick shower, he stood in front of his bathroom mirror scrutinizing his beard while holding small clippers in his steady hand.

"I see you there," Forrest whispered to a stray, wiry beard hair sticking up from his chin. Forrest liked order where he could have it. His straight, light brown hair was always cut short, though not severely short, and his full beard and mustache were precisely groomed to complement the length of his hair. His sister had realized when he first started growing a beard that it could provide years of Christmas presents, thereby solving her struggle to find gifts for a brother who only liked books but was picky about what books he liked. Thus, Forrest now had an impressive collection of artisan beard oils and trimmers.

Forrest smiled to himself in the mirror, practicing the first impression he hoped to give his students. Dimples peeked over the edge of his beard. No amount of facial hair could hide this boyish trait, but many female classmates had assured him over the years that it was a trait he did not want to hide. With his forced smile, faint laugh lines stemmed from his chestnut brown eyes. Those, at least, suggested the maturity Forrest desperately wanted to convey. His smile fell, and he headed to his room to dress.

When he had completed the defense of his dissertation three months earlier, he went out and bought the wardrobe of a serious academic. His pants were khaki, his shirts were plaid, and his sports jackets were patched with leather at the elbows. With his neutral palette and tweeds and leather accents, he cut an image that was almost a caricature of the quintessential professor. Dressed so, he looked just as professorial in a line at Wal-Mart as he did in front of a lectern.

Forrest walked to the front door of his apartment and picked up the briefcase he had carefully packed the night before. The briefcase was another post-dissertation-defense purchase, and, really, Forrest had not intended for the leather of the briefcase to so perfectly match his elbow patches. It was just a happy accident.

Leaving his apartment, the early morning Kentucky air was just starting to whisper of the approaching fall. He had rented close to campus because he preferred walking to driving when possible. From his front door to Hart Building, where the English Department was housed, was a twenty-minute walk for most, but with his long, purposeful strides, he easily made it in fifteen.

Halfway through his walk, Forrest saw Dr. Porter Finch a few paces ahead and ran to catch up with him. His new colleague looked like the headshot of a 1950s movie star, and Forrest had already heard that he was constantly running from moon-eyed undergraduates. Perhaps when they had developed more rapport, Forrest would kid him about it. But for now, Dr. Finch was to be pitied; a few years ahead of Forrest in his professorial career, he was beginning the stressful process of obtaining tenure.

"Dr. Finch. How are you doing this morning?"

Dr. Finch grinned and said, "Good morning. I'm fantastic, but you have got to start calling me Porter. Otherwise, everyone will assume you're a student."

"Good idea. I definitely don't want to be mistaken as an undergrad on my first day of teaching."

"When is your first class for the day?"

"In exactly six minutes. I timed leaving so that I would arrive precisely on time."

With his eyebrows raised and a smirk, Dr. Finch said, "So you're completely relaxed and going with the flow today?"

Forrest let out a gust of laughter that immediately dissipated some of the nerves that had built throughout the morning. "You're figuring me out quickly. I just wanted to avoid pre-class small talk."

"I remember my first day in my own class, not just assisting another professor."

"Yeah. How did it go?" Forrest was hopeful Porter's story would bolster his confidence. After all, even the most ancient professors had once taught their first day.

"I puked in the bathroom, marched into the class, and delivered one hell of a lecture on Ernest Hemingway."

"That's good, I think?"

"You're going to do great," Dr. Finch said as he gave Forrest two firm pats on the shoulder. "I'm heading to the faculty gym for a quick workout before my 10 o'clock, but come by my office this afternoon and tell me about your day."

"Will do," Forrest called out as Dr. Finch headed towards the athletics center.

***

Forrest stepped into the back of the class and looked around. He took a few more steps in and paused to survey the nearly-full lecture hall. These students were here to learn from him. He was going to tell them about some of his favorite people, about Mark Twain and Walt Whitman and Harriet Beecher Stowe. Everything he had done for the past decade had been leading to this moment.

Just as he was slipping from his reverie back into the present moment, Forrest heard a female voice with laughter behind it saying, "What's the point? All English majors become secretaries, right?"

Apparently, English major humor was not all that different in Kentucky from what it had been in the Northeast.

Forrest chimed in with his own laughter-laced voice: "I think we can do better than that."

The two female students who had been talking looked back at him with eyes round with shock. The one with wild, wavy strawberry blond hair blushed deeply, clearly realizing the identity of the eavesdropper. Forrest made a quick mental note that he should try not to mortify any more students that day.

Hoping to put her at ease, Forrest gave a small wink. After all, no one studied existential despair to the extent of the average English major without developing a brand of humor that was deeply sarcastic. He certainly was not going to take offense at her joke.

A few strides took him to the front of the class, to a podium that felt as though it had been waiting for him since his first day of college. He pulled some notes out of his briefcase and placed them on the podium. Forrest took a deep breath. With his practiced smile now coming more naturally to his face, Forrest began: "Good morning, class, and welcome to 19th Century American Literature. I am Dr. Graham."

CHAPTER 1

FALL, 2017

The weeks following the fall midterms were always filled with chaos in the PSU English Department as students ran in and out debating their grades and begging for an opportunity at redemption before finals. Lucy had managed to escape for a brief respite, but she did not dare stay away too long or she would never catch up.

Looking in the mirror of the ladies' bathroom, Lucy inhaled deeply, held it for a moment, and slowly exhaled. It was half-way through the afternoon, and she could not remember if she had yet been to the bathroom that day. She vaguely remembered doing so, but hadn't it been the day before?

Since graduating, Lucy had worked tirelessly as the office administrator for the English Department. There were three different offices for the department, each of which housed four professors. Lucy worked in the office that housed the department chair, Dr. Edith Rose, so their office was the central hub of the larger department.

When May of her senior year of college had come around, Lucy hadn't felt certain about much. However, she'd known she wasn't ready to fly the coop. College was still the first and only place she had ever been able to engage in erudite conversation without being thought unladylike, where feminism was an assumed value, and where her lack of feminine wiles and charm had not been counted as a strike against her.

So when the office administrator position opened up just as Lucy was preparing to walk across the stage, she quickly sent in an application thinking it would be a convenient stop-gap on her way to...something else. With her reputation among the department's professors as a student with an uncommonly strong work ethic, Lucy found the job was hers within the month.

There were numerous times over the years when Lucy had almost leapt to something new. She'd researched teacher certification and signed up for a few courses only to decide the timing wasn't quite right. Every couple of years, she would get the itch for further education, leading to a small stack of graduate school applications in the bottom drawer of her desk.

Every time she took a step to move on from her "temporary" stint as a secretary, something would give her pause. Porter would announce another baby was on the way in his growing family. Dr. Hubert would have another health scare. Forrest would ask her to stay late to discuss a new research idea. Edith would ask her opinion on a matter of campus politics. Somehow, she never pushed send on the email. She never clicked the "Submit" button. She never dropped the envelope into the mail.

To be fair, Lucy had not spent the past ten years nursing the crush that had flickered into being that first day of her senior year. In fact, Dr. Forrest Graham and his dimples had not in any way figured into her accepting the position. Well, at most, he and his dimples had only been ten percent of the reason. Hardly a deciding factor. What mattered was that today and for many years preceding, she and Dr. Graham had become colleagues with a great deal of respect for one another.

Still hiding out in the bathroom, Lucy repositioned a bobby pin only to watch it pop out, not up to the task at hand. Lucy's strawberry blond hair was naturally wavy. Unfortunately, it was not a swimsuit-issue, beach-hair kind of wavy. It was, rather, an unruly mix of waves and curls that never seemed to stay where Lucy put them...hair products be damned.

Most days, Lucy twisted it up on the top of her head in a bun looped with a scrunchie, grateful that the contraption had recently made its way back in style so she could purchase it at the drugstore without looking hopelessly bleak.

Despite waking up a teensy bit late this morning (How many times had she hit the snooze? Three? Four?), Lucy had been able to rush through her normal, minimalist makeup routine; nude lip gloss on her full, coral lips, a light brushing of blush over her freckled cheek bones, and mascara to bring attention to olive-green eyes. Lucy's mother had once said, "Darlin', a little foundation would go a long way to covering up those freckles." These many years later, Lucy had yet to add it to her shopping list.

Growing up, Lucy's mother had dressed her in the ruffles, bows, and bright floral prints of Southern Belles, fashion statements that had always complemented her mother's own petite frame. It wasn't until Lucy was in her late teens and fully grown into her father's height that her mother admitted Lucy would never be petite or a Belle. The boutique pieces that were her mother's second skin were patently unflattering on her daughter. Since then, Lucy dressed, or rather hid, in a closet of neutral colors. In general, it was a relief to escape the gingham sundresses and four-inch wedges of her youth, and Lucy appreciated the basic uniform.

Lucy buttoned and then unbuttoned the top of her navy-blue cardigan, debating if the hint of cleavage showing above her camisole should be hidden behind the sweater. With a short sigh and her lips pursed to one side, she buttoned it again.

Lucy was tall enough to be a bit too tall for the average guy. The skinny cut on her black dress pants likely drew attention to her height, but Lucy always wore black or nude flats to keep from being what her mother had called "offensively tall."

The one bold statement Lucy allowed in her appearance was her glasses. She wore a larger frame in a tortoise shell with just a hint of a cat-eye at the corners. They were Kate Spade and fabulous by any measure. While Lucy balked at perfectly curled and hair-sprayed hair, a thick mask of makeup, or fashion-forward clothing, she did appreciate a fine specimen of eyewear.

Peering into the mirror one more time, Lucy noticed a smudge on the bottom corner of her glasses. She took them off and did a quick cleaning using the hem of her cardigan. Putting them back on, Lucy swiped a few stray curls behind her ears in a futile attempt to tame the hair that had escaped her bun. The curls bounced right back.

Lucy took another deep breath, but this one did nothing to calm her. It was more a growl of frustration. Her hair was going to escape the bun, and the sweater looked ridiculous strained across her chest. She unbuttoned it again, and shook a little more hair loose, because what was the point? Conceding defeat, Lucy left the bathroom to return to the storm.

***

Forrest dismissed his class after what had been a very satisfactory lecture. Several students stayed behind to talk with him, and Forrest never rushed these after-class conversations. While Forrest loved the research part of his job, he found the teaching to be equally important and rewarding. On this particular afternoon, though, it was unusually difficult to not rush the students out. Forrest was distracted and eager to complete a task that had been hanging over his head.

Today, though, five students came up with questions regarding the midterms he had just returned. Four of the five were female. His colleague always kidded him about the number of female students who stayed after his classes, and Forrest cringed at the jesting. Now that Porter was a father of three, he was no longer the butt of these jokes, passing the baton to his unwilling younger colleague. Forrest was not blind to the truth: more than a few students had developed a crush on him during his first decade of teaching.

Fortunately, Forrest had become an expert at answering academic questions while deflecting all other forms of interest. Today, he was motivated to perform this exercise with even more efficiency than usual.

Ten minutes later, the last students left the class. Much to his mortification, the last one had both blushed and giggled on her way out. Finally free, Forrest focused on the task at hand.

Three o'clock on a Tuesday afternoon was perhaps a nontraditional time for a breakup, but it was a task he was ready to be done with. Four nights of sleep were enough to lose over a relationship that had run its course. Forrest left Hart Building and headed towards Rayburn Building, home of the science department.

For six months, Forrest had been in a relationship with Dr. Meredith Wray, a professor of biology. They had developed a routine that was predictable, a word Forrest usually liked. Every Wednesday night, she made pasta, and they had dinner (and a bit more) at her place. Every Friday, they went out for dinner and returned to his place.

And that was it.

Two evenings a week, they trudged through a few hours of conversation that had become painfully stale (they ran out of topics of mutual interest the first month). They then efficiently and with little passion fulfilled their mutual physical needs and went their separate ways until the next time. They were each content to ignore the other and focus entirely on their students and research projects and journal articles the other five days of the week.

It was not until this past Friday evening that Forrest had found their arrangement unsatisfactory. They were post-coital, laying on opposite sides of the bed. Cuddling was certainly not part of the deal. Dr. Wray began talking about her newest research project on the symbiotic relationship of insects and fungi. Being two college professors, it was not unusual for their pillow talk to turn to their most recent research or class materials. Romantic? No, but...

However, this time, something strange occurred. As Dr. Wray was enumerating the many ways in which insects benefit from the various properties of fungi, Forrest suddenly felt an overwhelming drowning feeling whoosh through his gut. He was so bored. So painfully bored. He did not want to be bored twice a week for another week. Or month. Or six months.

And more than the boredom, he felt guilt. Dr. Wray (goodness, shouldn't his mind use a first name when thinking of someone with whom he had been sleeping for six months?) was a nice person. A grand conversationalist? Perhaps not, at least not with him. But not a Friday or Wednesday had gone by that she had not shown kindness to him. She deserved someone who was not drowning in boredom two minutes into a discussion on plants and fungi. Odds were, she did not find the relationship between Walt Whitman's poetry and the Civil War all that engaging, either.

Halfway across campus to the science building, Forrest wondered if saying "the symbiosis of our arrangement has run its course" would be considerate of her interests or insulting to the extreme. Regardless, it was true.

If Forrest took a moment to be completely honest with himself, his and Dr. Wray's relationship was a reflection of all his romantic entanglements throughout his adult life. Forrest had never felt romantic love. At least, he had never felt the overwhelming passion that makes a man lose control. He had felt far more emotion reading about love than he had ever felt with a real, flesh-and-blood woman.

Fortunately, or unfortunately (Forrest could not decide which), he seemed to have a sixth sense for finding women who were unlikely to spark any great passion. For that matter, he had a knack for finding women who were unlikely to *feel* any great passion, either.

An objective observer would likely diagnose Forrest with run-of-the-mill momma issues, but the situation was much more nuanced than that. When Forrest was the age a person first develops memories, his mother walked out and never returned. She was a drug addict and died a few years after her departure.

Given that she had so easily left behind two children, Forrest doubted he had missed out on much by her absence. His sister, Gracie, had been more than willing to step in and nurture the brother who was only two years her junior. While Forrest suspected he was irreparably broken in the romance department, it was not because of a lack of motherly love during his childhood: Gracie had made sure he never wanted for affection or encouragement or care. Even now, at the age of 37, Forrest could always rely on Gracie's regular calls, visits, and invitations to her own home.

However, losing his mother had not been without cost. When Forrest's mother walked out, she had taken a bit of his dad with her, and Forrest had always suspected it was the bit that could have given his dad the necessary willpower to walk away from the bottle. Granted, his father's alcoholism had started well before he had lost the love of his life. But the hope of a cure seemed completely lost when she left. So Forrest had spent his childhood staring into the shell of a man left behind by a once-passionate love gone wrong.

Forrest arrived at the Science Department and headed up to Dr. Wray's office. The knot he had carried in his stomach since the previous Friday evening tightened its grip. Although he had cycled through this relationship process a few times by his age, Forrest hated breaking up with women. He hated being a disappointment. He hated seeing his own failure to be what another person wanted or needed.

But right as he approached the door with Dr. Wray's name on a plaque, Forrest thought of how mind-numbingly boring the next evening would be if he did not complete this unsavory task. He lifted a fist to knock, the sound jarringly loud in the abandoned hallway. He opened the door as she said, "Come in."

"Good afternoon, Mer..." Why couldn't he say this woman's first name? "...you. How's that research going? You really sounded on the cusp of a breakthrough on Friday." Had she though? He couldn't remember a word she'd actually spoken other than *symbiotic*, *insects*, and *fungi*. The whole evening was a blur, so he was impressed he remembered that much.

"Hello, Forrest." She looked distracted, shuffling through stacks of paper that seemed to be sitting on top of, well, stacks of paper. Her hair, always kept short for efficiency's sake, was meticulously styled, and she was wearing a lab coat, likely on her way to examine bugs. Or fungi. The coat swallowed her severely thin body. "It's unusual to see you on a Tuesday. How can I help you?"

"Uh, well, I never know how to start these things, but I, uh, just wanted to, uh..." He sounded like an idiot. Forrest did not like sounding like an idiot. When one is a professor, it really isn't on brand to sound like an idiot.

"Forrest? What's wrong?" She didn't sound worried. More impatient than anything else.

"It's just, well, I think we should break up." There it was. He got it out. He sounded like an acne-clad adolescent stuttering to his first girlfriend, but the words were no longer knotted in his stomach.

Dr. Wray finally stopped shuffling papers and looked up at Forrest. He did not see hurt in her eyes, for which he was thankful. What he saw instead was a dawning awareness. "Oh, well. I suppose you're right."

"Huh?"

"I agree. I believe the symbiotic benefits of our relationship, while very satisfactory during the past six months, have likely reached their limits."

He'd clearly missed an opportunity there. Who knew?

"I'm so glad we're on the same page," Forrest said, and he was. He had managed to escape a long, dull Wednesday night, and hurt feelings had been avoided. Apparently, when he had pegged Dr. Wray as someone who was unlikely to become overly-attached, he had judged correctly. Something about this thought depressed him, but he shrugged off the requisite questions it posed.

"I guess I'll head out now, let you get back to whatever it is you are doing with those stacks of paper. I'll see you around campus?"

"Of course. I'll send you a copy of *Scientific Monthly* when I get the insect and fungi research completed."

At that, Forrest smiled. She really was nice. She just wasn't the right person for him, or him for her.

"I would love to read it. Have a great day."

Forrest left Rayburn and directed his steps towards Hart Building. He felt lighter knowing he had finished the dreaded job of ending a relationship. Forrest wondered if "relationship" was even the right word for what he and Dr. Wray had been doing the past six months. Had he ever been in an actual romantic relationship in his life?

Forrest dismissed these uncomfortable wonderings and focused his mind towards the direction he was moving. In a few minutes he would be back at the office, and he could deliver the next section of his work in progress into Lucy's capable hands. She did all of Forrest's editing, and there was no one better at giving feedback or fleshing out half-formed ideas. Forrest was eager to sit across his desk from Lucy and think of nothing else except Walt Whitman, the Civil War, and poetry.

CHAPTER 2

H art Building was a Greek Revival behemoth of a building stationed at the heart of Paducah State University. Lucy's office set in the center of a third floor office suite, wreathed with four other offices, each belonging to an English professor who depended on Lucy to keep life in order, the department running smoothly, and, sometimes it seemed, the world spinning.

The office was filled with heavy wood furniture that looked as though it had been borrowed from a Humphrey Bogart film set. The lower half of the walls was wainscoted in a dark walnut panel, and the upper walls hadn't been painted in 50 years, the white paint now yellowed to depths rivaled only by the library's archived book collection. Renovations were for the business departments.

As soon as Lucy sat down after returning from the bathroom, the phone rang. Lucy inhaled for the long greeting: "Paducah State University English Department. This is Lucy. How can I help you?"

"Lucy, dear, how are ya today?" The voice that spoke was gravelly and dry, the result of far too much hard liquor poured over vocal cords. But it was still a voice that made Lucy smile.

"Mr. Graham, I'm just fine. How are you?"

"Oh, all's well down here in Mayfield. The farmers are getting their tobacco barns smoking, and it looks like today is going to be chilly." Between every few words, Lucy heard a wheeze as Mr. Graham inhaled. The mundane nature of the conversation thinly disguised a struggle beneath the surface as he reached for the end of a sentence, none of which was standard in her weekly phone calls with Forrest's father.

Lucy didn't feel it was her place to mention how weary he sounded. "Well, I'm glad to hear everything is good, if cold, in Mayfield. What can I do for you today?"

"I was just wondering how that son of mine is doing."

"Oh, he's up to no good, as always."

Mr. Graham laughed, which sent him into a fit of coughing.

"Are you okay, Mr. Graham?"

Finally, he said in a pant, "I'm fine, dear. Just fine."

"Dr. Graham is really doing well, Mr. Graham. He's just busy with the normal fall to-dos. He's grading midterms and sludging through these slow weeks ahead of Thanksgiving. And writing, of course."

"Anything new published?"

Mr. Graham always asked this, and Lucy always made sure to get him a copy when Forrest made it into an academic journal.

"Actually, yes. I was going to mail it out today."

"That is just wonderful. Just wonderful." Another wheeze came through the phone like wind through dry corn stalks. "I'm going to let you go, Lucy. Tell Forrest his old man said hello."

"Will do, Mr. Graham. You take care of yourself."

As Lucy hung up, Lily, an undergraduate with a messy bun that still, somehow, looked effortlessly stylish and fresh (the exact goal Lucy reached for and failed at each morning, not that she was jealous), walked out of Dr. Edith Rose's office. A large tear crept down the no-make-up-necessary cheek of the tragic heroine. Lucy immediately reached for the drawer where she kept emergency rations for Edith's victims.

"Here hon. I'm sure it wasn't that bad," Lucy said as she handed Lily a gold-wrapped dark-chocolate candy and triple-ply Kleenex.

"She said my project proposal was devoid of substance."

Tame, for Dr. Rose. "See, Lily, that is just a bit of constructive criticism you can certainly address."

"And that the grading of such a flat, meaningless paper would ruin her whole Thanksgiving break..."

"Oh."

"And that Sylvia Plath would have stuck her head in an oven far sooner if she had been forced to read said paper."

"Have more chocolate, dear."

Before Lucy could usher the wilted flower from the premises, a crash resounded from the closed door of Dr. Porter Finch's office. His wife, a journalist who was frequently on the road, was currently in...was it Chicago this time? Lucy couldn't remember, but what she did remember was that the nanny, claiming a migraine, had dropped the kids off an hour before, and Porter had his hands very full.

Lucy jumped out of her seat and began speed-walking backward towards his office while saying to the forlorn Lily, "I'm going to need to check on that. Lily, perk up. Everything will work out. Believe it or not, Dr. Rose will do all she can to make sure you don't fail."

Lucy turned around and walked into Porter's office, closing the door behind her. He was shushing his six-month old daughter in his arms while his two sons chased each other in a circle around him.

When Edith had first come to PSU the year after Lucy had begun working there, she had whispered to Lucy that Porter looked like a cross between Rock Hudson and Tom Hanks. He was a curious mixture of heartthrob and approachable; commanding but also able to not take himself too seriously.

Within Porter's office, bright primary-colored toys were strewn across the floor. Lucy immediately stepped on a Lego for which her thin-soled flats were no match. Massaging the offending foot while hopping on the other, Lucy regretted that there was no dignified way to recover from a Lego injury. Thankfully, Dr. Finch was much too frazzled to notice.

"I'm so glad to see you, Lucy. I decided to build a leaning Tower of Pisa with Billy and Luke using the books from my lower shelves..."

"Of course you did."

"...and just as we were finishing up, someone..."

Billy and Luke each yelled "It was him!" while pointing at the other.

"...knocked over the tower which woke up Anna..."

"Of course it did."

"...and I'm going to need someone to take Anna while I tidy up. I say all that to say, can you hold Anna?"

"I thought you'd never ask." Lucy reached for the wailing six-month old girl, cooing soothingly and bouncing her in an attempt to return quiet to the small office. Or, at least as much quiet as could be achieved with a six- and a four-year-old boy wrestling in the corner. Lucy set about straightening the pink headband with a bow barely smaller than the child's head. After the bow was put back in order and no longer obscuring Anna's vision like a pirate with an eye patch, Anna quieted. Lucy laid her cheek on the soft curls above the headband and inhaled deeply, telling herself that eggs were far from shriveled at the age of 32. Well, maybe not far. But they definitely were not shriveled.

Still using the baby-talk cadence that had calmed Anna, Lucy said, "So what exactly were you and Charlotte thinking when you had three children under the age of 6?"

"I can't speak for Charlotte, but for myself, I was thinking about those business dresses she wears to interview corrupt politicians."

"I officially regret asking that question. Anna is coming with me while I go remind Dr. Hubert about his appointment today."

"Thank you, Lucy."

Back out the door and once again safe from errant Legos, Lucy stuck her head into Edith's office on her way to Dr. Hubert's. Hoisting the baby an inch higher up her hip, Lucy said, "Edith, I forbid you from making any more students cry today. I'm running out of chocolate."

"It was a joke. I can hardly help that undergraduates have no sense of humor." Sitting in an obscenely large chair likely chosen for the purpose of intimidating others, Dr. Rose looked like a magazine advertisement for power suits. Her smooth black hair, styled straight and cut in a shoulder-length bob that slanted forward with a perfect level of drama, contrasted sharply with her ivory complexion. Despite her beauty and clear I've-got-it-together air, she was flashing Lucy a mischievous grin that reminded Lucy why she loved sharing an office with this powerhouse.

Lucy matched Dr. Rose's ornery expression with her own skeptical glare: "Sylvia Plath? Really?"

"In my defense, her paper was truly atrocious. And I managed to convey that fact in a manner that was both humorous and educational. You know if I don't push her, she'll be eaten alive next year in graduate school."

Lucy sighed as a half-smile sabotaged the stern expression she was trying to maintain: "Just promise me you will try to be nice."

Edith laid her hand on a small stack of treasured books that permanently resided on the corner of her desk.

"I solemnly swear on my first edition of *The Bell Jar* that I will not make any more students cry for the rest of today."

"It's 3:30 in the afternoon."

"Exactly."

Knowing she would not get anything more, Lucy conceded, "Okay. I'll take it. But you owe me more chocolate."

"I'll add it to the department's budget."

Edith flashed a self-satisfied grin as Lucy shook her head and laughed. Lucy turned with Anna toward Dr. Hubert's door.

Dr. Charles Hubert was the living legend of the PSU English Department. He had taught within Hart Building for forty-five years with no plans to retire anytime soon. He was a Shakespearean scholar. When he spoke, it was with the authority of a monologue delivered on the stage of the Globe Theatre.

In his prime, he had been an imposing force. He was towering. Old age had not robbed him of his impressive stature. However, age had put a few pounds on him, and his sweater vest worked a little harder these days to stretch over this girth. His head was completely bald, but he made up for it in eyebrows that were truly astounding. Lucy never understood how someone could simultaneously be so bald and so hairy.

Dr. Hubert was an exacting teacher, but those who graduated from the department inevitably formed a soft-spot for this university relic. Through her four years as a student, Lucy had feared and respected Dr. Hubert, knowing each time she signed up for one of his courses, she faced a grueling but enriching semester. As his administrative assistant, Lucy had lost all of the fear. Dr. Hubert, though gruff in manner, was completely loyal to his coworkers, including Lucy.

Once again readjusting Anna on her hip, Lucy gently knocked on Dr. Hubert's door and then pushed it slightly ajar. "Dr. Hubert."

"Hmm..." A groggy groan followed by a cough came from the small sofa he kept across from his desk. "Excuse me. Who's there?" Dr. Hubert's voice was always booming, even when he was just waking from an afternoon nap. Anna made a small jump in Lucy's arms.

"I'm sorry to wake you Dr. Hubert, but it's time for your doctor's appointment."

It took some effort, but Dr. Hubert began the work of swinging his long tired legs off of the edge of the sofa so he could labor through to standing. Lucy hated seeing him age. When had simply standing up become such a chore?

"Oh that doctor's appointment," Dr. Hubert growled. "It is such a waste of time. Yes, doctor, I know I'm fat. No, doctor, I don't plan on giving up donuts during my last years of life on this earth!"

Lucy wanted to look disapproving, but a smile undid the effect. "Be that as it may, do you want to tell Mrs. Hubert you skipped out on a cardiologist visit?"

"No, but I'd happily pay you to do it for me." A cascade of wrinkles gathered above his eyebrows as he looked hopefully to Lucy.

"You couldn't afford my asking price." Lucy would never overcome her fear of the formidable Mrs. Hubert.

Growling, he said, "I'm getting ready."

"Good, I'll go call an Uber. Mrs. Hubert is meeting you at the doctor's."

Heading back to her desk, Lucy conversed with Anna. "It is forty-five minutes after Dr. Graham's final class of the day, Anna. I wonder where he could be?" Not that she followed his every move or always knew where he was. It was just that he was nothing if not predictable. His hair and beard were always the same length. His clothes were always neutral tones and professorial. His smile was always easy. And he was always in the office within twenty minutes after class dismissed.

Just as she was finishing booking a ride for Dr. Hubert and covertly texting Mrs. Hubert to let her know the asset was moving without resistance, the front door swung open, and in walked Forrest. His hair was, shockingly, slightly disheveled on one side. Lucy just happened to know it was the side he ran his hand through when he was nervous. Any good secretary would know that.

But despite the evidence that he had been dealing with stress, he immediately smiled, the dimples flashing over his beard in a way that had made countless female students stay late after class. Never had questions on Ralph Waldo Emerson seemed so urgent.

"Hello, Lucy. Hello, Anna."

He reached over Lucy's desk and tugged gently on Anna's toe, garnering a toothless grin. Forrest and Porter had developed a brother-like bond during Lucy's time in the office, so Anna was as comfortable with him as she was with any uncle or family member. Looking up from the smile he had earned, Dr. Graham said, "Lucy, I've got something for you. The next section of the Whitman paper was completed in a blaze of glory at three o'clock this morning."

"That's wonderful. I'll come into your office in a minute. I just have to return Anna to her owner."

Lucy had just finished editing a particularly involved research project for Edith, but she was ready to take on a new section of Dr. Graham's work. His was always a little lighter than Edith or Porter's pieces - almost playful even though his works were meant for heavy, academic journals. Plus, while Lucy would go into his office to get a manuscript to edit, she fully intended to also find out the mystery behind his mussed hair.

***

Forrest walked into his office and removed his sports jacket, placing it on the back of his desk chair. Sitting down and leaning back in the chair, Forrest unbuttoned the cuffs of his white shirt and rolled the sleeves to just below his elbows. He felt lighter than he had in half a week, and he allowed himself a moment to simply enjoy the sensation.

Forrest loved his office. The room was lined with bookshelves filled with American classics and books about American classics. Inhaling deeply, Forrest imagined that the old-book smell coming from his books was no different than what must have surrounded Mark Twain or Henry Wadsworth Longfellow or Herman Melville in their own studies while writing their masterpieces. He was breathing the same air.

Around the perimeter of his desk stood four large whiteboards on easels, each with row after row of notes and ideas for future classes, research projects, and articles. Lucy always joked that this was the stream-of-consciousness section of the larger office.

The color-coding was of Lucy's doing. Years ago during a slow, hot week in between summer sessions, she had developed a system to catalog his ideas more efficiently. It was as if she'd walked into his cluttered mind and organized each item, closing the unnecessary tabs while putting what remained in tidy little rows. They had spent every day that week moving information around the office and discussing appropriate marker colors for each item.

But Forrest's affection for his office went beyond his little nook. He loved the entire cluster of the English Department. Before he walked into his specific office, he was in Lucy's territory. It always had fresh flowers, brewing coffee, and a lit scented candle. The scent usually mimicked some home-baked good, and it made Forrest wonder if he was now, in his late 30s, experiencing what life would have been like had he been given some *Leave It to Beaver* existence.

Forrest also loved the constant energy and commotion of the place: Porter's wild children with Porter's own child-like enthusiasm, Edith's raging at all manner of incompetencies or injustices, and Dr. Hubert's booming voice, making a simple observation on the weather sound like a dramatic monologue worthy of the stage. And, of course, Lucy keeping them all in line. There was also the revolving door of students worried about a grade, seeking guidance, or just wanting to sit and chat with Lucy while getting a chocolate.

Just as the tension was truly releasing from Forrest's shoulders, Lucy walked in. Tall himself, Forrest had always appreciated the way Lucy filled a space, so unlike the petite Dr. Wray. He supposed it was useful to be so small when one had to weave between microscopes.

"So, what do you have for me?" Lucy asked, cutting straight to the point.

She looked harried today, like the office had been keeping her particularly busy. However, Forrest couldn't help but think harried looked nice on her. Reddish curls had escaped from her bun and were framing her face, the tip of one curl coming perilously close to her full lips. This was not unusual. Lucy's hair was never what one would deem orderly. He must have noticed it today because it was such a contrast to Dr. Wray's perfectly coiffed hairstyle.

"Dr. Graham?" Lucy's voice cut into his thoughts.

"Yes. Sorry, Luce. My mind is wandering today something awful."

"I believe you have a paper for me to edit?"

"Yes. Have a seat. I'll get it out."

While Lucy relaxed into a chair opposite his desk, Forrest grabbed the printed pages from his old, worn leather briefcase, the same one from his first day of teaching.

"It is the next section from the Whitman paper. Like I said, I finished it at three this morning. Assume it will be awful." Forrest cringed as he handed it over. He would only hand a draft this rough into Lucy's competent hands.

"Ooh, goody. I'll get out the really big red pen."

"You take entirely too much glee in pointing out all of my mistakes."

"The student becomes the master and so on," Lucy smirked teasingly as she made a brief flip-through of the text, the papers making a flapping sound as Forrest chuckled.

"You will hear no arguments here."

"I should have time to read it tonight. I'm finally finished with Edith's project. When do you want to meet to discuss it?"

"If you are sure you can get to it tonight, would tomorrow night work for you? At least for the first section."

"Wednesday? I thought Wednesday was date night with Dr. Bugs."

"Porter certainly has a way with nicknames," Forrest sighed.

"And he never passes up the opportunity to supply one when you have a girlfriend."

What else could Forrest do but sigh again, this time with a little more drama. "True enough. But back to Wednesday. You are correct that Wednesdays are date nights. Or rather, *were* date nights with Dr. Bu..." Lucy smiled innocently while Forrest growled out, "Dr. Wray. They were, that is, until we broke up."

"When?"

"When what?"

"When did you break up?"

Forrest checked his watch. "Seventeen minutes ago."

"That's hot off the press. You could have given me warning, you know. I'm fresh out of breakup supplies." On a university campus with so many young singles roaming around, it would be irresponsible to not have a box of junk food and relaxation candles ready at a moment's notice. Unfortunately, Lucy's supply had recently been tapped out, and she had not been able to run to the store in a few days.

"Oh yeah, didn't you use them for Edith when she broke up with what's-his-name last week? Was it Tony? Oscar?"

"It was George, and the answer is sort of. Only I didn't use them for Edith. I used them for George. He was really torn up."

Forrest slowly nodded his head as the memory returned. "That's right. She broke up with him in the office, didn't she? Brutal."

"I ran 15 minutes late getting home that night. Poor guy. But back to the important topic, I can't say I'm surprised about your breakup."

"Lucy, I'm wounded." Forrest put a hand over his heart in mock pain.

Mortified, Lucy rushed to explain herself: "No, I don't mean I'm not surprised you and Dr. Wray broke up."

"Because I'm so well known for my long-term relationships." A little self-deprecation was a small price to pay to see Lucy frazzled. It made her cheeks flush to almost the same coral tone as her lips. Not that he *normally* noticed her lips. It was just that they were so much fuller and more animated than Dr. Wray's lips.

If he had not just seen and broken up with a woman with whom he had been involved, he definitely would not have been noticing Lucy's lips.

Lucy's mortification had quickly been replaced by mild irritation at being teased. "What I *meant* to say was that I knew something had you stressed out from the moment you walked into the office."

"Yes, and how's that?"

"Your hair."

"My hair? My hair is like a helmet. It always looks the same."

Lucy straightened up in the chair and leaned forward. Cleavage. Lucy had cleavage. Of course she had cleavage. She was a girl. Why was he noticing her cleavage now? Didn't she usually button the top of her sweaters? Forrest focused squarely on Lucy's face.

In a conspiratorial whisper, she said, "Not so. True, your hair is almost always in the exact same style, but when you are tense, you run your right hand through it, and it unsettles that side just a bit."

Forrest could not elevate his eyebrows any higher if he tried. "Really?"

"Really. I've worked here a decade. It's basically my job to know that."

"And no one has ever accused Lucy O'Shields of not being good at her job." Forrest smiled at her genuinely. She really was a master at what she did. He wanted to change the subject, though. Maybe if they moved on from the breakup talk, he would stop noticing that the one stray curl kept inching closer to the corner of her mouth. "Enough about my day. What happened in your day?"

"This afternoon, your dad called."

"And?"

"He didn't sound so good."

"Life-long alcoholics rarely do at seventy."

"True, but I don't know. He sounded worse than normal."

"I'll check on him this weekend. What did he want?"

"The usual. To check on you."

To this, Forrest tilted his head to the side, and gave Lucy a knowing smile that did not reach his eyes. She silently matched his expression, tilting her head just a bit, too. She knew.

"I know I suck at talking to my dad. I'm glad, Lucy, that he feels comfortable calling you."

"Of course. I don't mind at all. He's a sort of charming old guy."

"And don't say it's your job to chat with my lonely old man. It is far above and beyond your job."

"Aren't you flattering this afternoon?"

"For me, flattering is really a way of being." Forrest was impressed he had managed to get this line out without laughing.

"Would Dr. Bugs agree?"

At this, he snorted in a lost battle to hold in the laughter. Placing his elbows on the desk, he directed his full attention to Lucy: "Moving on. How about the office? How was the office today?"

"Well, the Tower of Pisa collapsed in Porter's office..."

"So his kids visited."

"Edith made no less than three students cry today..."

"It is the week after midterms, so naturally..."

"And I only had to threaten Dr. Hubert with tattling to Mrs. Hubert to get him to his cardiologist."

"It's the small victories that count."

Lucy guffawed at his deadpan expression. The laughter lit her green eyes, eyes that were remarkable by any standard. He really did prefer green eyes to...what color had Dr. Wray's eyes been? They weren't anything like Lucy's eyes.

At this thought, a sweat broke out on the back of Forrest's neck. Why did he keep thinking of Lucy in terms of a woman with whom he had slept? Lucy was not, nor would she ever be, in that category. Her lips? Her unruly hair? Her green eyes? And, for the love of Mark Twain, *her cleavage*? These were not parts of Lucy about which Forrest allowed himself to think. Sure, he had noticed. One notices such things after ten years in a smallish office. But Forrest had designated these parts to a locked box in a deadbolted closet in a forbidden corner of his mind. He was sure he had.

For the second time in a week, Forrest felt the uncomfortable stirrings of panic.

"If you don't stop abusing your hair, it is going to lose that helmet-like quality of which you are so proud."

Forrest dropped his hands to his lap, squeezing his knees tightly.

She continued, "Don't worry, I'll bring breakup supplies tomorrow night to the editing meeting."

"No need, Lucy. Really, I'm fine." Although, he was not entirely sure he believed this statement.

As she stood up, Lucy said, "It's no problem. Plus, Cheetos and M&M's will make all the red ink I'm going to use sting a little less."

Maybe it would be best if she thought he was stressed about the breakup. "Sounds good. Don't forget the Gummy Bears."

CHAPTER 3

A few minutes before Wednesday's lunch hour, Lucy left the office to go to a small cafe in downtown Paducah. It was a favorite spot among the locals for business lunches, something that Lucy rarely found herself doing. However, on this Wednesday afternoon, she happened to have an appointment with none other than the president of the university, Dr. Burke.

As Lucy walked towards her car to head to the cafe, she breathed in deeply of the fall air. To Lucy's thinking, fall in Western Kentucky was a gift. The air was lightly scented with hickory smoke emanating from tobacco barns. Lucy loved the anachronism that was Kentucky's tobacco barns. In a world where people regularly fly hundreds of miles in a few hours and purchase goods from across the globe with a push of a button, tobacco farmers were still lighting slow-burning fires on the floors of enormous barns where row after row of dried tobacco hung above. As Lucy drove to the cafe, she rolled down the window so she could enjoy the smoky air.

Lucy arrived at the cafe, still wondering about the purpose of the meeting. When she received an email from the president's office requesting the meeting, she hadn't hesitated to accept. Even though being president of a small university did not make someone all-powerful, there was something about the title of "president" that brooked no argument.

Arriving a few minutes before the president, Lucy ordered a cup of coffee for a pre-lunch infusion of caffeine. She was exhausted, the result of reading not only Forrest's paper on Whitman, but also several chapters from a biography of the American poet. Lucy did not like to appear ignorant when she engaged in a discussion with a colleague. Forrest paid her significantly for her editing, and she wanted to do a thorough job of the task at hand. Lucy did not always walk into a room confidently. She usually felt a little too big and unrefined for any given space. But she did engage in conversations with confidence. Where she might have doubted the value of her appearance, she did not doubt the value of her mind.

Looking across the small cafe, Lucy saw President Burke entering. He was well-acquainted with Lucy's father, a member of the Board of Trustees for PSU. She wondered if her father had a part in this mystery lunch. He had never been a particularly hands-on father, preferring to give his small but mighty wife the reigns over their daughter. Since Lucy's mom passed away soon after Lucy started her job in the English department, her father had been at a loss for how to connect with his daughter. Playing a little puppet-master in the background to try and benefit Lucy would have been in his playbook, his definition of basic fatherly love.

"Good afternoon, Ms. O'Shields. Thank you for having this lunch with me." President Burke's Southern drawl was thick as he greeted Lucy and sat down across from her.

"Of course, Dr. Burke. I was so grateful to be asked." Lucy was good at being polite. While her mother had failed at turning her into a frail beacon of femininity, she had taught Lucy manners.

Small talk about the weather and the upcoming basketball season and the appropriate amount of sweetness for sweet tea filled the time as they ordered their lunches and waited for the food to be brought out. Finally, Dr. Burke turned the conversation to PSU business.

"How are things in the English department?"

"Never a dull moment, as always." Lucy preferred to keep things vague. There was no need for Dr. Burke to know all the details of their little office (like exactly how many books collapsed to the ground with the fall of the Tower of Pisa or how many naps Dr. Hubert took in a week. Or a day).

"Oh, I'm sure. That is quite a cast of characters you have there. I never know what to expect next from Dr. Rose in our faculty meetings."

If Lucy wasn't mistaken, Edith had taken over last month's faculty meeting to deliver an impromptu lecture on the importance of living wages for the university's groundskeepers and cleaning crew. Lucy smiled sweetly and said, "She is charming."

President Burke gave a chuckle that almost sounded nervous. Edith had that effect on people.

The waitress came over with the day's lunch special of pork chops and baked potatoes for each of them. As she walked away, President Burke got to the business at hand: "Lucy, I invited you here today for a reason. There is an opportunity I would like to talk with you about."

"Yes?"

"Well, as I am sure you know, your work ethic and aptitude for office administration is legendary on campus."

"Legendary? Sir, I'm only 32 years old."

President Burke paused with his knife and fork in midair. "Hence, the legendary part."

"Well, color me flattered." Lucy was pretty sure a blush was doing just that.

"Mrs. Smith, the presidential office's administrator for the past forty years..."

With a nod of reverence, Lucy cut in, "Also a legend."

"Yes, well, she is retiring."

"Aah," Lucy suddenly knew what was coming, but she had no idea how she would respond.

"I'm here to ask you if you might consider taking over Mrs. Smith's post. I can think of no one else who could possibly fill her shoes."

"Dr. Burke. I am honored. Truly."

"But?"

Lucy knew there was a *but*. She just didn't know what it was.

"I don't know, sir. It is something I would need to think seriously about."

"I understand. Let me give you a few pieces of information that will help you make this decision."

"I'm listening."

"You will get a 25 percent pay raise..."

"That is very generous, sir."

"As well as a boost in retirement. It is a challenging, busy, high-demand job, but you strike me as someone who likes to be busy."

"That is true."

"You will be in charge of the running of the entire President's Office. I would give you a great deal of authority." He paused as if trying to remember any selling points he had omitted, then said, "And did I mention the 25 percent raise?"

Lucy laughed. The president had a sense of humor. Good to know. But so did the four professors whose offices wreathed her own.

As they finished their meal, President Burke gave Lucy a deadline of a few weeks to make her decision. While she was sincerely flattered by the offer, Lucy also felt nauseous at the thought of leaving a position in an office where she felt so much affection for her co-workers. President Burke seemed nice enough, but, really, who could compare with Forrest, Edith, Porter, and Dr. Hubert?

***

After a slice of Derby Pie and saying goodbye to President Burke, Lucy exited the cafe and headed towards her car. She glanced across the street from her vehicle and saw Miriam Howatch, her closest friend, coming out of the coffee shop across the street.

"Miriam!" Lucy called out to her. Miriam beamed when she saw who was calling her name and immediately started walking across the street to Lucy.

Miriam was still as outgoing, outspoken, and mischievous as she had been in undergrad, but her life had taken some unexpected turns. After graduating, Miriam had shocked Lucy, her family, her friends, the English Department, and (it seemed) the world by announcing that she would be enrolling at a seminary the coming fall. Lucy had always known that Miriam was fascinated by books that touched on theology, and she often brought religious themes to class discussions in the various English courses they had taken together, but Lucy had never heard Miriam even casually muse that she might enter the priesthood.

It took Miriam several years to go through seminary and the ordination process, and during that time, she had lived on the opposite end of the state. However, two years ago, Miriam had been called to be the Associate Rector at Paducah's Trinity Episcopal Church. As soon as she arrived in town, it was as if they had not been apart for eight years. The two had always kept in touch, so it was natural for the friendship to immediately pick up where it had left off. Lucy still felt a pleasant shock that her best friend finally lived in the same town as her.

Miriam was none of the things Lucy had learned to associate with religion over the years. When she was angry at an injustice, she did not shy away from the occasional profanity, she was inclusive to the extreme, and she reveled in the joys which life had to offer. Like wine. Miriam loved a glass of wine (or two) with dinner. She and Lucy got together at least once a week for dinner and wine and conversations that stretched deep into the evening.

As Miriam walked toward Lucy, she adjusted her crisp, white clerical collar. Even after a decade of knowing her friend was moving toward and then into the priesthood, Miriam still did not look like the image of "priest" Lucy had in her head. While in undergrad, Miriam had collected a small menagerie of tattoos. Lucy would go with her to the parlors on Friday nights and ramble on endlessly about the various couples who were beginning flirtations or spiraling apart in a stunning display of undergraduate drama. Miriam always said Lucy's chatter kept her mind off of the pain of the needle as the artist created the tree with roots that crept down her left forearm or the cascade of birds that flew across her right shoulder. Except for the tab collar, Miriam wore all black, and the black coupled with her tattoos felt more biker than priest.

And unlike the bald, overweight men Lucy had grown up seeing in the pulpit of her mother's Baptist church, Miriam was strikingly beautiful. She was about the same height as Lucy, but slenderer. She probably had that skinny gene scientists had just discovered. Lucy had read about it in the news while eating a brownie from the campus cafeteria, feeling unending jealousy towards the people lucky enough to be born in bodies that stayed thin regardless of brownie intake. Miriam had chestnut hair that was naturally curly, and she wore it cut above the shoulder. The curls bounced as she jogged the last few steps to Lucy.

Miriam leaned against Lucy's car as she said, "Hey, you. What are you doing downtown? I didn't think they let you leave campus."

"Well, since you asked, it turns out I'm a very important person, and very important people get to leave for business lunches."

"I feel like there is a story here. Do tell." Miriam still loved to hear about other people's lives. It was the sort of personality trait that served her well in her occupation. The only difference from undergrad was that Miriam now took confidentiality very seriously.

Lucy had already planned to confide in Miriam and seek advice. "President Burke asked me to a business lunch."

"That does sound important."

"And he offered me the job of being the administrative assistant in the President's Office."

"That's good, right?"

"I'm not sure. I was sort of hoping you could tell me."

"Explain."

"Well, I'd get a 25 percent raise..."

"Important people should make more money." Miriam could never stay completely serious for too long.

"Obviously. And I'd have a lot more responsibility and challenges..."

"You like challenges. But?"

Lucy's voice rose a step with frustration. "That's the thing. I know there is a 'but.' I know that when I talk about this, a 'but' is implied in my tone and probably in my eyes, too. You know how I get that weird, wide-eyed look when I'm confused."

"Your eyes do look a little odd right now." Miriam got the reaction she had been seeking; the stressed slant of Lucy's eyebrows relaxed as she laughed. Good friends remind you to not take yourself quite so seriously.

Miriam's face took on a more somber expression, and she said, "Luce, can I give you some advice?"

"That's your whole job, right?"

Using her best sermon cadence, Miriam declared, "Yes. Let me share with you my infinite wisdom."

"Go on."

"Seriously, as your friend, you've only known about this job for what, an hour?"

"More like thirty minutes."

"Exactly. Not long. You don't have to know what the 'but' is yet. It is enough that you know something is giving you pause."

Lucy's body slumped against the side of the car next to Miriam, and she said, "You know, Miri, when you're not being a total mess, you're really pretty wise."

Just as the words escaped Lucy's mouth, a man walking down the sidewalk called out, "Good afternoon, Mother Miriam."

Miriam waved and returned the greeting as he went by.

"But even if I think you're wise, I will never get used to hearing people call you 'Mother Miriam.'"

At this, Miriam bent over laughing, reveling in the irony of her career choice.

Once she collected herself, Miriam asked Lucy, "So, how many students are in love with Dr. Graham this semester?"

Since they had been in his first class together, the gaggle of adoring students around Dr. Graham had always been a source of humor for them.

"It's hard to know an exact number. A dozen maybe? I had to lie to one the other day who was trying to deliver him a book of Pablo Neruda poetry. He hid quietly in his office while I told the girl he was out and that professors aren't allowed to accept books from students."

"Is that an actual rule?"

"Nope, but I came up with it years ago when he bemoaned that he couldn't fit any more poetry books on his shelves."

"Shame on you, Lucy. Lying like that."

"I'm sorry. Should I have started the telling of that story with, 'Forgive me, priest, for I have sinned'?"

"It does have a ring to it, but I'll let it pass this time."

"I can't really ridicule those girls since I myself may have stayed up late with thoughts of trimmed beards and tweed jackets in my own undergraduate days." This was still a source of embarrassment to Lucy, but what was the point in hiding from Miriam what she already knew.

"Yes, but you never lurked. You didn't think of twenty completely inane questions about a footnote so that you could stay."

"That's right. When I stayed late, it was for legitimate, thoughtful questions I would have asked any professor, even an old, unattractive one who smelled musty. And if I had bought him a book, I would have at least made sure it was 19th century American." Lucy wasn't positive this was strictly true, but she knew Miriam was a loyal friend who would play along.

"Exactly. I only knew you had a crush on him because your blushing wouldn't let you hide it from me."

"It is a curse to be so fair and so readable. Especially when one is young and susceptible to all manner of crushes." Lucy still cringed thinking about her reaction to Dr. Graham that first semester. She was sure her face had darkened three shades the first ten minutes of every class. Her palms would get sweaty and she would feel horribly conspicuous, reassessing each day if the second row was really a good idea.

Curious, Miriam asked Lucy, "How did you get past that? You had it pretty bad for him."

"Good, old-fashioned exposure therapy. After the first year or so, we just became friends. He's easy to be comfortable around once you aren't hopelessly crushing on him." Lucy thought about their conversation the previous afternoon, how he had seemed stressed but had still taken time to ask her about the details of her day. Yes, it was easy to be comfortable with him now.

"Speaking of Dr. Graham, is he still with Dr. Bugs?"

Lucy smiled broadly. "Porter's nicknames do have staying power."

"I shouldn't have favorites, but he is definitely one of my favorite parishioners." In undergrad, Porter's youthful, energetic teaching style had made him a favorite with Lucy and Miriam. He and his family happened to be members of Miriam's church, so she had become reacquainted with him since moving back.

"Well, I'm sorry to say Dr. Bugs and Dr. Graham are no longer an item."

"Is this something people are sad about?"

"Dr. Graham didn't seem sad. More stressed than anything. Something about him seemed a bit off when he told me. Maybe he's sadder than he realizes." Lucy shrugged a shoulder.

Miriam squeezed Lucy's arm as she said, "I would love to stand here and analyze Dr. Graham's love life..."

"Let's not."

"...but I have to get back to the parish hall for a meeting with the bereavement committee."

"Fun?"

"You have no idea. Are we still on for Saturday?"

"Absolutely. I've got to get back, too. I have a mile-long to-do list this afternoon, and then Dr. Graham and I are working on some editing tonight."

A mischievous glint animated Miriam's face, making Lucy feel for a moment like they were saying goodbye before each heading to their next class. "Be careful, Luce. Dr. Graham's a free agent now."

＊

Lucy looked into the rearview mirror. Her glasses were, as always, smudged, so she did a quick cleaning before putting them back on and starting up the vehicle. As she began driving back to campus, Miriam's words reverberated through her mind.

Dr. Graham was a free agent. Although, in her mind she heard, *Forrest is a free agent.* In the office, Lucy mostly referred to each professor as Dr. Insert-last-name. There were students always in and out, so it made sense to keep things formal. In private conversations, though, she had long since started calling Dr. Rose and Dr. Finch Edith and Porter. It was a natural product of friendships formed over so many years.

Dr. Hubert, though, was always Dr. Hubert to Lucy. It wasn't for lack of friendship. Lucy loved Dr. Hubert no less than Edith and Porter. It was just that the very essence of Dr. Hubert was so professorial, it was hard to imagine calling him anything else. Even Mrs. Hubert called him Dr. Hubert. Lucy laughed to herself as she mused over when might have been the last time Dr. Hubert had been referred to as Charles. An angry high school basketball coach yelling across the court for him to block the other team's guard? His mother when dropping him off at his first college dormitory as she reminded him to wash his socks? A world where Charles Hubert wasn't Dr. Hubert seemed completely alien.

But Dr. Forrest Graham? He had implored Lucy to call him Forrest on numerous occasions. He insisted that they spent far too much time together to be so formal, and Lucy agreed. She really did. It was just that when she tried to say *Forrest*, she felt tongue-tied. Suddenly, all of the insecurities of the college senior crushing on the new professor flooded in on Lucy, and she would retreat back to the security of a formal title.

The reality was that Forrest had not suddenly become unattractive to Lucy the moment she accepted the job as department secretary. She hadn't flipped a switch on her attraction to him. But the professional relationship and, eventually, friendship they'd built had become more valuable, more tangible, with the passage of time. Miriam and Lucy were the only two people who knew there had ever been anything more in Lucy's thoughts and feelings toward Forrest. Perhaps the small formalities she kept in place were simple precautions to safeguard against that secret getting out.

Lucy's remedy to this problem was to avoid saying his name in one-on-one conversations as much as possible. Really, when one set their mind to avoiding saying a name, one realized how little names are necessary to the normal rhythm of a conversation.

Lucy was fully cognizant of just how strange this particular mental block was. She had no idea what separated Forrest from the others in her mind's categories. If she was color-coding her colleagues, why would *he* be a different color? And exactly how much would she have to pay a therapist to get to the bottom of this mystery?

Regardless, Lucy did not have the time or energy or desire to try and find out. She generally avoided ignorance, but she had a feeling it was preferable to the alternative in this situation. After all, she was already squirming with discomfort at Miriam's words.

This was far from the first time Forrest had suddenly been single over the past ten years. In fact, he seemed to go through breakups at least once every year or two. The relationships were always brief and spaced out by prolonged periods of singlehood. Dr. Wray had really achieved something impressive with a full six months. Perhaps that is where the discomfort was coming from. Lucy had simply gotten used to Forrest being in a relationship.

Lucy reminded herself (in her sternest internal monologue) that tonight was no different from the dozens of editing meetings they had shared over the years. That Forrest was no more or less available than at any other time in their working relationship. He was always permanently unavailable to the office administrator. Clearly. And she would be a normal person tonight who was perfectly capable of calling her colleague and friend by his first name without performing verbal gymnastics to avoid it.

And then her treacherous mind responded with a meek, *I think I can.* To which Lucy scowled the rest of the drive to the office.

CHAPTER 4

Forrest arrived at his office only a few minutes before Lucy's golden retriever, Clark, came barreling through the door with Lucy unceremoniously dragged behind while gripping the leash. Clark jumped towards Forrest, knocking him back a few steps in the process.

"Hey big guy." Forrest knelt down to greet the enthusiastic (and slobbery) dog as Clark's entire back-half wagged in delight.

Bending over to unhook his leash, Lucy said, "I had planned to take him back to the apartment after our walk, but we ran out of time. I hope you don't mind."

"Of course not. We always get more work done when Clark is here." Forrest tried to move his face a little further from the licking Clark was graciously bestowing.

"I'm not entirely sure that's true, but sure. Let's go with it," Lucy quipped as she draped the leash over a whiteboard.

Growing up, Forrest's dad had made sure his kids always had a dog. Over the course of Forrest's childhood, there had been three dogs, each some pound-rescue mix of who-knew-how-many breeds. Forrest figured it was his father's attempt to make up for his own inadequacies. If a single-dad couldn't escape liquor long enough to have an actual conversation with his kids, he could at least get the kids a dog. It was companionship by proxy.

Of course, the care of the dog had fallen on Gracie's shoulders and, when he got older, Forrest's. With all of his dad's flaws, the list of which was legion, Forrest could not fault him on this one point: each dog had in fact enriched Forrest's childhood and helped alleviate the loneliness that so frequently weighed on him.

However, as an adult, Forrest rarely set foot in his own apartment for more than sleeping, so he had avoided the commitment of a pet. After the uncomfortable questions that had arisen the day before as Forrest had dealt with his relationship (or non-relationship) problem, Forrest cringed to think what his refusal to get a pet might say about his overall commitment issues. Instead of heading to a pound, Forrest chose to spoil Clark whenever Lucy brought him around, which she did often, especially during the summer when the campus was practically empty.

Taking off her windbreaker, Lucy said, "We went for a long walk to burn off some of his energy, and then we stopped by Shipley's on our way here to pick up a few break-up supplies."

Finally done with the rather long and wet greeting process, Forrest stood up while Clark laid down next to his desk, panting with residual excitement. Forrest brushed hair off the sleeves of his plaid shirt. Having Clark there reminded Forrest that it was no longer the work day, so he undid his shackles, loosening his tie to his second button, undoing the collar button, and rolling up his sleeves.

Lucy was wearing black leggings, an over-sized PSU sweatshirt, and sneakers. She must have changed from her usual uniform-esque work clothes before her walk. Clothes were not something people usually noticed about Lucy because of her nondescript style.

Even more strands of Lucy's hair than usual had escaped from the wavy pony-tail that bounced with each movement. Her cheeks were glowing from the excursion of walking with an energetic dog. She looked like fall personified, blown in on a chilly gust of wind, and Forrest found the overall effect to be charming.

"While I appreciate your thoughtfulness, the break-up supplies really aren't necessary. I'm not as upset as I think a person is supposed to be after six months with someone." He had hardly even thought about Dr. Wray the whole day, finding it easy to transition back into his single life. "I fear that at 38 years old,

I have finally achieved poster-child status for the offspring of dysfunctional families."

Lucy lowered her voice as her eyes gleamed and whispered, "You probably shouldn't advertise that. Seeing as how you're a successful college professor with countless publications under your belt, all the parents will start being dysfunctional."

Forrest shrugged his shoulders and said dryly, "Only if they don't want grandkids."

Forrest smirked along with Lucy's giggle, but the truth of the statement did not escape his notice. Porter was only a couple years older than Forrest, but he and Charlotte had a houseful of children. Forrest was nowhere close to fatherhood, much less making a reasoned decision about whether or not that was a goal he wanted to pursue. He put off the thought in a way eerily similar to how he put off a trip to the pound.

Lucy glanced at Forrest as she sat down the Shipley's bags. "You seem more relaxed today."

"I think you will find my hair is perfectly in order."

"Yes, but the relationship with Dr. Wray was six months, so at the very least, we should commemorate the passing of an era."

"A very short era."

Giving him the same look a teacher gives to a student asking obstinate questions, Lucy retorted, "Well, we're commemorating it with Doritos and gummy bears. It's hardly fireworks and speeches."

"Good point. Toss the gummy bears."

Lucy started sorting through her bags, getting out the gummy bears as well as his paper. He noticed several rows of red scribblings on the back. Ouch. Next to the paper, she placed a small bag of dog treats. Looking at Forrest as if scolding him prematurely, she pointed to the bag of dog treats and said, "Dogs can't have gummy bears."

"Noted." Forrest caught the package of candy Lucy tossed his way as he said, "I got us sandwiches from that new coffee shop downtown for our dinner."

"Great. I'm starving. I saw Miriam coming out of that coffee shop this afternoon." Forrest's desk faced two small leather chairs. Lucy sat on one and propped her feet on the seat of the second chair, her long, stretched-out legs accentuated by her black leggings. Not that he had noticed.

"Yeah? Did she say if it is any good?"

"We actually didn't talk about it. We were discussing..." Lucy paused for a breath, a pause so short Forrest wasn't even sure it had happened. "We were discussing other things."

Usually, Lucy was an open book. Forrest figured there was a reason for her ambiguity, so he let it be.

"Do you want to eat dinner before or after editing?"

"Actually, disappointingly for me, I didn't have a terrible lot to mark up. You might be that rare human who actually gets more competent at all-nighters with age."

"We can't know that for sure since I'm so young."

Lucy side-eyed him with a slow, "Uh-huh."

Forrest smiled.

"I say that to say, since there isn't much, how about we knock out the editing and then have our sandwiches."

"Sounds good to me."

Lucy took her feet off of the other chair, and scooted forward as Forrest also leaned in. He passed a few gummy bears across the desk to Lucy and tossed a dog treat directly to Clark who jerked his head up, ate the nugget, and returned to his nap. They each mindlessly popped gummies into their own mouths as they looked at the marked-up text, and Lucy explained her recommendations. Forrest's eyes darted for a brief moment to her chest, thinking that the sweatshirt hid far more than the unbuttoned cardigan from the previous day. It was fortunate. He couldn't really afford more panic attacks this week.

The fruity scent of Lucy's gummy bear filled the small space over his desk as she talked. They were very close to one another, proximity-wise. It felt cozy in their little space. In fact, it felt warm. Possibly too warm. Forrest hoped he was not about to start sweating.

Forrest strained to focus on each word Lucy was saying. But just as Forrest worked to discipline his mind to register the information she was sharing, Lucy's small movements and habits, idiosyncrasies that were familiar to him after a decade of working side-by-side, kept catching his attention, demanding notice.

When she paused to gather a thought, she always bit her lower lip. As she resumed talking, the spot where her teeth had been would be briefly white and then immediately turn a more vibrant shade of the coral color her lips were naturally painted.

Forrest tuned in long enough to give a coherent answer to her question about possibly rearranging paragraphs on the third page. But then he saw how her left hand, the one she was not using to point at the text, kept brushing through the hair that had fallen out of her bun, pushing it behind her ear. Without fail, the stray hair popped out from behind her ear, once again framing her face. The action was as without thought as breathing, but it made him wonder what her hair must feel like to the touch.

And then her glasses slipped down her nose, something they probably did a hundred times a day. She pushed them up with her index finger as her deep, questioning eyes rose to his.

"Forrest, did you hear me?" The full attention of those round, owl-like green eyes was squarely focused on him.

Forrest shook his head, trying to clear the cobwebs (or in this case, green eyes and uncontrollable hair) from his thoughts: "I'm sorry. What did you say again?"

"I asked if you have any questions on that last bit."

"No. No, it all looks perfect. You're perfect."

Lucy immediately blushed from her neck to the roots of her hair. Forrest, still not entirely present in the moment, thought how lovely Lucy was when her lightly freckled cheeks blushed so darkly. Then, the realization of what he had said crashed into him like a bucket of ice water, and he reached for the only words he could to rectify the situation.

"Your *work* is perfect. As always."

***

Lucy schooled her face, immediately trying to camouflage the shock she had felt only a moment ago. For the briefest of moments, Forrest had seemed to call her perfect. Unfortunately, no amount of will power or determination could erase such a potent blush from a fair-skinned, almost-redhead.

Forrest picked up the red-inked transcript and rotated his swivel chair towards his computer. "I'll boot up my computer so I can make the changes."

With Forrest facing his computer, Lucy had a few moments to collect herself. *Please*, she prayed, *let me return to a normal color.*

He had meant her *work* was perfect. Obviously. It was a simple slip. And not of the Freudian variety.

And Lucy's work was perfect. She was very good at what she did. She took pride in each task completed, each paper edited, each crisis cured, each student served. But Lucy herself? No, Lucy was decidedly not perfect.

For just a moment, a voice, a soprano voice almost musical in its Southern lilt, began articulating insecurities from long ago. *If she would only learn to tame her hair. If she were just a little bit slenderer. Maybe a grapefruit diet? Why not try contacts, dear?*

Eight years had passed since an aggressive cancer had suddenly, with little warning, ended Lucy's mother's life. However, Lucy still remembered the exact pitch of her mother's voice, especially when that voice was writing plans for Lucy's improvement. It was always extra sweet when directed towards that task. Lucy did not begrudge her mother. She recognized that the "constructive criticism" had been a painfully misguided attempt at expressing concern and love.

Through years of late-night phone calls with Miriam after her mother's passing, Lucy had slowly begun to acknowledge the place this voice still occupied in her conscience. She had finally been able to name the voice (*Hello, Mom*), and on an intellectual level, she recognized that most of the information it spouted was simply untrue. Her hair was not a problem that needed solved. No amount of deprivation was going to make her solid, tall body frailer and more feminine. To think so was like saying she could shift shoe sizes. And, damn it, she liked her glasses.

It had been a while since Lucy had heard her mother's voice in her psyche, but Lucy was unsurprised at its sudden resurgence. After all, one could hardly forget a voice that was clearly still alive in one's head.

Forrest would likely be bereft to know he had in any way sparked self-doubt in someone else, especially someone with whom he was friends. And they were friends. It wasn't just Miriam who had helped Lucy lessen the frequency of her internal critic. It was also the people in the four offices around her own who regularly sung her praises, regularly reinforced her strength and intelligence and efficacy.

Sure, it might be nice to have an adoring man say she was perfect while gazing at her across a candle-lit table. Lucy's eyes shut tight at the unbidden thought. It *would* be nice, but having the unwavering admiration of friends and colleagues should surely be enough.

"Lucy, did you think I should move this sentence to the front of the paragraph or keep it in its spot at the end? I can't remember what you said earlier."

Lucy's eyes opened wide and her shoulders straightened as she came out of her reverie. She looked where he was pointing and said, "I would move it."

Without questioning her judgment, Forrest returned his attention to the computer, oblivious to the battle raging in Lucy. With skill obtained over a lifetime of practice, Lucy shut the door on the critical voice, hoping it would once again go dormant for a while.

Forrest pressed one last key with a gusto of finality, and turned his chair back towards her. "There, everything else can wait for tomorrow."

"Great! Should we eat something besides gelatinous candy made of ingredients I couldn't possibly pronounce?"

"That does seem like the responsible thing to do," Forrest replied as he pulled out the coffee-shop sandwiches. Lucy walked to the office mini-fridge and got them each a bottle of Sun Drop, the soda of choice in Kentucky. When Miriam had attended an out-of-state seminary, she had sent money each month to Lucy to ship a six-pack of Sun Drops her way.

"Let's not get too carried away with unprocessed food, though," Lucy said as she put the bottle of neon green liquid in front of him.

With food between them, the levity and ease they usually enjoyed returned.

After only a couple of bites, Forrest said, "I feel like I have sandwich all over my beard. This is the problem with beards."

"Yep. Your beard is definitely sandwich-flavored now." It was a ridiculous joke, but it had the intended consequence of making Forrest laugh. The laugh lines around his eyes had only recently become more noticeable, such a subtle sign of aging. They looked right on him. Anyone who worshiped Mark Twain with Forrest's enthusiasm was clearly an old soul. Aging for him was going to be a process of the external reflecting more accurately the internal. Also, Lucy had always loved how quick he was to laugh, and she now loved that his face held markings of this personality trait on the surface.

Lucy squirmed at the thoughts her mind was entertaining. She loved his *laugh lines*? Thinking about the other professors, Lucy tried to identify what she loved about each of them. No facial features came to mind. Although Dr. Hubert's eyebrows were certainly noteworthy, she wouldn't say she *loved* them.

Forrest said between bites, "I have to admit, despite your often-wacky sense of humor, I still sometimes think of you as the smartest student in class. In my over-a-decade of teaching, you still stand out as remarkable."

Lucy smiled at the compliment, but in the recesses of her mind, the thought passed that she would prefer he not think of her as a student. Of course, she, too, had a hard time moving on from their original dynamic.

"And I still have a hard time not calling you Dr. Graham."

Forrest set down his sandwich, and with mock anger said, "I know. Can you please tell me what that is about? We've been working side-by-side now for ten years." To emphasize the point, he tossed a chip into the air that Clark caught and swallowed in a single, smooth motion.

Lucy shook her head in exasperation and said, "Not sure. Your professorial prowess is so great, it has stunted my ability to move on in our relationship."

Yikes. What had made her use the word *relationship*. The teasing went out of Forrest's eyes, and he said, "I hear you call Porter by his first name all the time. He was also your professor."

Desperate to recapture the levity from a moment ago, Lucy said, "Don't know. Maybe if we tried a nickname. How do you feel about Forry?"

Lucy breathed an internal sigh of relief. It had worked. The dimples reappeared over the edge of the beard, and Forrest said through a chuckle, "I feel very bad about Forry. That is how I feel about Forry."

An impish grin crossed his face. "Here. I have a fantastic idea. Let's practice you saying Forrest."

Lucy's eyebrows rose in question, wondering what she had gotten herself into.

"I have chocolates." He reached for the entire bag she had brought in the break-up supplies. "I happen to know you love chocolates, especially after dinner."

"Guilty."

"Ask me for a chocolate, but say my name."

The air changed in the room. Lucy felt the tension rise. It was a challenge, but it wasn't just a challenge to her. It was a challenge to the structure of the working relationship or friendship or whatever one called what she and Forrest had.

Quietly but smoothly, Lucy spoke: "May I please have a chocolate...," Lucy paused briefly as she watched Forrest's head tilt in question. Then, frustratingly, her voice came out in a whisper, "Forrest?"

He thought for a moment, then said, "I don't think so. Whispers don't count. Try again."

Determined not to be defeated, Lucy sucked in a breath, looked straight into his challenging brown eyes, and said at a perfectly reasonable volume, "Hand over the chocolate. Forrest."

— • —

CHAPTER 5

As her lips formed his name, they puckered ever so slightly. Puckering was what lips had to do to make the f-o-r sound. It was basic linguistics.

Forrest had never been so glad to have his name. It was a really fine name when spoken by Lucy O'Shields.

A pause stretched out between them as Forrest processed the reaction his body was having to his name on Lucy's lips. There was a tightening in his abdomen, and his breathing shallowed imperceptibly. He had felt similar sensations earlier in the week, but this time was different. This was no panic attack. Forrest chose to not name the feeling, but rather, to be grateful for the expanse of desk wedged between them.

Realizing the pause was quickly approaching awkward-silence territory, Forrest said, "That wasn't the most polite way to phrase it. No 'please.' But seeing as how I'm a Southern gentleman..."

Lucy made a sound adjacent to a snort.

"I'll give in. Here's your chocolate."

He pushed the chocolate across the desk, purposefully leaving his fingertips on it. She reached across the other half, and laid her fingers on the chocolate, their fingertips touching for the briefest of moments. A shock ran up his arms.

Lucy unwrapped the chocolate, popped it into her mouth, and then said, "Thanks, Dr. Graham."

He rolled his eyes in exasperation as she giggled. The moment had passed. Forrest stood up to throw away the bags and wrappers from their meal. Never one to allow someone else to wait on her, Lucy stood up and joined him cleaning.

Still with laughter lacing her voice, Lucy said, "It's after 8 o'clock. Clark and I had better head home."

"I'm done here for the night. I'll walk you home."

"That isn't necessary. It's a short walk, and I have Clark to scare off the boogie-man."

They both looked at the dog, who had suddenly started whimpering in his sleep.

"Luce, I've known that dog for years, and I love him very much. But..."

"There's always a but."

"But, he is a total coward. I've seen him run from one of the campus stray cats. Odds are, he's whimpering right now because he's dreaming of nothing more ferocious than a squirrel."

"And your point is?"

"I'm not trusting Clark to get you home safely."

Lucy scowled in exasperation. "Clark and I have made this walk home - unescorted, in the dark - countless times."

"Clearly, I've been remiss."

Forrest was, like the vast majority of English professors, a feminist. If he had not been, he and Edith never could have coexisted in the same office for so long. Forrest's sudden chivalry would have elicited the middle finger from Edith, and Forrest wouldn't have faulted her for it. But he also knew that he would be escorting Lucy and Clark home. Period.

Lucy tossed the last Sun Drop bottle into the trash. "Fine. You win. But you have to wake up Clark."

"Fair enough." Forrest bent down and gently shook Clark's shoulder. The dog snored loudly and rolled back, even in his sleep seeing if the nearby human might rub his belly. "Come on, Clark. We've got to go, bud. You can do it. Let's wake up."

Forrest did not see Lucy bend over his shoulder, so he jumped an inch when she whispered into his ear, "Don't worry. I won't tell any of your students you baby-talk to dogs."

Forrest pursed his lips and turned his head to find her eyes surprisingly close to his own. "I'm sorry. Do you have a better way to get your dog to move?"

With a chummy pat on the back, she said, "Nope. Proceed."

A few more jiggles and pleas to get moving finally brought Clark back to the land of the living. Lucy held the leash and Forrest shut off lights as the trio left Hart Building.

The fall air was chilly but mild as they headed to the edge of campus towards Lucy's apartment. It would take about fifteen minutes to walk to her apartment and another ten to circle back towards campus and get to his own place. He hoped a brisk walk coupled with escaping the tiny confines of his office would alleviate some of the tension he had felt, so unusual for time spent with Lucy. She had always made him feel at ease with her off-kilter humor and attentiveness.

Tonight, though, there had been blushes and pauses and unspoken questions Forrest had not expected, and he had no idea what had caused them. Well, that wasn't entirely true. On his part, he was quite certain the thoughts that had invaded his mind the previous afternoon after his break-up with Dr. Wray had been at least partially responsible. But surely a few unruly thoughts in his mind didn't account for all of the subtle changes in this evening's meeting.

As the two walked together, each tall, their gaits matched easily. Soon, they were once again conversing like the old friends they were. Lucy said, "Are you looking forward to the basketball game next week?"

Basketball season was starting to crank up in Kentucky, and the PSU team was predicted to have a better-than-usual season. Lucy was adamant that the English Department needed to show their support for all aspects of the PSU community, so she organized for the entire office to attend a game together each fall. Lucy knew her way around campus politics. As Chair, Edith trusted Lucy implicitly on such matters, and Lucy had never failed to point the office in the right direction.

"I am looking forward to it. I think we're going to have a good season this year."

"Yes. That is what I've heard, as well. But I'll have to admit, I don't go for the game as much as I go for the experience of watching a bunch of nerdy English professors try to look natural in an alien habitat."

Forrest laughed. "There is that. But I think there is even more to it. I think you go because you don't trust Edith to not approach a coach about some player's late essay or poor mid-terms."

"Wow, it's like you know my job or something." Lucy bumped him with her elbow. The brief physical contact, though made in jest, had the odd effect of narrowing the gap between them. Lucy's warmth crowded out the night's chill.

"Do you remember the first thing you ever said to me?"

Forrest was surprised by the question, and by the hint of insecurity he had heard in her voice. Of course, he knew she had been in his first class. He could probably recite each student's name and recall the topic of their final essay. After, all, they were his first class. However, he couldn't remember an exact moment at which Lucy had entered his radar, or what he had said to her in that moment. "Let me think..." Forrest's eyes looked up as he contemplated the question. "I'm not positive, but it likely had something to do with Mark Twain."

In the darkness, Forrest could barely make out Lucy's facial features, but he sensed her smile. "Solid guess, but no. You might have started the class with that. In fact, I'm pretty sure you did start class with a Mark Twain quote. But you actually spoke a single sentence to me before class began."

"Why is this conversation making me nervous?"

Lucy looked down at her feet as if it was imperative she keep track of which was stepping forward at a time. She proceeded with the story, "Like I said, it was before class began. Miriam and I were talking..."

"There's a shocker." Forrest could not resist the opportunity to inject this little tease.

Lucy elbowed his arm again. If she was trying to reprimand him for his joke, the additional physical contact was not working. Lucy continued, "We were discussing upcoming appointments with the Career Center. Anyways, Miriam asked me if I was going to go, and I jokingly said, 'What's the point? Don't all English majors become secretaries?'"

Forrest didn't like the direction the story was heading.

"We didn't realize the new professor was standing right behind us until you chimed in, 'I think we can do better than that.'"

Forrest nodded his head like a slow-moving oil rig. "So I was an asshole?"

This time, Lucy didn't elbow him. Rather, she grabbed his wrist with her hand and stopped their walking. She faced him and said, "No, Forrest, that isn't what I meant at all..."

"I know, but I was sort of an asshole."

With her eyebrows slanted in consternation, Lucy said more emphatically, "No. The lesson here is not that you are an asshole. Not that there is a lesson. It's just that you said I was your smartest student, and here I am celebrating a decade of being a secretary. By and large, I'm proud of the job I do. I'm good at it."

"You're damn right you're good at it."

"But..."

"But?"

"But aren't you a little disappointed your star pupil became a secretary?"

"I could never think of you as a disappointment, Luce." The use of her nickname, one used only by the closest of friends, softened her whole expression. "Secretary is only a title. It isn't you, and it doesn't begin to describe everything you have done since you graduated."

As Forrest looked down at Lucy and felt her hand squeezing his wrist, he saw uncertainty. His words had not been quite enough to fix whatever insecurities she was battling. He really wanted to fix it for her. She released her grasp on his wrist, her hand falling to her side.

"When I'm teaching my students, and I walk them through four years of classes and then cheer them on as they walk across that stage, I'm not hoping they go on to fancy job titles. I'm hoping that whatever job they find themselves in, the education they received in our department helps them be a better person in that role. Better at their job. Better at just being. Better at working with those around them. So by my measurements, you are still my star student."

Lucy broke eye contact to glance down at Clark as he wedged himself between them and sat on their feet, confused that they had all stopped walking. But right before she looked down, Forrest could swear he had seen moisture in her eyes. Were words he had carelessly spoken over ten years ago causing her to doubt herself today? He rued the thought, and it made him desperate to see her eyes one more time, to see if they still looked so broken.

Gently, Forrest placed his index finger beneath her chin and guided her face back towards his line of vision. Then, with almost reverence, Forrest pushed up the glasses that had slid down her nose a smidgen when she had glanced down at Clark. There, now he could see her eyes. His hand returned to the base of her chin. He didn't want her to look away again. Not just yet.

Lucy's eyes were staring wide-eyed into his own, and what he saw there caused him to inhale deeply, just short of an actual gasp.

He didn't see hurt there anymore, thank Walt Whitman and all of his leaves of grass. The insecurity seemed to have been banished, at least for a little while. The emotions of just a moment ago had left her face raw, and what was exposed in the rawness was longing. Could it be longing for him? Was it possible that the blushes and awkward silences had been a product of attraction? Forrest doubted such a seismic shift had occurred in two days. Which led him to ask, had it been there before? Had it been there, unnamed and untapped, for years?

"Lucy?" Just as Forrest was about to say something or ask a question or lean forward or just do something (he hardly knew what), he heard a deep voice call out from down the block.

"Forrest? Lucy? What are you guys doing out?"

Jogging towards them with a stroller was Dr. Porter Finch.

***

Lucy and Forrest each jumped back a step, partially to create distance and partially because an extra exuberant Clark had bolted forward, barking a greeting to yet another friend. Lucy must have let go of his leash at some point, but she could not possibly identify when or why.

Lucy was stunned. In the minutes that had preceded this moment, she had forgotten that a world existed outside of the bubble in which she had stood facing Forrest while he had seemed to stare straight into her soul.

Her mind was racing, lobbing questions at herself faster than she could possibly process them. What had she seen in Forrest's eyes just now? More importantly, what had he seen in her eyes? Had he read there in a single moment everything she had kept hidden for the past decade? And where had that feeling come from, the feeling that had washed down her body? It was everything she had known about desire, but it was also more than she had ever felt. And when had her treacherous body started desiring Dr. Forrest Graham, for the love of all that was holy? She would blame Miriam and her ridiculous "free agent" comment for sowing seeds Lucy had no intention of reaping. And finally, where had Porter come from, and what would he think of what he had seen? It was dark. Perhaps he would think (Lucy frantically reached for a plausible explanation) they had been drawing on each other's body heat because they had forgotten heavy jackets?

Willing her mind back into the time and space where she stood, Lucy smiled as she greeted Porter with an enthusiasm the situation did not warrant. "Hey Porter! It's great to see you! Forrest was just making sure Clark and I made it home after some editing on campus!" Why was every sentence coming out with exclamation marks? She was not, nor had she ever been, an exclamation-mark kind of girl. English majors could fail a whole course for the use of a single exclamation mark. *Breathe, Lucy. Breathe.*

Thankfully, Porter was happily distracted by Clark. The dog's tail-wagging had blown into some kind of bizarre rotating dance that Porter encouraged with petting and ear-scratching. Good boy, Clark. He was giving Lucy a few more minutes to compose herself and, hopefully, tone it down a bit.

"So, it's an editing night?" Porter looked up from Clark, darting his eyes back and forth between Lucy and Forrest.

Forrest said, "Yes, you know, the Whitman piece I told you about?"

"Oh, yeah, that's right. How'd it go?"

"Fine. Fine. It's all going fine" Forrest's usual self-confidence and calm seemed to have abandoned them in the dark, and if Porter's eyebrows were to be trusted, he had noticed. Lucy decided to shift the conversation.

"So, what are you and Anna doing out past dark?"

"My mom came over to help put the kids to bed while Charlotte is out of town. She is focusing on the boys, while I'm putting Anna to bed. Last I saw, Billy and Luke were running naked around the dining room while she pretended to be a pirate chasing them. Seemed like a good time to leave." Porter was grinning as he told the story. He was not the sort of parent who bemoaned the antics of his children. Rather, he relished the chaos, having never completely outgrown the playfulness and orneriness of childhood.

Relieved to be talking about Porter's children, Lucy asked, "And how exactly are you putting Anna to bed? While jogging?"

"Oh, that. While babies in commercials can be laid down directly into a bed and fall peacefully asleep, my children demand a bit more effort."

Seeing Lucy and Forrest's confused expressions, Porter continued, "Specifically, Anna likes to fall asleep in the stroller while it is moving quickly. The strategy she and I have worked out over these past 6 months of her life is that I jog clockwise around the block twice, counter-clockwise once, and then back to two laps of clockwise. It works like magic."

"Funny," Forrest said, his usual ease seeming to have returned. "I always thought magic made things easier. Wave of a wand - a little incantation, and poof! You get whatever it is you're going for."

Donning his professorial confidence, Porter said, "Oh Forrest. On the topic of parenthood, trust me. Five laps around the block is a wave of the wand compared to pacing with a screaming baby for half the night."

Forrest raised his hands in defeat. "Clearly you are the master. I, on the other hand, have never raised a houseplant, much less a baby."

Snorting at the truth of the statement, Lucy shook her head. "Speaking of bed-times, I think Clark and I are ready to go curl up with a book."

Forrest questioned, "At eight thirty? Really?"

"Do you know who I work with? I'm exhausted."

Forrest and Porter spoke at the same time. "True, you have a point there." "Good point. Very good point."

Porter said, "Since Lucy and I are headed to the same place, I can walk her the rest of the way if you want to go ahead to your place, Forrest."

Forrest looked directly into Lucy's eyes for just a moment, not long enough for Lucy to discern what she saw there. Was he disappointed they had been interrupted? Did he wish to walk her the rest of the way?

"Yeah, I think I'll head on home. Are we still on for the Kentucky game this weekend?"

Porter beamed. "Absolutely. I'm ordering an obscene amount of junk food from the Corner Bar, and I fully intend on us both making ourselves sick while cheering on the White and Blue."

At Porter's enthusiasm, Forrest's dimples made an appearance. Lucy couldn't look away. His dimples and his beard and his warm, brown eyes seemed to invite stares when he smiled. "Sounds perfect." There was that word again, but once again, he was not directing it at her. "I'll see you both tomorrow at work."

Forrest turned around and walked back towards campus to his apartment. Porter and Lucy started walking towards their homes, which, incidentally, were in the same place. Lucy lived in the apartment above Porter's garage. Before starting a family, Porter and Charlotte bought a historic home in a classic, two-story design with deep front porches on both levels. The home was a few blocks off campus. It was a relic of the early twentieth century, and it came with a detached garage with a quaint apartment built above in the same style as the house.

Porter had been as excited about his new home as a child receiving their first bike, and as was often the case with Porter, his enthusiasm had been contagious. When Porter mentioned that the new house had a garage apartment in need of a little updating, Lucy immediately volunteered to live in the space and fix it up. They agreed on a financial arrangement that suited them both, and Lucy was liberated from the cookie-cutter apartment of her college days, free to turn the small garage apartment into a space that reflected her aesthetic. She loved coming home.

On the last short leg of the walk home, Porter and Lucy chatted about the upcoming PSU game that the department would be attending, Charlotte's most recent travels and what story she was covering, and how quickly Anna had gone from newborn to six-months-old. It was so easy to talk to Porter. There was no tension in the air, no penetrating looks that made her wonder if she was hiding her feelings well enough or what those feelings even were and why she felt compelled to hide them.

As they came closer to the apartment, Porter said, "Forrest sure keeps you busy editing. I need to be publishing more."

"Yes, with all of that spare time you have," Lucy tilted her head towards Anna, looking perfectly peaceful in her jogging-induced sleep.

"I do sort of have my hands full." Porter's eyes softened as he, too, looked at Anna.

They finally arrived at the base of the stairs that went up to Lucy's apartment. Lucy turned to Porter to tell him goodbye, but she paused at the contemplative look that had come over his face. He said, "Forrest dedicates himself so much to our profession because he's afraid. He's afraid if he doesn't, he'll become like his dad."

Lucy was silent. It was not like Porter to analyze someone else's motivations or behaviors.

"I'm glad he has you. I'm glad you're there with him."

Lucy knew that Porter's analysis was true, that Forrest's tireless work ethic was motivated by what he was running from. She had been friends with him too long to not understand something so central to his personality. But she had never heard another person acknowledge this reality. The quiet lingered as they thought about their mutual friend, then Lucy said, "I'm glad I can be there for him, too."

And just like that, the cloud of seriousness lifted from Porter, and he said, "Well, goodnight. You'd better get some sleep. The odds of the kids' nanny not getting another migraine tomorrow are pretty low."

Lucy laughed as she and Clark started up the stairs, calling back to Porter, "Goodnight to you, too."

Opening the door to her apartment, Lucy sank into the comfort of the living room. Despite the slight sting of shame that she was in her early 30s and still renting a garage apartment, Lucy loved coming home to her cozy quarters filled with an eclectic mixture of antique-shop finds and a few clean-lined, modern pieces. The Grahams granted Lucy wide-ranging freedom to decorate the interior of her apartment so long as her choices were period-appropriate. Lucy's closet-size kitchen was a sunny, daffodil yellow, her bedroom sky-blue, and the wall behind her sofa was accented with floral wallpaper that sparked joy the instant she opened her front door. After the evening she and Forrest had just had, she wanted to lay on the sofa, pick up a book, and escape the questions that were churning from the moment before Porter burst into their space.

But her mind would not allow her to escape. Instead, she busied herself in the kitchen preparing a cup of chamomile tea, the questions once again flying like debris across a window. Why, she wondered, had she not told Forrest about her meeting with President Burke? The opportunity had been wide open. Why had she blushed at their teasing, a dynamic they had managed for years without awkwardness? And why, in the dark street, had her body seemed so ready to step right into his? Why had his eyes looked like he would have welcomed her?

During her senior year, Lucy would have been lying if she claimed not to have felt the desire of a young woman for a man hopelessly beyond her reach. From the second row of the lecture hall, it was safe to indulge the occasional fantasy about the tall, handsome teacher with dry wit, chocolate eyes, and a magnetic smile she could never turn her eyes from. She had wondered more than once what his beard would feel like if it were to brush along the hollow of her neck.

But for ten years, she had denied the college-student within herself the luxury of fantasizing about her professor, and it had worked. Lucy had established a working relationship built on mutual respect and a friendship built on affection and compatibility. The dichotomy of the relationship had always worked because they had never entertained the possibility of anything more. Romance and (mercy) *sex* were off the table.

After her tea was finished, and she crawled under the ruffled white duvet of her bed, Lucy closed her eyes only to see Forrest looking down at her. Her mind had captured every detail of his expression from that brief moment when he had guided her to him, his finger so warm and gentle beneath her chin. Not forcing. Merely suggesting, asking, maybe even hoping.

As she relived the moment, her body once again reacted with the same need. But this time, in the privacy of her home, Lucy was able to recognize that the desire was not a resurgence from college-student Lucy. This was entirely different. This was the desire of a woman for a man who she knew, truly knew. A man who saw her and treated her as an equal.

At the realization, Lucy jolted up in bed. She walked to the couch, slumped down, and cradled her head in her hands, trying to run beyond the edge of the fog.

Lucy was the secretary; Forrest, one of her bosses. While he treated her as an equal, she was not an equal. And even if she ignored the uncomfortable dynamic of being a secretary dating a boss, there was the rest of the office to worry about. They had built a quirky little family, a family Forrest needed. He needed each and every one of them, because he had made that job his life. It was the fuel that kept him from sinking into his past.

Lucy was now able to answer one question from the past two days. She now knew why Forrest's name was color-coded differently from the other English faculty in her mind. She was, simply put, attracted to him. But she knew that it was an attraction she must never indulge for the sake of the life they had built in Hart Building.

Looking at the clock, Lucy saw it was only 10 o'clock. She dreaded the long, sleepless night ahead of her.

***

Forrest opened the door to his apartment about an hour after he had left Porter and Lucy. He had felt restless, too restless to return immediately to the bare, colorless confines of his apartment.

Forrest's apartment looked exactly like what it was: a place avoided for all purposes but to provide a roof and a bed when its occupant needed to sleep. Home was the book-lined shelves of his office, the antics of his co-workers, the tree-lined walkways of Paducah State University. It was Porter's house for games and movies and Dr. Hubert's house for Sunday lunch. His apartment was not a home. It was sleeping quarters.

Forrest set his shower as hot as he could tolerate and walked into the steam. He scrubbed hard on his hair, harder than was necessary. Then he thought about Lucy knowing he was stressed by simply looking at his hair. Smoothing down his hair with even more vigor than he had scrubbed it, Forrest wondered how she had known his nervous tick when he had not known it himself.

Each task Forrest undertook in the bathroom, he did roughly and clumsily. Water sprayed all over his mirror when he shook out his wet toothbrush. The towel overshot the hamper by several feet when he tossed it. He jiggled the handle of the toilet so violently when it wouldn't stop running that it popped off, delaying bed by ten minutes while he fixed it.

When he finally walked into his bedroom, the nervous energy that had been driving him all evening began to dissipate. He sat heavily on the side of his bed and stared at the only ornamental object in the white and gray room. It was a picture frame, silver with "Paducah State University" embossed at the base and filled with blue and gold resin. Along the other edges of the frame were paw prints for the PSU Wildcats.

The frame and the picture within it had been a Christmas gift from Lucy the previous year, probably bought from the campus bookstore. The picture was of the whole office and Porter's boys, all scrunched together on a bench of the basketball stadium's bleachers. It was from their annual basketball game the previous year.

Edith was on the far left of the photo looking formidable. Forrest recalled that the picture had been snapped just moments after she had yelled at the refs for a bad call, hence the scowl. Next to her was Dr. Hubert, wearing his PSU baseball cap backwards, with Billy propped on a knee. The backwards cap was likely Billy's doing. Luke was sitting on Porter's lap while reaching across to poke at his brother. And on the right end were Lucy and Forrest, looking perfectly at ease while sitting side-by-side.

Lucy had walked into his office in the quiet following the English Department holiday party with a gift bag stuffed with decorative paper. After he opened it, they sat on opposite sides of the desk, just as they had done hours ago. Together, they laughed at the memory of Edith ostentatiously miming the appropriate signals for the call the refs *clearly* should have made. If he remembered right, they had marveled at how big Porter's boys were getting and how another Finch baby would soon join the office.

It had been a perfectly normal conversation, the type one might have whispered with a sister after a too-heavy turkey dinner while the rest of the family napped.

Maybe the breakup with Dr. Wray was affecting Forrest more than he realized. It felt like he was losing his grip. What had he been thinking tonight flirting with Lucy? Why had he looked into her eyes that last time? Hadn't he realized how dangerous it was? How much there was to lose? In truth, he hadn't realized the danger until he'd seen her eyes looking into his own with undisguised longing.

Dr. Wray was a decent person, and he wasted six months of her life. And before her, more women than he cared to count had wasted three to six months with a guy who was incapable of giving them more than the barest level of intimacy. Lucy deserved better. She deserved better than a Graham. If he insisted on being the noble gentleman and walking her home in the dark, the least he could do was protect her from himself.

Thankfully, Porter had interrupted. Forrest still did not know what would have transpired had Porter not arrived, but he had no doubt Porter had saved him from a grave mistake. Tomorrow, Forrest would go into his office and treat Lucy like the dear friend and work colleague she was. He would move on from tonight and never look back.

CHAPTER 6

For the most part, Forrest had succeeded at his Wednesday night resolution. The rest of the week had gone fairly smoothly. Yes, Lucy had diverted eye contact a few times, and he had given a wide berth anytime their paths had crossed (it never hurt to maintain personal space). But by five o'clock on Friday, Forrest had nearly convinced himself that he'd overblown any changes he'd felt earlier in the week between himself and Lucy.

Now it was the weekend, and Forrest was driving down the road from Paducah to see his father in the small town of Mayfield. He wore a thick flannel shirt in brown and red plaid with an old, worn pair of jeans and work boots, ready for a morning of labor in the chilly fall air. When he called his dad earlier in the week to check on him, his dad mentioned that his yard was drowning in leaves. Lucy had been right about his father sounding tired. Forrest volunteered to drive down Saturday morning to rake and bag leaves. That evening, he and Porter would be watching the game, so Forrest was glad for physical, outdoor activity earlier in the day. Hopefully, it would burn off the nervous energy he had felt all week.

Forrest pulled into the driveway of the home in which he had grown up. The old two-story house was looking shabbier than usual. White paint chipped off the board and batten siding, and the dark navy trim only thinly disguised the rot around the windows. Although his store of good memories in this house was low, Forrest hated seeing the disrepair.

In the front yard, two large maple trees stood in the front, practically bare of leaves. The raking would keep him busy. Forrest wanted to get started soon, but first, he would check on his father.

As he unlocked the door with the same key he had used in high school, Forrest called through the house, "Dad, you up? It's Forrest."

"Hey son." His dad's voice, coming from the kitchen in the back, sounded like sandpaper. Forrest wondered if he had just awoken. Walking through the dark, paneled hallway to the kitchen, Forrest found his father unshaven and disheveled, his gray hair standing up on one side and pasted to his head on the other, and his yellowed hands shaking as he reached for the steaming mug in front of him. He looked desperately tired to Forrest.

When one's parent is an alcoholic, one becomes accustomed to seeing them out of sorts. This felt worse, somehow. Forrest's father had always been an alcoholic, but a functioning alcoholic. Today, he did not look as though he was functioning. Forrest promised himself he would call Gracie on the drive home.

"Hey, old man. How's it going?"

His father brightened a bit at seeing him. "Oh, I don't know, son. Your old man is tired today."

"I'm sorry to hear that. Have you seen a doctor recently?"

"Oh, no need. No need." The gruffness and faltering of his voice compelled Forrest to argue, but his father was not one to be persuaded on such points as pertained to his health. Forrest chose to remain silent. Maybe Gracie would know what to say.

"If you're sure?" Forrest could not keep the question from his voice.

"I am." His dad stared at him for a moment, and then smiled as he said, "And don't you go calling Gracie to get her all worried. I'm fine."

Forrest couldn't help but smile at his father's intuition.

"Have some coffee. I made it extra strong this morning."

"No, thanks. I stopped at the Coffee Bean on my way over."

"Oh, that milked-down junk isn't coffee."

"But it tastes good."

His father barked. Forrest was sure it was meant to be a laugh.

"How about I have a cup after I get the raking done?"

"That sounds fine. I'll have a bologna sandwich ready for your lunch."

Forrest steeled his stomach as it lurched at the word. There was no escape. He would be having bologna and tar-black coffee for lunch. "That'd be great, Dad."

Forrest headed to the garage where he collected the rake and a few bags. He went into the yard, and began working. Three hours passed with his mind blissfully empty of anything but the scraping of his rake and crunching of the leaves beneath his boots as he shoveled more into each bag. Finally, the yard was pristine (in great contrast to the house, the more cynical part of Forrest bemoaned), and he had hauled away several loads in his father's truck.

As he walked into the kitchen, his father was setting two plates onto the green Formica table. Each plate had the promised bologna sandwich with white bread, the kind that stuck to the roof of one's mouth. It had been years since Forrest had eaten such fare. The coffee shops and cafes Forrest frequented were all about artisan breads, ciabatta, and sourdough.

Next, his father set down two cups of coffee. Sure enough, it was pitch black. Forrest noticed his father's hands shaking less as he placed the cups. He must have had a shot of whiskey with his morning cup to take off the edge. Forrest withheld judgment. He had learned at an early age that judging his father for alcoholism was a burden heavier than he cared to bear.

"Have a seat, son. Tell me how Lucy's doing?"

Of all the parts of Forrest's life upon which his father could inquire, he was unsurprised his father had chosen his secretary.

"She's wonderful. Although, you talk to her as much as me. You probably know more than I do." Hyperbolic? Yes, his father's weekly calls hardly equaled the hours he and Lucy spent within the close confines of their office. But, damn it, he didn't want to talk about Lucy O'Shields with his father right now.

"Yes, but she always talks about you, never herself." Of course she didn't. Lucy hardly noticed her own existence because she was always so busy keeping everyone else's in order. Forrest remained silent.

"She's a good girl, that Lucy. Never acts like she doesn't have time to talk to me. Always tells me what project you're currently working on. Of course, I don't know who the hell Walt Whitman is, but I appreciate she thinks I might."

"That does sound like Lucy."

"You don't suppose you and she might..."

"Not an option, Dad." Forrest's tone was unmistakable, and his father raised a palm in surrender.

"Whatever you say, son. I'd just like to see you settled, you know, like your sister."

"Marriage and family didn't work out so well for you, though, did it?"

Forrest saw his father flinch at the words. "I suppose you're right."

"Trust me, Dad. It's not for me." Forrest hoped his father heard the apology in his voice.

***

"Miriam, as a minister, could you please thank God on my behalf that it is Saturday night?"

As if to put a fine point on the request, the microwave beeped, signaling that the popcorn was ready.

Miriam was already sipping a glass of wine on Lucy's sofa with Clark stretched across, his head lying on her lap, snoring. It was the one day of the week that she did not wear a clerical collar, and she looked relaxed in her seminary t-shirt and yoga pants. The hand that was not holding wine was mindlessly pulling at her individual curls, then releasing them as they sprang back into place. Lucy supposed if her unruly waves ever decided to become perfectly smooth curls, she would fiddle with them as well. Miriam said, "That good of a week, huh?"

Lucy carried the bowl of popcorn to the antique traveling trunk she used as a coffee table in front of her sofa. She picked up the wine Miriam had poured for her and sank into one of the robin's egg blue wingback chairs that sat across the trunk from the couch. Really, by the end of the week, things felt normal enough she almost wondered if she'd only imagined the events of Wednesday evening. Almost. She said, "It wasn't an awful week or anything. Just weird. And stressful."

"Tonight's movie has no start time. Do tell."

The two-word invitation to share elicited a string of words Lucy had not realized she was holding in. They spilled forth in rapid, clumsy sentences. "I had all the normal job stuff this week. Students crying. Legos on the floor..."

"Legos? In a college English Department?"

Lucy didn't seem to hear the question. She continued, "...books crashing..."

"That I can believe."

"...doctor's appointments to remember. And then President Burke had to offer me that stupid job..."

"Oh, have we decided that's stupid?"

"I haven't a clue. And then Forrest picked the day after he broke up with Dr. Wray..."

"I assume you mean Dr. Bugs?"

"Yes, he picked *that* day to notice I never actually call him Forrest to his face. So now I'm trying to call him Forrest without being weird or anything..."

"It is his name."

"...and I had an editing meeting with him, and it was productive and all, but it was weird..."

"Weird?"

"...Yes. Weird. And then he walked me home because it was dark, and then he looked at me funny."

"Funny how?"

"I don't know. Just funny. But this thing happened when he looked at me. I felt a zing. A little zing. Like, an itty-bitty little zing."

"Itty-bitty? Did you just use the word itty-bitty outside of a nursery rhyme?"

"And then I spent the rest of the week in the office that I love and where I am damn good at my job..."

"Damn good."

"... but I felt awkward there, like our office space was tiny and I was Alice in Wonderland during that scene where she's huge. Do you know what scene I'm talking about? The one where's she so big?" Lucy's eye grew shockingly wide as she expressed how very big Alice was.

"Yes. Quite large. Proceed."

"Which is all so stupid. Because I am not that person. I'm not 21 and I'm not a school-girl and I don't blush when some guy makes eye contact with me."

There was a pause.

"So, yeah, it's been a long week."

"I'd say so," Miriam said, and then she took a rather large gulp of her wine. "I feel like you told me this lovely story because you would like to talk about it? Which leads me to the question, where do we start?"

"Not sure. That was a lot of sharing I just did." Lucy smiled sheepishly. Only Miriam was ever privy to stressed-out Lucy, and she had just been given a heavy dose.

"Okay," Miriam hesitated for a moment. "The new job possibility. Why is it, I believe the word you used was, *stupid*?"

"Because there are a dozen practical reasons for accepting it and twice as many impractical reasons for declining. I don't know how to weigh those kinds of pros and cons. It is an impossible equation."

Miriam and Lucy discussed the various arguments that had been running through Lucy's head since Wednesday's lunch. Lucy knew the raise would be wonderful, and she feared turning down the possibility of this upward movement would close the door to future possibilities. At the same time, she was content in her current position. Happy even. On Sunday evenings, she didn't start dreading the coming of Monday morning or bemoan the weekend ending, or at least not usually. She supposed this weekend was the exception that proved the rule.

Miriam reached over for a handful of popcorn, earning a snort from the sleeping Clark. As she did so, she said, "So, like I said Wednesday, you have time to make this decision. It does sound like you've figured out what the 'but' was

that you kept sensing after lunch that day. Simply put, you like your job. There
are worse problems you could have."

"I know. I shouldn't complain."

"I wasn't meaning to guilt-trip you, Luce. It is okay to complain. This is a
tough decision. Just give yourself some grace, okay?"

"That is not generally my way of being, but I'll try?" The implied question
and the uncertainty of her expression communicated her doubt that she could
go easy on herself in this instance. Miriam decided to move on.

"So, why is the name thing a big deal?"

"I've been asking myself that question for the last ten years. Saying Porter?
Easy. Edith? No problem. Dr. Hubert? Irrelevant since his first name has basically been lost to posterity."

"Dr. Hubert is probably the name on his birth certificate."

Lucy laughed at the joke, grateful for Miriam's wit chipping away at her
anxiety. Or was it the wine? It was both, Lucy thought. Definitely both. She
continued, "But there is something about Forrest. Maybe it is because my first
encounters with him were all fogged up with me being crush-y. Is that a word?"

"If it isn't, it should be. Continue."

"Yes, so I wonder if I've used Dr. Graham all of these years to keep the wall
up that originally made my feelings so inconsequential. Maybe, it was just a
misguided attempt to protect a vulnerable 21-year-old who knew she had an
impossible crush."

Miriam nodded her head slightly, but her face held a hint of skepticism. "That
seems possible. Even likely. That is probably exactly why you kept saying Dr.
Graham those first few years. But once you had moved past the schoolgirl crush
phase, why did the formality linger?"

"Habit?"

"Perhaps. And now, that leads us to our final point of discussion. I for one
enjoy a good zing. So what do you think happened there?"

Lucy's voice took on an air of certainty she didn't feel but wished to convey.
"Likely, it was his dimples. Occam's Razor, right?"

"Okay," Miriam sigh was long-suffering as she said, "but being that I have never, ever been one to stop at the simple answer..."

"Oh dear, no. Why do I come to you with my problems?"

Miriam chose to ignore this question. "Let me pose a possibility other than dimples. Not to say his aren't amazing. When I was in his class, I never wrote a comma in my notes without thinking of them."

Lucy laid a palm over her heart in solidarity. "So say we all."

"But. But what if you did get over the school-girl crush only to develop something more substantial and mature a few years later?"

This thought had already crossed Lucy's mind, but she wasn't prepared to admit it in front of a witness. So, she guffawed in a decidedly unladylike manner that would have mortified her mother. "That's ridiculous, Miriam. We have been average, run-of-the-mill friends and work-colleagues for years."

"Yeah, Luce, it's completely normal to spend the weekend reading..." Miriam turned her torso to grab a thousand-plus page book that she held up as she said, "*Walt Whitman: The Civil War Nurse and Master of Romantic Era American Poetry* so that you can chat with your boss over your lunch hour."

Knowing Miriam had made a point that was hard to argue, Lucy tried to justify the door-stop-sized book waving in front of her: "I'm interested in Whitman. Always have been. I love leaves, and I love grass, Miriam."

"And one other point."

Lucy steeled herself, knowing Miriam rarely made a point that wasn't spot-on.

"Why do you think you have hardly dated at all over the past ten years?"

"Oh, I don't know. Maybe it's that I'm always standing next to someone in a clerical collar."

"Touché."

"And I have had remarkably bad luck the few times I have dipped my toe in the dating pool."

"The professional accordion player was..." Miriam searched for a word, but when nothing came, she said, "well, he was something."

"How about the one who got in a fight with the waiter over the done-ness of his steak?"

"I concede that you have had some legitimately bad luck. But all I'm saying is maybe you haven't tried too hard for the same reason you aren't jumping on that new job. Maybe you're content with something, or should I say someone, who is already in your life."

Lucy had no comeback, no little joke to deflect or denial to insist upon. Miriam's hypothesis was solid.

"You're pretty quiet over there. Did I hit too close to the target?"

"Well, you are Mother Miriam."

Miriam grinned as she said, "Speaking of which, if you think it is hard to get a date sitting next to someone in the collar, try being the one wearing it."

"I'd rather stare at Hugh Grant."

"Amen, sister." Miriam picked up the remote and pushed play.

***

To walk to Porter's house from Forrest's apartment, Forrest came up to the house from the back. This meant walking by Lucy's garage apartment. She had deep-purple mums sitting next to her door at the top of the stairs. Next to her vehicle was another small sedan. Forrest wondered who it might belong to. And then he told himself that it did not concern him. And then he thought of how her hair always managed to escape confinement and frame her face in a mess of waves. And then he said a thank you in his head to college football and the distraction it provided.

As he rounded the corner, Forrest saw his friend sitting in a rocking chair on his fern-lined front porch, rocking Anna while watching Luke and Billy play a violent game of tag around the azalea bushes.

Once he was within hearing distance, Forrest called out, "Hello, Porter." Billy's eyes immediately darted to Forrest, and he started running as fast as he could directly towards him. Once he was a few feet away, Forrest planted his feet firmly, preparing to take a hefty blow. However, he still wasn't prepared for the gut punch he received as Billy yelled, "You're it," and ran away. Thankfully, Luke, still young enough to not entirely understand the game of tag, desperately wanted to be "it." So with a short jog off the sidewalk and a quick tickle, he was able to tag the giggling boy and head to the porch.

"And that is how Finches say, 'Welcome to our home.'" Porter's joke did nothing to disguise his pride.

"Billy has a pretty good arm on him. Took my breath for a moment."

"Yes. He got it from his mother."

"Obviously."

Forrest took the rocking chair across from Porter. Porter said, "So, how has your day been?"

"Pretty good. I'm actually a bit sore. I spent all morning raking leaves for my dad."

"Oh, yeah. How's he doing?"

"I don't know, Porter. He seemed old, really old today. Of course, he is old. But it was different today."

"I'm sorry. Nothing quite prepares you for how hard it is to watch your own parent age."

They sat in silence, allowing Forrest's worry some space. Although Porter was usually jovial and light-hearted, he was also good at being present for the hard moments. It was one of the many aspects of Porter's friendship that Forrest had come to value over the years. Finally, Forrest said, "Well, when does all the junk food arrive?"

Porter looked at his wrist watch, "Any minute now. Charlotte offered to run and pick it up. She said I deserved delivery after taking care of the kids on my own last week."

"She's been on the road a lot lately, huh?"

"This is how it is every election season. It's prime-time for journalists. She'll be gone some this coming week, as well."

"Does that mean what I think it means?"

"It does if you're thinking the kids will be at the basketball game on Thursday."

Forrest grinned. "I'll get the office betting pool going on whether Billy or Luke will be the first to run onto the court."

The entire office took great enjoyment in how active and clever and downright mischievous Porter's kids were. Because of how much time Charlotte was out of town, the kids were frequently in Hart Building, wreaking havoc. Consequently, they had become the English Department's own mascots.

Porter said, "My money is on Anna. She started to crawl this week."

"That seems too soon." Time had never moved so quickly to Forrest as it had since Porter and Charlotte started a family. Counting time through the lens of how much Billy had grown or Luke was talking or Anna had changed made it seem infinitely faster.

Forrest said, "This whole year is flying by. I can't believe basketball games are starting up."

"Yes, and Lucy strategically does an early-season game so more people will notice we're there. We should change her title to PR director."

"Always making sure we're not forgotten so our funding isn't forgotten."

"Yes, I'm afraid us old, dusty professors forget to think of such things."

Just as the words came out of Porter's mouth, Charlotte drove up with the food. Everyone went into the house to eat and watch the game in the family room that was connected to the kitchen. The boys chased each other around the island, while Porter and Charlotte took turns rescuing Anna from various poor choices.

Stating the obvious, Forrest said, "She's a climber, I see."

Charlotte picked Anna up to point her in the opposite direction from where she had been heading. Her crawling motions never even paused as she was lifted. Charlotte said, "Yes. And do you know how many bookshelves are in the home of an English professor and journalist?"

Although it was counter-intuitive, Forrest never felt more relaxed than he did on the evenings he spent in Porter's house watching games or movies with the closed captions on because no one could hear over the children's racket. At 38, he doubted family life was in his future, but he was content to be Uncle Forrest to Porter's children.

After the game ended, Charlotte and Porter put the kids to bed while Forrest cleaned up the food and dishes from their, in Porter's words, "junk food extravaganza." A half-hour later, Porter came down.

"Well, that is two boys, a baby, and one wife asleep. Poor Charlotte is exhausted from all of the traveling. Thanks for cleaning up, man."

"No problem. Thanks for having me."

"Of course. You know you're always welcome." Porter grabbed a beer and sat down on one of the stools at the kitchen island. Forrest was leaning against the opposite cabinets, finishing the Sun Drop he had opened earlier in the evening. Porter said, "So, Forrest, when I was jogging the other night, I couldn't help but notice you were standing awfully close to Lucy. And she didn't seem to mind. Would you like to talk about that?"

Forrest was momentarily shocked by the question, but he recovered quickly enough. "Just a trick of the lighting, Porter."

Porter swallowed a gulp of beer and - with no fanfare - said, "Bullshit."

"I'm serious, Porter. I can see how it might have looked like something. In my recently-broken-up, addled mind, I was even tricked for a moment. But upon further reflection, I can see clearly that it was nothing. The rest of the week, we were fine."

"Bullshit." Porter was being quite the conversationalist this evening.

Forrest's hands ran roughly through his hair. "What do you want from me, Porter? What am I supposed to say?"

Porter held the beer bottle tightly with both hands. "I want you to be honest with yourself, Forrest. What made you look at Lucy the way you looked at Lucy? It may have been a while since I was single, and seeing as how I almost always have spit-up somewhere on my person, I'm probably not the first person who comes to mind when you think of romance. But I'm not blind. I know what I saw. So I ask again, what made you look at Lucy that way?"

Forrest rested his elbows on the counter and his forehead on the palms of his hands. Was Porter right? Was Forrest deluding himself? The possibility was too unsettling, so Forrest persisted, "I don't know. Probably just my break-up. You know how weird a break-up can make you act."

"But a break-up with Dr. Bugs? You haven't seemed too bothered by it. Considering I've never had a conversation with her that didn't revolve around entomology, can't say I'm surprised."

"She wasn't that bad."

"Not bad. Just boring. At least to people like us. I'm sure she's a real kick at the Environmental Sciences Department Christmas party."

Forrest couldn't help but laugh as he said, "You're right. I wasn't that upset. It just brought up some weird thoughts about Lucy that caught me off guard. That's all. But now, I've worked through it. I have it under control. And you don't need to worry about her or me. We'll be fine."

Porter's head tilted slightly, an eyebrow cocking. "Forrest, I'm not worried. No wait. Let me reword that. I'm not worried about you and Lucy becoming something more. You two are fantastic together. It's part of what makes our office so wonderful. What I'm worried about is this control you speak of. You can't control raw attraction, Forrest. And trying to isn't going to end up in anyone being happier. I worry about you denying yourself - and Lucy - a chance at something more. Especially if there is something there. A spark, or whatever you want to call it."

Forrest picked up a dish from the drying rack and rubbed it with his towel. He didn't know where the dish went, so he set it down and threw the towel onto the counter. "Porter, it just wouldn't be right. That isn't the nature of our relationship." Forrest spoke with a conviction he did not feel, and odds were, Porter could tell.

Porter said, "She's not your student anymore. You know that, right? We are well beyond ethical concerns."

"It's not that." Forrest didn't enlighten Porter on what was in fact the obstacle. He didn't know himself. He just knew Lucy deserved better, and that he wasn't the right person for her.

"Okay." Porter held his palms up. "I've said my piece, and I'll drop it. If you're sure, I trust you."

"Thank you."

"So, how about that fourth quarter?"

Yes, football. Forrest was grateful for the subject change. The fact that Porter had seen something between Forrest and Lucy made it much more difficult to pretend there was nothing there. But even with the outsider perspective, there was little clarity in Forrest's thoughts of Lucy. What he did know, though, was that the boundaries he had set were more important than ever. Especially, if he was doomed to feeling attraction to Lucy O'Shields.

— • —

CHAPTER 7

F orrest stood with Porter and his children, Edith, and Dr. Hubert outside of the basketball stadium. They had agreed to meet at seven o'clock for the game, and it was now five after.

"It's sort of refreshing having Lucy be late instead of one of us," Edith said as she spun Luke around in a circle for the dozenth time. "Although, if she doesn't get here quickly, I will look drunk walking into the game as dizzy as I'm getting."

"More, Aunt Edie. More."

"Come on, kid." Luke's feet lifted from the ground as he swung around again.

Forrest craned his neck towards the parking lot. A large group of students, a few of whom he recognized, were heading in their direction. In the back, barely discernible except by someone who was searching, Forrest saw a straw-berry-blond bun bouncing on top of its wearer's head. Lucy was speed-walking, weaving her way through the horde of students. Eventually, the students turned to go into the stadium, and it was just Lucy walking towards them. As she got closer, the light of the sidewalk lamps gleamed off of her glasses.

Lucy was wearing dark-blue jeans that sculpted to her legs, emphasizing how tall she was. Had she always been this tall? Do women grow in their early 30s? She definitely was not this tall when he met her 10 years ago. She had on a simple PSU t-shirt just barely tucked into the front of her jeans. For the second time in only a week, Forrest noticed how much he enjoyed seeing her out of her work clothes. Forrest shook his head and pulled at the front of his own PSU t-shirt. What he had *meant* to think was that he enjoyed seeing her *in* more casual clothes. She looked relaxed and comfortable in her own skin. Her work attire was always so formal and muted, so unlike her personality.

On one shoulder, Lucy lugged a beach bag that looked as though it would burst at any moment. Getting closer to the group, Lucy said, "Who wants face paint?"

Right as the question was spoken, Forrest noticed two small blue paw prints on her cheek, just below the rim of her glasses. Billy and Luke ran up to her.

Billy tugged at her already encumbered arm as he said, "I want some Lucy!" At the same time, Luke was glued to her leg moaning, "Me first, Woosy."

In the excitement, Anne started kicking violently, wanting to join her brothers. Porter tried repositioning her as she flailed in his arms. "I'm already tired," he grumbled into Forrest's ear.

Lucy said, "Alright, boys. Let me get the things out."

She set her bag on a nearby bench and started passing out foam fingers and pom poms until she got to the face paint at the base of the bag. She looked to Billy and asked, "What would you like painted on your face?"

"A pirate ship stranded on a beach with flying whales attacking it."

Lucy looked to Porter.

"You asked."

"Let's edit that a bit, Billy."

"She's good at editing, Billy. Trust her." Forrest winked at Lucy over the boy's shoulder.

After much debate, Lucy and Billy settled on a whale with an eye-patch. It had nothing to do with the game, but, as Lucy said, "He is the son of an English professor..."

Finishing Billy's blue whale, Lucy moved on to Luke who was perfectly happy to go along with her suggestions. "How about a basketball, Luke? An orange circle is more in line with my artistic ability."

Dr. Hubert walked up to the bench, watching curiously as Lucy began on Luke's basketball. He had on his normal buttoned-up shirt complete with a bow-tie and cuff-links. However, he had pulled a PSU jersey on top. Speaking slowly and deliberately, Dr. Hubert said, "I never did such things in my youth.

But now that I'm nearly 80, why the hell not? Lucy, dear, put this bald head of mine to use."

Lucy looked up to him beaming. "Yes, sir."

As soon as she completed the boys', Lucy painted a spread-out paw print across the expanse of Dr. Hubert's bald head. The whole office, including Porter's kids, gathered around. It wasn't everyday Dr. Hubert had a paw print painted on his head.

Holding up a compact mirror from her purse, Edith said, "Here, Dr. Hubert. Take a look."

In his professorial tone, no different from when he was explaining to his students the various schools of literary criticism, Dr. Hubert said, "It is absolutely marvelous, Lucy."

Forrest said, "I don't think we could possibly look more festive. Are we ready to go in?"

Billy and Luke darted towards the door, each jabbing a pom-pom towards the other as if they were swords. Porter said, "This should be interesting," and the group walked in.

People paused as their crew walked by, opening a path for them like the Red Sea for the Israelites. Mouths gawked and eyes bulged, mesmerized by the image of Dr. Hubert. Graduates from the past 50 years had taken English courses from him.

Forrest paced his steps to Lucy's, who was in the back smiling at her handiwork. Leaning over to her, he said, "You out-did yourself. We look like we belong on a mega-tron somewhere."

"Porter told me the kids would be here. I wanted them to have fun. It was nothing, really."

"It was a little more than nothing." As the compliment left his mouth, Forrest noticed Edith was waving a giant foam finger. "Although, who gave her a weapon?"

She'd obviously heard him, because she turned around and, smiling angelically, said, "It would be more fitting for me if it was a different finger pointing up there, wouldn't it?"

Lucy burst into laughter, and Forrest wished he had been the one to make her laugh. Then he chastised himself for such a petty thought. Just as Lucy was collecting herself, they arrived at their seats and started arranging themselves.

Dr. Hubert and Porter, who was holding Anna, were on one end with Billy between them, Dr. Rose sat in the middle, and that left Lucy and Forrest on the other end with Luke separating them by a seat. As they situated themselves, Lucy said, "Edith, I just noticed you are wearing the other team's colors. Why do I have a sinking feeling that was intentional?"

"I'm making a statement, a peaceful protest, if you will. That coach of theirs is always demanding I lighten up on my grading. This is just a reminder that I don't lighten up."

Forrest said, "That'll show him."

"Actually," Edith said, "he likely won't notice, but it makes me feel better."

Lucy said, "I don't know about that. He sure does find a lot of excuses to come see you."

"He just has an obscene number of players who seem unwilling to read basic English. That's all."

"Oh, Edith," was all Lucy needed to say. It would be futile to tell Edith that even though she was a hard-ass, guys still noticed she was stunning.

Just then, Billy yelled in a voice that easily carried across the bleachers, "I've gotta pee. And poop. I've gotta pee and poop."

The chatter around them quieted slightly, and Forrest was both shocked and delighted to see Porter flush. It was rare for Porter to ever be fazed.

Porter leaned forward to speak down the row. "Who wants a baby so I can take Billy? Or you can have Billy? Billy is definitely on the market, as well."

He was clearly expecting Forrest or Lucy to volunteer, but before they had a chance, Edith eagerly said, "I will. Take Anna, that is." She reached for Anna, faced the baby towards her, and started bouncing her on her knee like an expert. Lucy, Forrest, and Porter all gawked.

"What? A feminist can still like babies."

"That's right Edith," Dr. Hubert chimed in. "As you all know, my wife, the venerable Mrs. Hubert..."

"All bow," Forrest whispered across Luke into Lucy's ear.

"...was the original feminist."

"Absolutely, a woman before her time," Edith agreed.

"And she still loved every moment with our babies."

With these words of affirmation, Edith turned to the baby and began cooing, "That's right, Ms. Anna. And one day you're going to grow up to be big and strong and smarter than the vast majority of men, and Aunt Edie is going to buy you a copy of *The Awakening*, and we're going to have a nice long talk about patriarchal oppression."

Once again, Forrest leaned over to Lucy, almost close enough for her stray hairs to tickle his nose. "Words never before spoken in baby-talk."

Lucy choked on a giggle. Forrest smiled with satisfaction. This time, *he* had made her laugh.

***

The game proceeded as well as Lucy had hoped. The score was reasonably close, so none of the adults got bored. And with lots of popcorn and candy, they were able to keep Billy and Luke relatively close to the group. Anna was given free rein to crawl over the laps of the adults, passing back and forth between arms that were tired by the final buzzer.

Several times throughout the game, Forrest leaned over to comment on the game or make a joke or tell her which players were good students. It felt normal, like they had made their way back to their equilibrium from whatever strange place they had occupied the previous week. Occasionally, Miriam's words crept into Lucy's thoughts. Was she subconsciously hung up on Forrest Graham? Whatever the case, Lucy was grateful for a return to normalcy, for the reemergence of their easy friendship.

This did not, however, erase her awareness of Forrest. In the decade since she had known him, she had rarely seen him not in a button-up shirt and sports jacket of some sort. But, apparently, he was feeling the school spirit tonight, because he had changed to a PSU t-shirt and jeans. The fabric of the t-shirt clung more than the starched shirts he normally wore. She could see that despite being very slender, his arms and back showed the smooth, defined lines of muscles.

As he watched the game, he would occasionally run his fingers and thumb down each side of his beard. It was a habit he did frequently. For as much time as she had stared at that beard, it seemed odd she didn't know how it felt beneath his fingers. Was it coarse or smooth? Prickly or barely textured?

The buzzer went off, interrupting Lucy's musings. The game was over with a PSU victory, and it was time to arrange how everyone would get home. Lucy volunteered to drive Dr. Hubert home since he was not supposed to drive after dark.

With a petulance not unlike Luke when they had denied him a third candy bar, Dr. Hubert said, "My eyes are fine. I don't need to be given a ride."

"Of course, Dr. Hubert. But do you know what Mrs. Hubert would do to us if we let you drive home this late?"

With only a mild growl, he said, "Oh, all right."

Meanwhile, it was agreed that Forrest would go home with Porter to watch the boys while he put Anna to bed. Lucy and Forrest had both been in the Finches' house at bedtime enough times to know it was a two-person job. It was good Forrest had volunteered.

Edith said, "I will see you all tomorrow. I'm heading over to the gym to work out."

Lucy knew her eyes were probably comically large as she said, "At 9:30?"

"I know it's late, but I've got to wind down. You know. The crowds and all."

"Have you ever tried a glass of wine?"

Edith turned toward the gym, waving a hand in their direction as if dismissing Lucy's question. "Goodnight."

Lucy and Dr. Hubert walked to her car. "It was good to be out tonight. You young people keep me fresh."

Lucy decided to not mention that most of them were solidly middle-aged. She supposed that from Dr. Hubert's perspective, the thirties were basically adolescence. "I'm glad you had fun tonight. Your face paint will make this year's department picture truly epic."

"Yes. Like Beowulf."

Lucy laughed. She'd forgotten to be careful about the use of the word "epic" around an English professor. "I confess to hyperbole."

As they approached Lucy's car, Dr. Hubert's eyes widened.

"Lucy, your car does not look as though it will fit me."

Lucy drove the most compact of cars. Unfortunately, Dr. Hubert needed a significant amount of room. With a bit of grunting and Lucy shouting instructions slowly and deliberately, they were finally able to get his seat back as far as it would go and buckle his seatbelt.

Once they were on the road, Dr. Hubert said, "Now that it is just the two of us, I'll give you ten dollars to pull into the Dairy Mart and get me a cone without telling Mrs. Hubert."

Lucy thought for a moment. "Where is this idea coming from?"

His bushy eyebrows came together, erasing the small gap between them. "Extreme deprivation, my child. Extreme deprivation."

Resistance was moot. "How about you keep the ten and just buy me a cone, too."

By the time the two had their ice cream, turned on the interior car lights to ensure no evidence lingered...

"Oops, you dripped a bit."

...and dropped him off at his house, a half-hour had passed since the game ended. Lucy calculated that Forrest and Porter were likely reaching wit's end. Two men against two children and a baby were not good odds. She parked at her apartment, but went to the Finches' back door and let herself in as she called out, "Yoo-hoo. How's it going?"

Just then, Billy ran into the room in his pajamas. He immediately placed a finger over his lips, which Lucy mimicked to confirm her silence, and he crouched behind the family room sofa.

Within a few seconds, Forrest walked in and winked at her. His dimples were on full display as he said, "Lucy, you have arrived just in time. I keep losing track of the Great McFarty Face. And I, Evil Poopy Pants, must find him." His shoulder lifted imperceptibly, and his face clearly conveyed without speaking a word that these names were not of his choosing and he was still not sure how he had become part of this game.

As seriously as she could, Lucy said, "I'm so sorry, but I don't help evil villains, and certainly not ones with poopy pants. Nothing personal. Just a policy I have."

No longer able to contain himself, Billy burst into a fit of giggles, and Forrest ran behind the couch and scooped him up.

"It's time for bed Great McFarty Face."

Barely able to catch his breath, Billy said between giggles, "I want you and Lucy to read my bedtime stories."

"Of course," Lucy said. "What are we reading tonight? *Crime and Punishment?*"

Billy screamed, "No!"

"*Great Expectations?*"

"No!"

Forrest chimed in, "*Moby Dick* is more my style?"

"Guys, no!"

Lucy and Forrest listed off several more classics much to Billy's consternation until they made it to his room, where Billy stacked a small tower of books for them to read. Lucy and Forrest each squeezed on one side of Billy's pillow on his twin-sized bed, and Billy propped between them. They took turns reading the books, neither eager to tell the boy no.

The last book in the stack was the classic, *To the Moon and Back*. It was Forrest's turn, so it was his deep voice that spoke the father's words of love to his young bunny. Billy felt warm between them, and his eyes began to look heavy as the book proceeded. Lucy felt a small lump form in her throat. She swallowed it down quickly. Where had that feeling come from? That momentary sensation that she was looking through a window into a possibility that was so remote it felt hopeless, and yet just possible enough it hurt.

As Forrest read the final words, he looked at Lucy, and for a brief moment, their eyes met without immediately darting away. He swallowed, and then smiled, but the smile did not reach his eyes.

"Goodnight, Forrest and Lucy."

The groggy whisper broke their moment of eye contact, and they each gingerly stood up so as not to disturb Billy, whose eyes were already shut. In silence, Lucy followed Forrest down the stairs and into the kitchen where Porter was opening a can of beer, the hiss of the can loud in the sleeping house.

"We did it," Porter said with a satisfied grin. "All three asleep at the same time. So, you two are pretty much my favorite people right now."

Forrest shrugged. "Well, we only had to take care of the Great McFarty Face, so really it was nothing."

"Be that as it may, I'm still grateful."

There was a momentary pause, Lucy and Forrest a bit abashed at Porter's gratitude. Then, Forrest said, "Oh, I've been meaning to ask, Porter, if you still have that Whitman biography I loaned you a while back?"

Immediately, the image of Miriam holding the tome up in the air Saturday night flashed to Lucy's mind. "Actually, I borrowed it from Porter. It's at my place."

CHAPTER 8

Forrest looked to Porter and saw a gleam in his eyes that made Forrest very nervous.

"Oh yeah. I remember that now. You should go home with Lucy and get it, Forrest."

Forrest turned his face enough that he was certain Lucy would not see and glared at Porter.

Porter grinned in return. "Would you mind, Lucy?"

"Of course not." Forrest turned to Lucy. Was that a blush creeping up her face? In the lamp-lit room, it was difficult to tell. What he did know was that he did not want there to be awkwardness between them, and if he refused to step into her apartment just long enough to grab a book, it could cause damage to their relationship.

Making all of these calculations in only a few seconds, Forrest said, "Thank you. I'd appreciate it. I was going to look over a chapter tonight before I went to bed."

They both bid Porter goodnight as they walked out the back door towards the garage. Forrest was behind Lucy, and he looked back at Porter before he shut the door. Porter raised up his beer bottle in silent cheers to Forrest, to which Forrest shut the door just a fraction too hard.

"I don't believe you've ever seen my apartment, have you?" Lucy asked as they crossed the yard.

"Nope. Never."

"Porter and Charlotte have let me have free rein over it. I've loved learning how to fix things up. It was in pretty rough shape when they bought it."

"My dad has always been handy, but he never really taught me. I think he was afraid if he did I would end up not going to college."

"Well, good news. Fixer-upper skills were not on my mother's agenda for me, either. But you can learn a lot these days with the Internet."

"I'll keep that in mind if I ever decide to take the plunge and buy."

This chatter carried them to the second-floor landing that led into Lucy's apartment. She unlocked the door, and they walked inside. Lucy turned on a lamp near the door. Before Forrest had time to take in the space around him, Clark came clumsily bounding out of a door on the opposite side of the living room.

"I probably should have warned you. This is how Clark greets me."

Clark was so excited to see them both there that he couldn't decide where to go. He ran back and forth in the space that now felt impossibly small, alternating between barking and whimpering.

Forrest began, "Dogs really know how to make a person feel sp..." Just then, Clark's feet slid on the hardwood floors, and he clunked into the side of Lucy's knee. She fell towards Forrest, and he instinctively caught her in his arms.

Immediately, Forrest realized that somewhere in the falling or in the catching, Lucy had turned towards him, and her full breasts were pressed against his chest. Like a lightning bolt, he felt it all over his body. A jolt of awareness of just how perfect she felt crushed against his body. And then his mind, blast his stupid mind, imagined how much more perfect it would be if they were just like this, but with no school-logoed sweaters or t-shirts separating them.

"Oh my goodness. I'm so sorry, Forrest. I'm so sorry."

Suddenly, Lucy was talking in the stream-of-consciousness style she did when she got frazzled.

"Everyone told me to get a lap dog. This apartment is so small. But I, of course, said damn it to practicality and got an 80-pound golden retriever. An abysmally trained one, I might add. I'm so sorry, Forrest."

"Yes, you said that." At least all of the apologizing was causing her to repeatedly say his first name.

In the dim lamp light, Forrest saw a cloud of awareness pass over her green eyes. In her mortification at her dog's behavior, Forrest suspected she had not realized just how much of their bodies were pressed against each other. And then he realized that he had definitely held her longer than was necessary.

"He seems to have calmed down a bit," Forrest said, his voice coming out gruff as he stepped away squeezing Lucy's upper-arms with his hands as if he was setting her back on firm earth. "And I like your abysmally-trained behemoth. You don't need to apologize to me. Ever."

In an attempt to control the sensations still running through his body, Forrest looked around. "So this is where Lucy O'Shields and her noble Clark live. It looks like you. I like it."

"Thank you. We like it, too." She turned on a couple more lamps she had spread throughout the living room. The space glowed like a Grandma Moses painting. "Would you like something to drink?"

"Water would be good. Really cold water."

"On a fall night?"

"Yes. Really cold." Anything to knock his body back under his control. On the wall opposite the front door, Forrest noticed three rows of beautiful wooden bookcases, nothing like the particle board ones from the department store that were in his apartment. "These are beautiful bookshelves. Where did you get them?"

"Well, one night when Miriam was over for supper - we get together about once a week - I mentioned that I needed new bookshelves, and I hated to buy the same cheap ones we always had in our dorm rooms. So Miriam, being Miriam, watched a bunch of YouTube videos, and she and I spent a weekend building them."

"That does sound like Miriam. She has always been resourceful."

"Sometimes I call it resourceful. Sometimes I call it relentless. Depends on my mood."

Forrest smiled. Miriam had been a fantastic student, and now she was back in town, and he heard only good things about all she was doing. Porter talked about her as if she was the best thing to ever happen to Trinity Episcopal Church. She was always advocating for marginalized groups and delivering sermons that pushed boundaries where boundaries needed moved. Lucy's friendship with her seemed to be a place from which she gleaned confidence, and so in Forrest's book, Miriam was the best kind of friend for his Lucy.

It also struck Forrest that Miriam's car might have been the one he saw Saturday evening when he had walked to Porter's house for the game. His smile broadened. Maybe he could ask her? But no. There wasn't a way to do that without coming across stalker-ish. Also, he had no idea why he cared so much. She could have anyone she wished over on a Saturday night.

Lucy's quiet voice cut into his thoughts: "While I'm very proud of the bookshelves, I'd rather you ignore the actual books on the shelves."

"And while I respect your wishes, I don't think I'll be able to resist."

Lucy closed her eyes in resigned horror. "I did invite a book junkie into the house. Go ahead."

Forrest took a finger, and began running it slowly over the spines of books. "Jane Austen. Anthony Trollope. The Brontës. There's nothing to be ashamed of here."

"Keep going."

He moved to the next row. "Aah. *The Governess and the Duke. The Rake and the Wallflower. Once a Duchess.*"

"Bingo."

"I had no idea." He was flummoxed in the best possible way. Lucy liked paperback dime-store romances. It was her secret, and he now knew one of her secrets. Was he giggling? That couldn't be dignified for a middle-aged professor.

Lucy's brows creased in warning, and a finger pointed directly at him. In the same voice she used when Dr. Hubert forgot his medicine or Billy and Luke left toy cars in the front of the office, Lucy said, "Yes, I like romance novels, but you will not tell anyone, or I'll divulge the mystery-novel stash you keep behind your desk."

"You wouldn't."

Her face said she would.

Finally catching his breath, Forrest said, "But really, Luce, you shouldn't be ashamed. Nor should I, for that matter. There is nothing wrong with a little escapist literature."

"In my experience, shame is an integral part of womanhood."

Lucy had spoken the words in jest, but something, maybe it was the tilt of her head or the way her mouth shifted to the right, something told Forrest the joke was tinged with truth. And then, in the pit of his gut, Forrest felt anger swell. He was not used to anger. Fear? Regularly (especially here lately). Doubt? Occasionally. But anger was foreign to him. The anger was not directed towards Lucy. It was towards anyone and everyone who had ever made Lucy O'Shields feel ashamed.

He wracked his brain for something to say, something that would take away that shame. Frustrated with his unending legacy of ineptitude when it came to communicating with women, he turned to the only thing he really knew; he turned to Mark Twain.

"There's no shame in enjoying a good love story. Most of the great American writers were cynics about love, of course. But that's why Mark Twain's my favorite. He and his wife lived one of the great love stories of American history. After she died, he wrote an ode to her, *Eve's Diary*."

"I've never read it."

"It's amazing. And she edited all of his writings. Did you know that he used to put things he knew she wouldn't like into his writing just to see her reaction?"

"Is that why you refuse to adopt the Oxford comma? You enjoy seeing me stress?"

"You'll never know." Whatever he had seen in Lucy before seemed to have passed. He could always count on Mark Twain, he supposed. Forrest said, "Maybe my next article can be on Mark Twain and his wife. Now that I know your favorite genre, I'll write you a romance." Forrest realized only after speaking the myriad ways his words might be interpreted. He added, "So you won't be bored."

"Your writing doesn't bore me, Forrest. I love that I get to edit. But since I do clearly have a depth of experience in romance - books, not life - I'm sure I'll be exceptionally good at editing it."

She was being cheeky, but Forrest wanted to reinforce the truth of her words. "You always do an exceptional job."

Ever since Forrest had first had Lucy as a student, he had been able to sense that she needed to be told when she had done well. Perhaps it was the easy blushing or the talking that got whisper-quiet when she was uncertain, but he had known. So he frequently complimented her work. However, he was beginning to wonder if compliments on editing and her work at the English Department were enough to blunt the shame and insecurity she carried with her.

Not realizing he was going to, Forrest suddenly asked, "Why do you always edit for me?"

***

Lucy was surprised by the question. *Why did she always edit for him?* It was not something she did in her capacity as the English Department's secretary, and she didn't need the extra income he paid her. She did it, simply, because she wanted to.

"I like editing. I know it sounds strange, but I like it for the same reason people become dental hygienists or quality control specialists. I love finding little flaws and moving stuff around and finding a better flow. I like fixing problems. Underneath it all, I enjoy editing for the same reason I sincerely enjoy my job. I like anticipating what people need before they realize it, finding the areas that are missing something or altering a situation where things aren't running smoothly. I'm extraordinarily competent and meticulous to the extreme. It's a gift. A boring gift. But a gift."

"Boring is in the eye of the beholder."

Lucy quirked her eyebrow in question.

"In other words, I'd have to disagree with your assessment."

Lucy felt that her apartment had never been quite this small. Forrest kept giving her compliments, and with each one, the walls closed in a little more.

It was all Clark's fault. She would be able to dismiss the compliments as basic politeness had it not been for the brief moment when she was quite sure every inch of her from the chest down had been pressed against every inch of him. It wasn't that it felt divine. Whether or not it did was completely irrelevant. It was just that it had been so disconcerting.

And when Lucy was disconcerted, she spewed words. As she apologized a thousand times for her dog (her dog who would not be receiving treats for several days), her mind had screamed for her to shut up. But as soon as she did shut up, she became instantly aware of him and all the parts of him that were touching so many parts of her.

Which all led to this moment. This moment in which a man simply telling her she was not boring (how low could her compliment threshold possibly get?) was sending her into a crimson hot flash. Suddenly, she desperately needed water. Frigid cold ice water.

"Ice water," Lucy squeaked. "I forgot to get you ice water." She turned around and walked to her kitchen.

Forrest followed, saying, "No problem. Can I help?"

Oh, good grief, Lucy thought. Her kitchen made the living room look positively spacious. "No, thank you. I've got it."

He leaned against a cabinet, one foot crossing the other. His long legs easily stretched halfway across the kitchen, seeming to engulf the space. One arm crossed his abdomen, while the other hand rested beneath his chin, the thumb aimlessly rubbing back and forth through his whiskers. He looked like Huckleberry Finn all grown-up, pensively recalling his days on the raft.

"What has you smiling?"

Lucy hadn't realized she was smiling. "Oh, nothing really."

"I believe the saying goes a penny for your thoughts. But given inflation, I'll make it a dollar."

He would be relentless. She might as well go ahead and relent. "I was thinking about your beard. It's a nice beard. Very Americana."

"Americana? So basically, I am what I teach?"

Lucy grinned as she mindlessly wiped already-clean counter tops. "We've clearly spent too much time together reading-slash-writing about American literature."

"What makes you say that?"

"I was just thinking to myself that you look like what I'd imagine Huckleberry Finn would look like all grown up."

A laugh sputtered from him, and he said, "I'm going to choose to take that as a compliment."

"As you should."

Bewildered that she'd complimented Forrest's looks through a comparison to Huckleberry Finn (of all people), Lucy refocused on the task at hand. She opened the dishwasher to grab glasses, but noticed it was empty. She'd forgotten that before running out the door to the game, she'd put up the clean dishes. That meant all of the glasses were just above Forrest's shoulder. Of course they were.

"Excuse me, Forrest. I just have to reach..." Physical proximity was unavoidable. Forrest tilted to give her room, but she still brushed him with the side of her torso, warmth radiating off of him. A spark of heat spread directly from him to her center.

Extra ice was in order.

Turning to the fridge, Lucy figured her best chance for regaining composure would be to make normal, everyday conversation. What could be more mundane than talking about parents?

"So, how's your dad doing? I haven't heard from him this week. Didn't you go over there Saturday?"

"Yes, I raked his yard for him and hauled the leaves away. Afterward, he and I sat in the kitchen and talked. He made me the same lunch he made me for the vast majority of my childhood." Forrest's face took on a look of distaste. "Bologna sandwiches."

"Your favorite, clearly."

He looked directly into her eyes to check for sarcasm. He must have found it there, because he said, "Oh, yes. The finest in culinary delights."

"Other than fixing a less-than-favorite lunch, how was he doing?"

Lucy carried the glasses of ice water to the small dining table that separated her kitchen from her living room space. It was a round Formica table from the 1940s that she'd found at a local antique fair. Around it were four metal chairs, each with olive green leather cushions. It was a favorite piece in her apartment because of its retro flare. They sat opposite each other as Forrest began voicing concern.

"Not good, I'm afraid. He was shakier than usual. His voice sounded like gravel, and he was moving slowly. He never offered to help me outside. Not that I minded, of course. I was fine doing it myself. It's just unusual for him to not insist he can help. But the worst thing I didn't even notice at the time. It's just looking back on Saturday that I keep thinking about it."

"What's that?"

"His skin. I'm sure I'm just being paranoid because of how much he has drunk over the years, but he looked, I don't know, yellowish. Just off, I guess."

"I'm sorry, Forrest. Should he see a doctor?"

"I called Gracie Sunday afternoon to ask her opinion. She drove down there Monday to see for herself. She is trying to encourage him to set up an appointment, but he's being ornery. He insists it's just regular aging, but I don't know about that."

Lucy had met Gracie a handful of times over the past ten years. She would occasionally stop by campus to see Forrest if she was driving through town for a work trip or to take their father to a doctor's appointment. Just from the few times Lucy had seen the two together, it was clear they shared a significant bond. Forrest only had good things to say about his sister. Lucy sometimes wondered how someone who so clearly could maintain a wonderful familial relationship with a sister could not maintain a romantic relationship for more than six months. She would never ask Forrest this question directly, but she supposed it wouldn't hurt to ask a question indirectly.

"You and Gracie seem close. You're lucky to have her right now. Have you always been close?"

"Yes. Although, the nature of our relationship has changed throughout the years. Originally, it was more paternalistic. She was trying her hardest to be a replacement for my mother, and at times," his eyes squinted as if it was painful to say the words out loud. "And at times, she was also trying to replace dad, too. He was never a mean drunk. He didn't hit us or anything. But, there were times when he was just absent. Even if he was bodily there, he wasn't there."

"So Gracie would be there?"

"Yes. And now she is married with two beautiful children and she refuses to ever let me spend a holiday alone."

"Whether or not you want to?"

"Whether or not I want to." Forrest winked as he took a drink of water.

"But Gracie agrees with you? She's worried, too?"

"Unfortunately, yes." They were quiet for a moment, and then Forrest said, "It must have been hard going through your mother's sickness without a sibling to support you."

Lucy thought back to that dark time in her life. She had been 25 years old, in her third year working for the English Department.

It had been a quiet, summer Friday in the office when her mother called to invite her over for lunch the following day, saying she needed to talk with Lucy. It wasn't unusual for Lucy to be summoned by her mother in this way. It might be that one of the boys with whom she had grown up had just broken up with a girlfriend and was back on the market. Or a women's magazine had a diet that promised an astonishing ten pounds gone in three days. Or her mother wanted to announce the most recent engagements of girls from her class to amp up the pressure to "at least start trying to find a man."

On the next day, a humid, sweltering Saturday morning, Lucy had driven south of Paducah just across the Tennessee border to her parents' rural home. She was fully anticipating an uncomfortable conversation about her weight or dating prospects. What she'd found, though, was her mother looking even smaller than normal but still dressed to perfection in a crisp white-collar shirt tucked into a tight and flattering pencil skirt. Lucy's father had also been there, his complexion that day as pale as her mother's shirt. Typically, he allowed Lucy's mom to guide conversations, but that day, his silence was like the ominous tune scoring a dramatic film.

Lucy's mother placed a salad in front of Lucy and her father, but she refused to have one herself. Lucy made a joke about how a salad for lunch would hardly cause her pants to not fit. And then her mother had said, "I'm not hungry. Apparently, telling one's daughter that one has terminal cancer takes one's appetite."

Thus, Lucy had found out her mother was no longer invincible. She'd always looked so petite, as if a wind might carry her away. It suited her mother to camouflage her fierceness in fragility. Her version of femininity worked best when the illusion was maintained that the female might need rescuing at any moment. However, that year, it was no illusion. And over the coming six months, it felt as though the wind did just carry her away.

About six months later, she died of an aggressive lung cancer. Her mother had quit smoking in public or socially decades before when it went out of vogue, but she continued the habit in secret in the family home's garage and on walks in the nearby woods. Lucy always figured it was a weight management strategy, pure and simple. There was nothing her mother had feared more than gaining a few pounds, and she had seen many of her friends quit only to put on ten or twenty pounds through the process. It probably never occurred to her that the smoking might cause something worse than the weight gain she would face if she quit. In fact, knowing her mother, she had probably thought that since she wasn't smoking in front of people, it didn't even count. Her mother had lived her life building an image for others to see. What happened behind the curtain was hardly real to her.

Lucy shook her head, trying to escape the reverie that consumed her anytime her mother's illness was mentioned. "I'm sorry, what did you say, Forrest?"

"Just that it must have been hard when your mother got sick. Not having siblings."

"It was hard in the way it's always hard to lose a parent. But I didn't feel alone. You and Dr. Hubert and Porter and Edith wouldn't allow that. Never have four absent-minded professors been so solicitous." She smiled. This was the part of the memory that made it bearable. "Dr. Hubert would sneak me little shot glasses of Kentucky bourbon anytime I looked sad or had received more bad news. It's really a wonder he didn't turn me into an alcoholic that year." Just as the words left her lips, Lucy realized the insensitivity of her quip. Her eyes wide, she immediately said, "I'm so sorry. I'm such an idi-..."

But before she could finish her self-admonition, Forrest dismissed her apology with a wave of the hand. "You are *not* an idiot. It's fine - really. Besides, Dr. Hubert does keep a fine stash of Kentucky bourbon. Wasn't it Edith's first year in the department?"

Relieved Forrest was - as ever - not easily offended, Lucy answered, "Yes, she was fresh off of her Harvard defense. I was so intimidated by her back then."

"She still terrifies me."

Lucy rolled her eyes as she laughed. "Yeah, right. We all know there's no bite behind that bark."

"But the bark is deafening."

Lucy sipped her water. "The funny thing is, I think she was more afraid of me than I was of her because she didn't know what to do with a woman going through losing her mother. She ended up making gestures of sympathy that were completely incongruous with what you'd expect from her."

Forrest's thumb was moving back and forth across his water glass, drawing lines in the condensation while he listened to Lucy's musings. "Like what?"

"She got me one of those really hokey stuffed bears they sell next to the greeting cards that said 'Thinking of You.'"

"You can't be serious." Forrest looked as though he had just received proof the moon landing was indeed a hoax. "A stuffed bear?"

"Yes. A stuffed bear. Coming from her, someone I didn't expect to notice my pain or care, it was really special. I actually broke down crying and hugged her."

"I know I shouldn't laugh right now, but that was probably her worst nightmare."

"I know, right?" And then they were both laughing, a deep, cathartic laugh. Lucy took her glasses off for a moment to wipe at a tear. She wasn't sure if it was from laughter or one of the other myriad emotions the conversation conjured. She slowly put them back on.

At some point over the past seven years, Lucy had arrived at a spot where she could take joy in memories from her darkest chapter, and it was due to her co-workers, of all people. "And then there was Porter and you. Candles and flowers kept popping up around the office until it was a level of cluttered that would daunt Marie Kondo."

Forrest slapped both hands onto the table, and said, "You knew that was us?"

"I suspected. Now I know."

"We didn't know what else to do. But we knew you liked those two things, so we came up with a rotation where we kept you well supplied."

"I'd say so. I'm still burning through the candles."

"I preferred buying the flowers. I've always hated buying them for girl-friends. I never know what they'll like, and it feels cliché, like I'm checking a good-boyfriend box. But that year, when it was my turn to get them for you, I'd go to that little flower shop across from the campus book store."

"Woodley's Florals?"

"That's the one. And I'd walk around and buy whichever stood out that day. I didn't worry, because you always seemed to like them."

"I didn't just like them. I loved them. I could feel you guys cared. It helped."

"Good." It was a simple reply, but it brought Lucy's eyes directly to his. She didn't know why he struggled to buy flowers for women with whom he was romantic. She didn't know why it was easier to for him to buy them for her. But she suspected it was because there was something good between them. Something simply good.

Forrest broke the eye contact first, taking a final few gulps of his ice water. "I'd better be on my way. The book?"

"I'll grab it for you."

She got up and retrieved the book from where Miriam had left it Saturday night. Forrest stood up and stretched, yawning. The hem of his t-shirt rose an inch above the waist of his pants, and Lucy glimpsed a dusting of hair, the same light brown as his beard. It was a mere inch of skin, but Lucy was certain that if she were ever to see Forrest without a shirt on, she would find him beautiful. She looked down at the book, running her thumb over the embossed title.

"Thanks for the water and the talk. It was nice."

He reached out for the book. She gave it to him, careful to not brush hands this time. "Of course."

"I'll see you tomorrow at work." He was opening the door to head out.

"Alright," Lucy said. "Goodnight, Forrest."

His hand paused on the door knob, one foot over the threshold. "I like that you're saying my name now. Thank you."

The door shut.

Lucy looked down at Clark, who had awoken just in time to see Forrest leave. His eyes looked into her own, their expression mournful, as if Forrest leaving had left a gaping hole in their living room.

"Come on, Clark. Let's go to bed."

Not that she was going to be able to sleep.

CHAPTER 9

F orrest arrived at the office five minutes after noon with his mind singularly focused on the sandwich sitting in the office fridge for his lunch. His stomach had been growling so loudly, he was sure the first three rows had heard it throughout the lecture he had just delivered. He'd skipped breakfast that morning, having overslept after reading three chapters instead of one in the Whitman book he retrieved from Lucy's place the night before. The extra reading wasn't because the book was a page-turner. Even to an expert in 19th-century American literature, it was the sort of book that generally aided in sleep. But Forrest had found himself wound tight after his conversation with Lucy.

It wasn't particularly unusual for he and Lucy to talk, and for the most part, the things she had shared about her mother's passing had not been news to him. After all, he had been there from the day she heard the diagnosis to the graveside service. All of them had been.

No, it wasn't the content of the discussion that had kept him awake. It was the electricity he had felt in the air much of the evening. It was how much he'd wanted to make her laugh or make her see herself through his eyes. Though he wanted to deny it, Forrest was forced to acknowledge that he was seeing Lucy differently

He'd always known she was beautiful, always suspected she didn't know it, but now her beauty had become intoxicating, keeping him up late into the night no matter how many pages he read. He deeply wished she was cognizant of how vibrant her unruly, strawberry waves were and how rich was the green of her eyes. He wanted to thank her for only wearing clear lip glosses that didn't hide her perfectly tinged lips from his view.

And Forrest wouldn't even allow his mind to start enumerating the many desirable attributes of the rest of her body. He didn't tower over her like he did most women, and when she'd fallen into him, each part had lined up perfectly with him. Those were the thoughts that were strictly off limits.

No, he couldn't allow it, because Lucy was so much more than any of the women he had casually dated over the years. Each break-up had been a mildly irksome loss at worst, and more often, a relief. Losing Lucy would be cata-strophic, and Forrest was not a man prone to hyperbole.

As he entered the office, Forrest was surprised to find their normally bustling office apparently abandoned. He saw a sticky note with Lucy's handwriting stuck to his door, so he went to retrieve it. It said, "Forrest, your dad called, and he has a doctor's appointment next Friday. Good, right? I'm out for the rest of the day. See you tomorrow, Lucy."

It was good. Forrest felt a small tension release.

He then headed towards the office mini-fridge to get his lunch. As he bent over, Forrest heard whispers coming from Dr. Hubert's office. Obviously, the office was not empty after all. Curious, Forrest decided to poke his head in and see who was still around. He walked over and knocked gently. The whispering stopped instantaneously.

"Hello?" he said.

Dr. Hubert's booming voice vibrated through the door, "Come in."

When Forrest opened the door, he was surprised to find not only Dr. Hubert, but also Edith and Porter gathered around his desk. They all wore the expres-sions of cheerleaders who had been caught gossiping about the coach.

"What are you all up to?"

Porter's eyes darted back and forth between Dr. Hubert and Edith, both of whom were ignoring him. Dr. Hubert had picked up a student's paper from his desk and was staring at it intently without his eyes moving in the slightest. Edith was suddenly engrossed in her cuticles.

Forrest expected Porter would be the easiest to break. "Porter? What's going on?"

"Nothing. We're just chatting. Weren't we?"

Dr. Hubert cupped a hand around the back of his ear to signal he hadn't heard a thing. The old man could hear better than any of them.

Forrest looked to Edith whose face hid nothing of the battle that was clearly taking place within. Looks like he'd miscalculated. Edith would cave first.

"Come on, boys. Let's just tell him. We don't even know if it is anything to worry about."

"What are you talking about?"

"It's just Lucy," Edith said.

"What about Lucy might not be anything to worry about?" He was worried. Worst-case scenarios stampeded through his mind. Was she moving? Ill? Had some ridiculous online dating app paired her with a sleazy jerk?

Porter said, "Edith had the quarterly department chairs' meeting today, and she overheard Dr. Burke's secretary announcing she is retiring and that they're hopeful Lucy would be taking her place."

Forrest felt something worse than panic. It was a squeeze right in the center of his chest, a hurt. What would this office look like without Lucy in the center of it? As sad of a commentary as it was on his personal life, this office was his life, and it was a life he liked. Trying his very hardest to not sound like a petulant child, Forrest said, "That can't be. She would have told me. We talked last night after the game. She was with me and Porter. Tell them, Porter. She didn't say anything about leaving us."

Porter glanced at Dr. Hubert and Edith again, but his expression looked somehow guilty. "You're right, Forrest. She didn't say anything. But it may not be a done deal, or she may not be ready to tell us. It's likely she hasn't even made the decision. We just don't know."

"And guys," Edith said, "we can't ask her. Do you hear me, Forrest?"

"Why not?"

"Because, Porter's right. She might be thinking this through. She's probably trying to make a decision, and she doesn't need us influencing her thinking. This is for her to decide."

"Yes, but we should let her know that we don't want her to leave. That we love her being here." It was official. He had crossed into petulant-child territory. But what else was he to do when they were all looking at each other as though he was a child? Why was Edith lecturing him on what to say or not say?

Dr. Hubert had been silent, but Forrest knew it wasn't because he couldn't hear. Surely, he would understand the gravity of the situation. "Dr. Hubert?"

Dr. Hubert crossed his hands along the top of his broad stomach, leaned back in his chair, and shut his eyes. Dr. Hubert often shut his eyes when he was about to say something important. He was known to have delivered entire lectures without opening an eye. "Forrest, son, you know perhaps better than any of us how brilliant our Lucy is. She deserves promotions and money and accolades and all of the good things a career can offer. All, unfortunately, things we do not have the capacity to give her."

"Of course she does," Forrest said in almost a whisper.

"If she feels this job opportunity would open doors or be fulfilling or offer challenges she would be eager to meet, we must give her our full blessing."

He was right, of course. Forrest wanted Lucy to have all the good possible, in her career and every other arena of life.

The professors sat in silence, each one processing Dr. Hubert's words. Finally, Porter said, "We all know she is too good for this job. She should be no less than the chief-of-staff for the White House."

Edith smiled ruefully as she said, "Yes, but we also know that this office does not run without her."

"Can you even imagine the job posting we'd have to write to have any chance at replacing her. All applicants need a background in child care, editing, trauma counseling..." Porter eyed Edith significantly. She rolled her eyes in return.

Then, Dr. Hubert said, "And geriatric care."

They all were briefly stunned before laughing. Clearly, his wisdom did not stop at self-awareness like so many.

As the laughter died down, Porter said, "As much as I worry about how we will manage without her - and believe me, I'll be losing sleep over it - I'm more worried that one day a dream job will come knocking at her door, and she'll turn it down because of us."

His eyes singularly focused on Forrest, making Forrest squirm. Lucy's devotion was spread equally among them all. Surely, if they were holding her back, the fault didn't lie solely at Forrest's feet. Unable to bear Porter's scrutiny any longer, Forrest averted his eyes only to find Edith and Dr. Hubert also staring at him.

"What?" He threw up his hands. When had he lost all impulse control? "I promise. I won't say anything to her."

"Alright," Edith said. "It's agreed. We all stay silent and hope for the best. For Lucy. Whatever is best for Lucy."

They each nodded in agreement, even as Forrest wondered why he'd been the center of their collective focus.

***

Lucy left the office a little before lunch. Forrest had been in the office about an hour that morning, and they seemed to have reached an unspoken agreement that all was fine. Just fine. Things were completely normal. Lucy was content ignoring whatever bothersome tingles she had felt in her apartment the previous evening.

Lucy still hadn't made a decision on the President's Office job, and for reasons she preferred to ignore (just set them over there with the tingles), she had yet to tell anyone in her office that the prospect was on the table. As of now, she was quite certain that she, Miriam, and President Burke were the only people privy to the knowledge.

Needing to get away from the office and any residual tingles she might or might not be feeling while sharing that space with a certain professor, Lucy took off the afternoon. She planned to lunch with her father, a ritual they had every time he came to town for university business. Later in the afternoon, she'd head over to Trinity Episcopal to help Miriam. Thanksgiving was just around the corner, and Miriam was panicked over the chaotic state of her church's food pantry. Lucy planned to spend the rest of the day and perhaps into the evening at the church helping Miriam completely take apart and then put together the pantry in preparation for the holiday rush.

But first, lunch. Her father was driving up from Tennessee for a PSU Board of Trustees meeting, and Lucy hoped to use the time to determine just how much her shiny new job offer had to do with her father's position.

Lucy wasn't sure she'd learn anything that might bear on her decision. However, she felt like she needed to know. Nepotism made her uncomfortable, and she supposed a part of her just wanted to be certain she had earned the job offer on her own merit.

Lucy arrived at the same cafe where she had lunched with President Burke. As she was turning off her car, her father pulled up next to her and parked. They both got out of their cars and greeted each other in front of the cafe.

"Hello. How's my Lucy?" he said as they embraced.

"I'm good, Dad. It's nice to see you."

It was good to see him. Although they only lived a little over an hour apart, they didn't see each other often. Lucy always got the sense that her father didn't quite know what to do with her. Perhaps it was that she was female or her bookish nature (he was a business man through and through) or how different she was from the Southern-Belle-type women to whom he was accustomed. Whatever the cause, meaningful conversations and deep connection were elusive in their relationship.

However, they shared the harrowing experience of the six months that led to Lucy's mother's death. And although he had not been the world's most attentive father, he had always been kind to Lucy. If he were a more emotive, outspoken person, Lucy suspected he would have curtailed some of her mother's more drastic attempts at improving Lucy (weight loss shakes for a high school student's breakfast?). Unfortunately, his withdrawing personality was no match for the battle engine that had been Lucy's mother.

Small talk surrounding the weather, PSU sports, and the afternoon's Board meeting took them through the walk to their table and waiting for their food. Since her father was there for a board meeting, he was dressed in a suit. It looked good on his tall frame. Lucy's body type and reddish-hair had both been gifted from her father. She was happy to note that he looked healthy and strong, but this thought was immediately followed by concern for Mr. Graham. With each phone call, his voice seemed weaker and more gravelly.

Once the food arrived, Lucy decided it was time to dive into her question.

"Dad, I had something I needed to talk with you about."

"Anything, sweetheart."

"Dr. Burke met with me a couple of weeks ago."

"Yes?"

"And he offered me the job of running the President's Office. It comes with a significant pay raise."

Her father's eyes lit up. "That's wonderful, Lucy. Just wonderful. No one deserves it more than you. There isn't a single time I step on that campus that I don't hear someone sing your praises."

"It *is* wonderful. An honor, really. I was just wondering, Dad, if maybe you had anything to do with the job offer. It sort of came out of the blue."

He set his utensils down, giving Lucy his full attention. "Lucy, I confess Dr. Burke did tell me about the job, but only after he'd asked you."

Lucy pushed up her glasses as a smirk lifted one side of her lips. "So the surprise you just expressed was entirely feigned?"

He picked up his fork and stabbed a tomato. "Yes. How'd I do?"

"Oh, very convincing, Dad."

"Thank you. You know, I starred in my high school's production of *The Music Man* many years ago."

"So you've said a time or two." Or a thousand.

His smile clearly conveyed that he was reading her mind.

Lucy was glad to hear the offer came before her father knew of the position. At least nepotism was, for the most part, off the table. Lucy would be worried the offer was still only connected to her father's status if she were not confident in the job she'd done and continued to do for the English Department.

They ate a few more bites in silence, and then her dad asked, "Lucy, will you take the job?"

The hesitation in his voice gave Lucy pause. It was not in her father's nature to push his opinions on her, but she realized she very much wanted to know what he thought. "I feel like you have an opinion, Dad. I want to know what you think I should do."

"Lucy, you are so gifted. You should be moving up whatever ladder you happen to be standing on. I hope you take it because you deserve no less."

"Thank you, Dad." His compliment was sincere, and so was his wish for her future. While it had not been in his nature to stand up to her mother's more harmful traits, it was not because he had shared her opinions. Lucy suspected that for all the flaws her mother had seen in Lucy, her father had seen only the good. As much as she mourned the loss of her mother, she was grateful that she was finally hearing her father's voice in her life.

"You never answered my question, though. Are you going to accept the job?"

Lucy wanted to run her hands through her hair like Forrest did when he was stressed, but her bun would never survive the assault. Instead, she put a hand on each side of her face and said, "I just don't know, Dad. I don't know."

"What's causing you to hesitate?"

"I love the people I work with. I love my job. I'm not a huge fan of the unknown, as you might remember."

They both smiled. Lucy had never been an adventurous child. She was always too careful and mindful to throw caution to the wind.

She continued, "I still have a couple of weeks to decide. I can't imagine that anything would happen in the next few weeks to alter my decision. Unless the heavens open up and an angel tells me what to do, I'm sort of stuck making a decision with a lot of good points on both sides."

"Whatever you decide, I'll support you, Lucy. Just make sure you're not holding yourself back because you don't trust yourself or you're scared. If you take this job, you will be wonderful. Okay?"

"Okay, Dad."

Yes, his voice was good to hear.

***

Lucy pulled into a parking space in front of the vivid red door of Trinity Episcopal Church. It was a Gothic-inspired behemoth of a building. A particularly whimsical architect built Trinity Episcopal Church in the 1920s with the goal of making Western Kentuckians feel they'd walked out of their American landscape directly into an ancient, Anglican cathedral in the motherland.

The grounds were immaculately manicured, and Lucy weaved through the stone walkways to the parish offices, the entrances of which were in the inner courtyard. Lucy pushed on a heavy, solid-wood door cut into a pointed arch. Black brass hinges stretched dramatically across the wood planks.

A secretary greeted her with an overly-friendly smile. "Hello, Lucy. How are you today?"

Lucy came around enough that the staff knew her, but she was unsure of their names. Southern church ladies had always made Lucy nervous. They were so often reflections of the woman Lucy's mother had wanted her to be. However, Lucy reminded herself that anyone overly judgmental was unlikely to last in a church where Miriam Howatch was leading. Unable to recall the woman's name, Lucy said, "I'm good, thanks. Is Miriam in her office?"

"She's already headed over to the food pantry. Do you know your way?"

"Behind the kitchens?"

"That's correct! Let me know if you girls need anything."

Lucy thanked her and headed back across the courtyard to the fellowship building that housed the kitchen and food pantry. Lucy was not a regular member in the way Porter was, but on the Sundays Miriam delivered sermons, Lucy often came to hear her friend. Knowing Miriam as well as she did, she could listen to a sermon and hear all the places where Miriam was tempering herself. She could hear where Miriam would have used profanity in normal conversation to emphasize a point, or where her sermons were translating her rage over an injustice into a measured but forceful message to which her congregants would be more receptive.

Miriam was a justice-oriented individual, and it seeped into everything she did. But where she might rant and rave about racial discrimination or poverty on a Saturday night, her sermons were highly controlled, structured to deliver the message in a way that was affective without alienating. She stepped on toes, and Lucy knew Miriam dealt with more blow-back than she told Lucy about, but she was very good at preaching a gospel of love and justice with a precision that brooked no argument.

When Lucy arrived, Miriam was already busy carrying food out of the pantry and laying it on the tables in the fellowship area. There, they would inventory and sort before rearranging it all. Miriam's sleeves were rolled up on a sky-blue clergy shirt with a tab collar. Just beneath the rolled sleeve, Lucy saw the roots of the tree that was tattooed on her upper arm. It had taken a few Friday nights over the course of their senior spring semester for Miriam to have that tattoo completed.

"Are you ready for some help?"

Miriam had not heard Lucy approaching, and she startled slightly. "I am ready for you, but this place is a disaster. You might not be ready for me."

"Bring it on. I could use something to get me out of my head for a bit."

"Well, in that case, do I have some grunt work for you." Miriam pumped her arm, looking like an oddly devout Rosie the Riveter. Lucy chuckled as she entered the pantry and lifted a heavy box of canned corn.

For the next few hours, Miriam and Lucy worked companionably side by side, carrying food into the fellowship hall, organizing it, and documenting the church's inventory. Then, it was time to take it all back into the pantry, but to return it with a level of organization that made Miriam and Lucy both feel they had accomplished something significant.

After the work was done, Miriam called in a pizza for delivery, and they opened a bottle of wine. Thankfully, the stereotypes about Episcopalians and wine are deeply rooted in truth. There were always a few bottles lying around.

Sitting at a table in the large, empty fellowship hall, Lucy stared at the loaves and fishes mosaic beneath the point of the vaulted ceiling. Ornamentation had not been spared in the non-worship spaces. There was no spot in Trinity Episcopal Church where one did not feel transported to a different time and place, a place where reverence was shown tangibly, where the spiritual and the physical were intrinsically connected. Except for the pantry, that is. The pantry was a pretty normal pantry.

"What are you smiling about?" Miriam asked as she returned from the front of the church where the pizza had been delivered.

"Nothing, really. Just enjoying the space. I was thinking about how divine it all is."

"Well, it wasn't all divine until the past hour. Now, though, the pantry is truly divine."

Lucy snorted as she reached for a slice of their favorite spinach alfredo pizza. "You're right. The whole place was a dump until we organized the pantry"

For Miriam, bulldozing her way through a seemingly insurmountable task was the best way to spend a day. Being her friend could be exhausting with so much energy pulsing through her at all times. But Lucy admired her friend's intensity. It was a direct contrast to the ideals of femininity she herself had never been able to achieve. Unlike Lucy, Miriam never even reached for such ideals. She'd rejected the entire premise from the beginning.

Having the space to themselves, they each used a chair to prop their feet up as they ate their pizza and sipped on wine. They talked about the sermon Miriam was currently writing and Lucy's most recent thoughts on her job prospect.

Lucy said, "Did I tell you I talked to my dad earlier this week?" Lucy and her father talked on the phone about once every week or so. Although she missed her mother, she was grateful that in her absence, she now got to hear her father's voice more often.

"Oh yeah? Did he know about the job offer?"

"Apparently, Dr. Burke told him after he'd offered it to me. I know it's vain, but I was relieved the offer didn't originate with my dad."

"It's not vain. What does he want you to do?"

"Take it, for sure. He said all sorts of nice-dad stuff about how gifted he thinks I am, and how I should be getting paid more, and so on." Although Lucy's tone was making light of the conversation, she appreciated his affirmation. When her mother had been alive, he'd been quiet in the onslaught of her constant criticism of Lucy. Now, he seemed to be making up for the lost time.

Miriam said, "Did the conversation give any clarity? Do you know what you're going to do?"

"Nope." Lucy didn't have much more to say than that. She and Miriam had already thoroughly hashed out the pros and cons. Now, Lucy was waiting for the clouds to part and a divine message to be delivered in indisputable terms.

Miriam set down a half-eaten slice of pizza and wiped her fingers on a napkin. She said, "How was the basketball game last night? I was sorry I missed it this year. It's always fun to see a bunch of English professors outside of their natural habitat."

"Oh my goodness. I forgot to tell you. Dr. Hubert let me paint a Wildcat paw print on his bald head."

"No! And I missed it? Stupid deacon's meeting."

Lucy laughed. "You probably shouldn't say that too loud in a church building."

"I've said way worse, and lightening hasn't struck yet."

"That I believe."

"Was there anything else I missed out on?"

Lucy thought about Forrest's leather and pine scent lingering in her apartment for hours after he left as she lay sleepless on the sofa. "Forrest liked the bookshelves we built."

Miriam's eyes bulged. "Why was Forrest Graham in your apartment?"

"To get the Walt Whitman book. It was nothing, really. We just sat for a while talking and then he left."

Miriam sipped from her wine glass and pursed her lips in thought. "No itty-bitty zings?"

Lucy didn't respond immediately. No, there had not been itty-bitty zings. That was not what she would call what had happened when she'd found herself pressed against his body or when they had brushed against each other in the kitchen. Nor was it the appropriate label for the moments of shared laughter or reminiscing about her mother's death. Bigger words, words rife with meaning and significance were needed. Words that she could not yet identify and that she wasn't willing to share even with her dearest friend. Finally, she said, "No itty-bitty zings this time."

Miriam's eyes were knowing. Without words, she communicated her awareness that the answer was incomplete, but that she wouldn't press further. For all of her aggressive energy, Miriam never turned it towards individuals, towards manipulating or pressing others. Instead, she exhausted it on messy pantries. Lucy rested in her grace, appreciating the space to not speak.

Finally, Lucy said, "I need to head home. Clark is probably about to explode."

"With desire for companionship or pee?"

"Take your pick. I'll see you Saturday night?"

"Absolutely. My place this week. What are we watching? It's been a while since we watched *Pride and Prejudice*."

Lucy thought for a moment. "No, let's do something else. Maybe...*Saving Private Ryan*?"

"That isn't our normal fare."

"No, but a change of pace sounds nice."

And now was just not the time for Elizabeth Bennett, Mr. Darcy, and a thousand zings.

CHAPTER 10

L ucy sat at her desk clicking through tabs of Gap shirts she'd pulled up for consideration. She was rewarding herself with a fifteen-minute break after spending the entire morning teaching Dr. Hubert to navigate an online discussion board. She turned down the shot of bourbon he'd offered her in thanks (it was mid-afternoon!) and the caramel candies (Miriam had made pasta for their weekly dinner the night before - big bowls of pasta), and opted for retail therapy, instead.

It had been a week since the basketball game. This morning, Lucy had awoken in her robin's-egg blue bedroom, crawled out from under the tufted white comforter, tip-toed across the chilled hard-word floor, opened her antique wardrobe, and found nothing that interested her in the slightest. Why was there only navy blue, gray, and black in there? Being best friends with a priest hardly made one a nun. At 32 years of age, the rebellion she'd been raging against Southern femininity was starting to lose its steam. Not that she was going to go purchase a halter-top dress with cherries printed on it. But a pink or (*gasp*) teal blouse might be nice.

Unfortunately, she had no choice this morning outside of drab or a little less drab. She settled on a gray turtle neck, black pants, and nude flats.

"What are you looking at?"

Edith's voice made Lucy jump in her chair. Lucy swiveled the chair around to face Edith's doorway. "Clothes. I think I might want to wear an actual color."

Edith stood up straighter and clapped her hands together, looking positively giddy. "*I think I might* is way too many qualifiers. Come with me. You'll wear color today, Lucy O'Shields."

The only thing that made Edith this gleeful was control. "You're making me nervous."

Edith swept her hand towards her office and said, "Just come with me."

Lucy acquiesced, walking slowly past Edith into the office. Edith shut the door behind Lucy as she said, "I have the perfect top."

Lucy wanted to clear up a few things. "Two things. First, why do you have extra tops in your office? And second, let me be crystal clear: you are not giving me a shirt."

Edith waved a dismissive hand. "Consider it a loan. I had an order come in today, and one of the shirts would be perfect for you. The coloring, the cut. Trust me."

Edith was always immaculately turned out. She was professional at all times, but she allowed her individuality and self-confidence to shine through her wardrobe choices. She was unafraid to add a statement piece or juxtapose something overtly feminine, like lace or florals, against something structured and masculine. It was a gift enviable by any standard, and Lucy decided that if she was going to trust someone to pick out clothes for her, it should be Edith. After all, Miriam had probably not looked at clothes without tab collars in half a decade.

Edith bent over in her massive chair, digging underneath her desk. Finally, she pulled out a plastic shipping bag bulging to its limit. "I cannot resist cold-weather clothes, and 'tis the season." Her childlike enthusiasm made Lucy grin. She was considered the ultimate hard-ass by her students and colleagues outside of the English department. Lucy supposed she and the rest of the office were in on the ruse. For reasons she did not know, Edith needed to project invincibility to the world outside her inner-most circle. Lucy was just glad to be on the inside.

After digging for a while, Edith pulled out a small plastic bag from within the larger package. "Ah hah! I found it."

"Resistance would be futile at this point, right?"

"Absolutely. Don't even try." Edith used a pair of scissors to open the smaller bag and remove a tag. She held up an emerald green top in a satiny fabric. There was a v-neck Lucy immediately feared would be cut too low, but other than that, the style was elegantly simple: long sleeves subtly gathered at the wrists and a hem that was slightly lower in the back and would be flattering un-tucked with her skinny black pants. "Here. I'll step out, and you try it on."

Lucy held the shirt up at her shoulders and looked down at the beautiful color. "Are you sure, Edith? Shouldn't I be doing something more productive?"

"As chair of the department, I declare this to be productive."

"Who could argue with that?"

"I'll be at your desk. There's a mirror on the back of the door because I'm vain, and I have a debilitating fear that I will one day walk into a classroom with the back of my skirt tucked into my panties."

Removing her glasses, Lucy laughed and shook her head as Edith shut the door. She took off the turtleneck, careful to stretch the neck around the messy bun that set atop her head. There was no need to loosen even more tendrils of hair than already curled at her neck and around her temples.

Next, she put on the green shirt, grateful she had worn a black camisole and bra under her sweater that morning. With a little shake, the shirt fell smoothly. Lucy slid her glasses back in place and stepped in front of the mirror. Sure enough, the v-neck was cut low, but it was not uncomfortably so. The dark green contrasted sharply with her fair skin, and Lucy refused to impose forced modesty on her inner-monologue. She shushed the voice telling her the shirt would make her stand out too much, bring attention to her flaws. Instead, she acknowledged that the shirt was flattering and sexy-but-not-too-sexy and that she looked lovely. Beautiful would be hyperbolic. Lovely, though, was fair.

"Are you coming out?" Edith could not hide her emotions if the future of feminism depended upon it. She was always an open book of anger or excitement or cynicism or joy. This time, impatience laced each word.

Lucy opened the door, and then blushed deeply when she saw Porter, Dr. Hubert, and Edith all looking at her. They had congregated around her desk, the men in the two chairs that faced her desk and Edith propped on the corner opposite her computer. They all ignored her mortification at being the center of attention as compliments filled the space.

"You look wonderful, Luce."

"That color is perfect for you."

"I nailed it." That input, obviously, from Edith.

Lucy said, "Thank you all, but what are you doing here? I mean, working obviously. This is your place of work. But what are you doing here, in my office, during this ill-advised fashion show." She was rambling. And blushing. It was unlikely to stop anytime soon.

Dr. Hubert said, "Just on my way from the bathroom. Or was it to the bathroom?"

Lucy looked to Porter. "In between classes. Stopped by to pick up some lecture notes, and Edith told me she was in the middle of a makeover. How could I run out after that declaration?"

Lucy glared at Edith. Edith giggled.

"Well, as much as I appreciate all the compliments, I have work to do. I'll just step back in here and change."

"On no you won't." Edith's voice was the voice Lucy had once heard her use to scare some frat boy who had referred to Emily Dickinson as a "chick." Edith continued, "That color looks amazing with your strawberry-blond hair and skin tone. You are glowing. I refuse to take it back. It would pale in comparison on me, and you know I don't like paling in comparison."

"Edi-" Lucy was just about to argue when the office phone rang. She said, "We'll get back to this," as she picked up the receiver. Then, she delivered her standard phone greeting.

"Lucy? This is Gracie. Forrest's sister, Gracie."

A pit opened at the base of Lucy's stomach. It felt ominously similar to that lunch on her mother's patio.

"Hello, Gracie. Is everything okay?"

"I'm afraid not. I probably should have called Forrest's cell phone, but I figured he was in class, and I thought it might be better coming from someone in person. Especially you, Lucy. It would be better coming from you."

Lucy's face must have shown her anxiety over what the hell "it" was because Porter said, "Lucy? Is everything okay?"

Lucy held up a finger to the concerned faces of the other three and said, "Gracie, what is going on?"

"It's dad. The hospital just called. He collapsed in his home. Thankfully, a neighbor came over to check on him, and she found him un-unconscious," Gracie's voice broke on the word. "They aren't sure how long he had been laying there. They haven't been able to get him to wake up. They said we need to come. Forrest and I. He may...He may not make it." Each word of the final sentence clearly took great effort.

"I'm so sorry, Gracie. Forrest should be in the office in the next ten minutes. His class is wrapping up right now. I'll let him know, and I'm sure he'll get on the road right away." Lucy felt she had to say it again, even though it was futile: "I'm so sorry, Gracie."

"Thank you, Lucy." They exchanged a few details about where Forrest should go and the hospital room number, and then Lucy hung up. She looked at her coworkers, and their somber expressions told her they had mostly heard or guessed at the content of the conversation. She filled them in anyways. "It's Forrest's dad. He's collapsed. They don't know if he's going to pull through."

As always, Edith's mind jumped to action. "Someone should go with him. He won't be in a state to drive."

Lucy agreed. "Edith is right. Porter, maybe-"

And then, Porter surprised Lucy by not volunteering to be the one but, rather, saying, "Lucy, it should be you."

Lucy prepared to argue. After all, Porter and Forrest were like brothers, and while she couldn't openly admit it, the feelings Forrest had recently stirred in her made her feel uniquely unqualified to be a rational, rock-solid presence for him in a crisis.

But then Dr. Hubert said, "Lucy, dear, it should be you."

Dr. Hubert looked at her directly, somehow communicating compassion underneath those bushy eyebrows. He had gone to dozens of doctors' appointments he desperately wanted to skip because Lucy told him he should go. She could have argued with Edith or Porter, but never Dr. Hubert.

Lucy looked down at the green shirt, feeling a pang of guilt for the levity of moments ago. She said, "Okay. I'll go."

Just then, the door opened, and Forrest walked in.

***

Forrest was relieved to see the clock finally move to 2:45. His class wasn't officially over for another five minutes, but it was close enough. He dismissed his students and began gathering his lecture notes.

His Tuesday and Thursday afternoon class was a core course required for all freshmen. Consequently, it was a large class not easily accommodated in the smaller rooms of Hart Building. Instead, he taught in a large lecture hall across campus. Today, he was grateful for the walk back to Hart, optimistic the crisp fall air might alleviate the blues he'd been feeling.

Apparently, his lecture had been affected by his glum mood, because no students stayed behind to ask questions or share ideas. This was an unusual occurrence for Forrest, but he was fine being left alone today. He left the building and headed towards Hart.

Distraction had plagued him now for weeks, ever since he had walked out of Dr. Wray's office feeling so relieved only to walk into his own office and straight into the epiphany that Lucy was, in fact, a woman. An available, alluring woman. The night of their editing meeting and the basketball game had each produced close-calls that still made Forrest sweat. What if Porter had not jogged onto the scene? Or if Lucy had not had the good sense to stand up straight and pull away after Clark had pushed her into him?

Forrest was a sober man. It was a virtue he'd cultivated with single-minded purpose for most of his adult life. He rarely drank, and when he did, it was never more than a finger of bourbon with Dr. Hubert. He stopped eating when he was full, he always drove the speed limit, he was perpetually monogamous, and he never became romantically infatuated. Infatuation was no different than addiction or drunkenness. It allowed forces outside of oneself to dictate one's behavior. Forrest had never given such power to another person.

And in doing so, Forrest had not only protected himself. He had protected others, those people who could have been hurt in the process if he, Forrest, had not done a damn good job of maintaining control.

As the thoughts roiled in Forrest's mind, he acknowledged that, yes, he had control issues. But he also knew better than most the price of abandoning control. His father had never had control over his alcoholism, and the romance he'd shared with Forrest's mother had been tumultuous and passionate and icy-cold in turns, by all accounts. Gracie, being older, remembered more than Forrest, and she'd shared with him memories of their parents being openly affectionate throughout the day only to have vicious, substance-driven fights in the evening.

It was hard for Forrest to comprehend these stories. They didn't mesh with the man his father was within the realm of parenthood. He had never been intentionally cruel to Forrest, cruelty being incongruous with his nature. All Forrest could figure was that his relationship with Forrest's mother had driven him completely outside of his normal self, and in the end, their family had been broken. Forrest and Gracie had been collateral damage in their soap opera.

For the past twenty years of adulthood, it had been relatively easy to protect himself and others. Perhaps it was from the thousands of stories he had read in books, but Forrest was an intuitive person. He'd been able to identify women like himself, people who were also not looking for passion and romance but merely convenience. He had staved off love and all the hurt and danger it entailed.

Forrest knew Lucy better than just about anyone but Porter. Lucy was not built in the way of his past partners. Lucy was meant to fall in love with some incredibly lucky guy who would spend the rest of his life being treasured by her. She treasured people. She treasured Forrest and Porter and Edith and Dr. Hubert. She treasured her best friend from college over a decade after graduation. She was all in within each friendship, and that is how she would be when she fell in love. She would be all in, and the man with whom she fell in love had better be worthy, damn it. Forrest could not bear such responsibility. It was contrary to how he had very intentionally structured his entire life.

Even admitting that there had to be boundaries in their relationship, though, Forrest was still nursing the sting of Lucy not telling him she was considering another position. Such secrecy was unusual between them. He'd thought it was, anyways.

In her apartment last week, sitting at the small table watching her mind drift to the memories of her mother's illness, Forrest had felt humbled that she'd shared memories so personal. No other woman had ever been so vulnerable with him, not emotionally. It felt important. Although he'd been there with Lucy during the whole episode she'd recounted, there was so much he had not known about her perspective.

In her apartment, that tiny space that was so very Lucy, there'd been several times when she said his name, and the hesitation he normally heard in her voice had been gone. It was the smallest of changes in their relationship, but it was noteworthy. Perhaps, they were moving into a more comfortable friendship, one in which she would not feel compelled to hide a job prospect from him. It couldn't be more than that, but Forrest wanted their friendship to stay strong. He needed her in his life.

Forrest arrived at the building and walked into the English Department. Standing in the middle of the office was Lucy, dressed in a rich green he had never seen her wear. She looked stunning, and he paused, staring in silence for a beat too long. Forcing himself to look away, he noticed that Edith, Porter, and Dr. Hubert were all congregated around Lucy's desk, and all four of them were looking at him.

"You guys look like you've seen the ghost of Mark Twain. What's going on?"

Their eyes darted between each other, but then Edith stood from where she'd been leaning on Lucy's desk and said, "Forrest, your sister just called, and your father is very sick." Edith was speaking in a gentle, almost maternal tone that was as disconcerting as the content of what she was saying. In that instant, it struck Forrest that this was a profoundly serious moment.

Forrest looked to Lucy. "How serious is it?"

"Forrest," Lucy's voice quivered on his name. "Forrest, it's serious. Gracie said you need to go now. The doctors are concerned there won't be much time left."

While Forrest had been zeroed in on Lucy, Dr. Hubert had approached him from the side. He put a heavy hand on Forrest's shoulder. Forrest was certain he drooped an inch beneath the weight, although he wasn't certain if it was the weight of Dr. Hubert's hand or the weight of the moment.

"Son," Dr. Hubert said. "I am so sorry you must face this moment. If there is anything Mrs. Hubert or I can do to help, do not hesitate to call us."

"Thank you, Dr. Hubert."

Behind Dr. Hubert, Porter stood up. "Forrest, we all talked, and we don't want you going to Mayfield alone. Lucy is going to drive you there."

"No, really, that isn't necessary. I'll be..."

Before he could finish, Lucy said, "Forrest, please. I want to go. I want to help."

Forrest considered the best way to turn her down. He knew that if things ended poorly, he would be messy. He wouldn't be controlled. He didn't want Lucy to witness such a moment.

Porter, knowing Forrest well enough to know his current line of thinking, said, "Forrest, there are moments in life when you shouldn't be alone. Let Lucy go with you. Edith, Dr. Hubert, and I will split your classes tomorrow. Let us help you."

The will for resistance drained from Forrest. Edith, still in a warm and nurturing voice that seemed like someone else, said, "You'd do the same for any of us."

Forrest looked to Lucy. "I'll just put my briefcase in my office, and we can leave."

— • —

CHAPTER 11

T he drive from Paducah to Mayfield was particularly beautiful in early November. The trees were a menagerie of warm colors, vivid oranges, golds, and reds with even a few spots of burgundy and pink. Knowing the wool blazer Forrest wore would keep him adequately warm, Lucy rolled her window down an inch, just enough to allow the hickory-scented fall air to act like the scented candles she burned in their office, hopefully alleviating the tension in the car's atmosphere.

Forrest hadn't spoken a word since they left campus. It had only taken a moment for them to prepare, and he'd almost jogged to her car. The skin above his beard was pale, and his mouth was set in an unmoving line. Periodically, a hand would go up and brush through his hair or smooth down his already smooth beard. Finally, he must have tired of even that movement because he propped an elbow on the base of the window and rested his head on his palm.

Lucy abided the silence simply because she had nothing to say. She wished she could text Miriam and ask what one should say when driving a friend to the possible deathbed of their father. Miriam would know. It was an average Thursday morning for her. Unfortunately, texting and driving was not an option, so the silence remained except for the sound of the air whooshing through the slit of the opened window.

Lucy thought back to her mother's illness. What had she wanted people to say to her? For the life of her, Lucy couldn't remember. She remembered the presence of those who cared about her. She didn't remember their words.

About twenty-five minutes into the drive when they only had five miles to go, Forrest spoke, his voice sounding unused: "What exactly did Gracie say? What do you think we're driving to, Luce?"

Lucy relayed the specifics of her conversation with Gracie and emphasized that his father would likely be unconscious.

"He was so close to that damn doctor's appointment, Lucy." It was supposed to have been that morning. Both hands brushed hard through his hair. Lucy resisted the urge to reach over and smooth down the hair he'd disturbed.

"I know, Forrest. I'm so sorry."

"You have nothing to be sorry for. You were the one who brought it to my attention that he sounded sick. I might not have forced the issue otherwise. Did they say what they think caused him to pass out?"

"Not that Gracie said. Here's our turn."

The hospital loomed in the distance, and Lucy suddenly wished Mayfield were a little further from Paducah. She wasn't ready to walk into a hospital and watch a friend go through the profound grief that still, seven years later, haunted her. For reasons she didn't understand, though, the entire office had deemed her the only choice for accompanying Forrest through whatever lay ahead. Lucy parked the car, silence sitting heavy in the absence of the engine's noise. "Let's go, Forrest."

***

Forrest and Lucy walked into the waiting area for the ICU. Lucy had written down directions from Gracie, and they had no problem navigating the typical-hospital maze. Forrest was, as ever, grateful for Lucy's unending wealth of competence and cool-headedness. It was obvious why the office had chosen her to accompany him.

He texted Gracie as soon as they parked, so within a few minutes of arriving, Gracie walked out from the patients' area. She was tall and lean, like Forrest, but her blond hair was several shades lighter than the light brown of Forrest's hair. Her arms spread wide as she approached him.

"Forrest. I'm so glad you're here."

They embraced for several moments before Forrest stepped back. Gracie was still squeezing his upper arms as she said, "Forrest, dad's actually showing signs of waking up. Which is really good news."

He smiled at her final words. Her desire to point out what was good news was a harkening to their childhood when Gracie had helped Forrest focus on the little bits of good they had.

Suddenly, Gracie noticed Lucy over Forrest's shoulder, and opened up her arms again, "Oh, Lucy. How kind of you to come with Forrest."

Forrest watched Gracie hug Lucy. They were alike in many ways. Both were naturally nurturing to others and exuded a warmth that made the area around them feel a little safer and nicer. Each had, in their own ways, built a home in which Forrest had lived.

As the hug ended, Lucy said, "None of us wanted him to drive alone. But don't mind me. I have a good book, and I'll be fine sitting here in the waiting room while you two go to Mr. Graham."

"Actually," Gracie said, "I need to use the bathroom and call George to check on everyone at home. How about the two of you go back there. The doctors are about to make afternoon rounds, and I want at least one of us there to hear what they have to say. I'll text you when I'm done, and Lucy and I can trade places."

"Whatever you think," Lucy said, but her skin suddenly looked exceptionally colorless next to the dark green shirt. Forrest thought about all of the hours Lucy must have spent in hospitals during her mother's illness, and he wondered if the bleach smell and fluorescent lights and outdated textured wallpaper were reviving old anxieties.

Forrest spoke up. "That's fine, Gracie. Tell George I said hello." He thought about his brother-in-law and niece and nephew. George was a stable (if slightly boring) accountant who loved Gracie to distraction, and Chloe and David were, at twelve and ten, starting to spend more time in their rooms when Forrest came for a visit. He missed the days when they hung to his legs throughout his stay. They were a beautiful family. Gracie deserved no less.

As Gracie walked out of the waiting area, Forrest and Lucy looked to each other. "Shall we go?" Lucy asked.

After pushing a button and being granted access, Forrest and Lucy walked towards the room number Gracie had given them. As they walked in, Forrest was stunned by the number of machines hooked to his father's emaciated body. His father had not been a small man in his prime, but he looked like a shell of himself lying among the tubes and computer screens and equipment of which Forrest feared knowing the various functions. Each would tell the story of something essential failing.

Forrest was paralyzed in place for several seconds, perhaps even minutes, when Lucy's hand reached over and their fingers intertwined. He squeezed her hand, unwilling or unable to release her.

A nurse walked in and said, "Oh, you must be Mr. Graham's son. Your sister said you'd be here soon."

"Yes." Conversation and full sentences alluded him.

"Will the doctor be here soon? Could we get a full report on what is known about Mr. Graham's condition?" Those were the questions Forrest had meant to ask. Lucy's voice was shockingly strong. Forrest looked to her and saw that she was no longer pale.

"Yes, ma'am," the nurse said in a thick Kentucky accent. "Any moment now. I'm just recording some vitals for the doc."

Forrest prepared himself for a long wait, knowing that when a hospital said it would be any moment, it was typically many, many moments. He slowly crept a few steps forward, reached out, and touched his father's arm. The skin felt brittle, like the leaves Forrest had so recently raked from his father's lawn.

Much to Forrest's surprise, the doctor arrived within five minutes. He was tall and imposing and exuded confidence as he walked directly to the end of the bed and grabbed the chart. He talked as he moved around the room. "Hello, there. I'm Dr. Dennis, and I've been working with your father since he arrived..." he looked down at his watch, "two hours ago. You must be his son?"

Forrest, still confined to monosyllables, said, "Yes."

Dr. Dennis said, "And you are Mrs. Graham?"

Forrest knew Lucy was ready to correct the doctor. She released his hand, cold air butting up again the skin she'd abandoned. However, before she could clear the misconception, Dr. Dennis was moving on, clearly trying to get through yet another consultation.

"Your father is experiencing the symptoms of Alcoholic Hepatitis. I suspect he has had it for a while. Unfortunately, that means he is in the late stages of this disease. It is possible that he will make a turn-around over the next several days, although I can't make any promises in regards to future quality of life. We will just have to address problems as they come at that point. However, for the next 24 hours, we are taking a wait-and-see approach. I'm very sorry to lay this all on you at once, but I find honesty is best with a challenging prognosis."

Forrest allowed a moment for the information to sink in, and then he said, "I appreciate your honesty."

"With the fluids we're giving him in his I.V., we're hopeful that he might wake up. The nurse said he was showing some signs of movement. Those are encouraging signs."

The doctor read a few monitors, made a few notes, and was on his way, leaving with the same purpose and drive with which he had come.

"Forrest." Lucy took his hand again, and they sat down. Under their gazes, his father's head turned in their direction, as if he sensed their presence. Then, an unmistakable movement in his eyes sparked a flicker hope in Forrest's chest.

He scooted his chair closer to the edge of the bed, weaving through the wires and tubes to take his father's hand. After several blinks, his dad's weak eyes focused on Forrest.

"Dad?"

"Forrest? Son? What's happening?"

The words were so quiet, so weak, Forrest had to strain to hear him. Forrest's other hand reached down to his knee, pressing his fingers deeply into his own flesh, willing himself to sound steady and calm. He explained to his father what had happened, as well as an abridged version of what the doctor had said. He would leave it to the professionals to communicate all the details. But his father was no fool.

"So the drinking finally caught up to me."

"I'm afraid so, Dad."

"I'm so sorry, son."

Forrest's fingers pressed deeper into the flesh of his knee, then he felt Lucy's hand on his shoulder. The slight movement caught his father's eye.

"Lucy? You're a sight for sore eyes." Despite being unshaven and wiry and lying in an ICU bed, his father lit up at the sight of Lucy. The words even came out above a whisper.

"Mr. Graham, it's good to see you, but I sure wish it weren't in these circumstances. You have to get better for all of us, you hear?"

Forrest smiled. She knew exactly what to say.

"Seeing you here with my Forrest..." His words sputtered, lacking the strength to complete the sentence. Slowly, he raised a hand to his chest, patting his heart to convey his meaning.

Just then, Forrest's phone dinged. "It's Gracie."

"Oh, of course," said Lucy. "I'll go out so she can come back. She'll be thrilled to see you awake, Mr. Graham. There is a two-person limit. I might go find the cafeteria and get some coffee, Forrest."

Forrest said, "Thank you, Lucy. Thank you for being here."

Lucy smiled, put a hand on his shoulder, and squeezed. She waved goodbye to Mr. Graham as she walked out, and he returned the wave with another tired smile that just barely managed to touch the wrinkles at the corners of his eyes.

***

Gracie joined Forrest a minute later, and the family of three enjoyed a short talk about Kentucky college sports and Thanksgiving plans, Forrest's father only contributing the occasional grunt of agreement or one-word answer. Soon Forrest saw that his father's head nodded periodically. Within a short ten minutes, he'd fallen back into a deep slumber, and Forrest and Gracie were left staring at their father from the rock-hard seats of the hospital's chairs. Forrest relayed what the doctor had said.

Gracie wiped a tear from her cheek. "I suspected as much. His coloring is awful. It was inevitable, I guess. So many years of drinking."

"I guess so."

The whirring of the various machines filled the silence.

Grace spoke first. "I'm glad Lucy is with you. Are you two...?" She didn't finish the questions, the words fading as she spoke.

"Lucy is my friend, one of the dearest friends I have."

"And that's all?"

"That's all." Forrest glanced at Gracie, and he saw that she was holding something back. "What?"

"George and I were friends before we started dating. He's still my best friend."

"And I admire your relationship. I love how George treats you and he makes you happy and takes care of you. But I'm not going to be Lucy's George."

"Because you don't want to or because you don't trust yourself?"

That hit entirely too close to the mark. Gracie knew him like a mother, a really attentive mother. Lying to her would be futile. She would see it for what it was and call him on it. So instead, Forrest kept quiet. Why speak when she knew the answer simply by looking at him?

"You know George and I have you listed as the kids' guardian if anything were to happen to us."

"Yes. Which, incidentally, is the one choice you've ever made that made me question your judgment." Forrest was surprised that he was able to joke around in the present moment, but Gracie just punched his arm, behaving very much like the sister she was.

"Ha-ha, Forrest. But in all seriousness, I wouldn't have put you in that position if I didn't trust that you could love my kids well. You do know that, right?"

"I know. And I do love them, Gracie." When Gracie had first approached him about the will she and George were making, her trust in him had been enough for him to consent to the remote possibility that he might one day need to parent her children. But romance was something entirely different.

For two more hours, Gracie and Forrest sat vigil by their dad's side. He occasionally woke up long enough to mutter a question or apologize for how tired he was, but mostly, he rested. Throughout the time, Forrest intermittently texted Lucy to see if she wanted to head home and if she was doing okay. Each time, she texted back assurances that she was fine and would wait for him.

After consulting one more time with the doctors, Gracie and Forrest went to the waiting room to confer with Lucy. She was reading a paperback book, and Forrest smiled when he saw that the words *Duke* and *Rake* were printed in the cursive, metallic title.

"Hey you." Lucy jumped at the sound of his voice. It must have been an engrossing scene.

"How's your father doing? Any updates?"

Gracie said, "The doctors say he might get out of ICU and into a normal room by tomorrow. But they also said we should stick nearby for tonight. I guess the first night after an episode like he had can be particularly dangerous. But since we got to speak with him, I'm more hopeful."

"That's good to hear."

"I was thinking I would stay here tonight with dad and, Forrest, you take the house. Tomorrow night we can switch if we need to."

Forrest suspected Gracie needed to stay nearby, and he should get sleep so that at least one of them was well-rested for whatever came tomorrow. "That sounds fine to me."

Lucy said, "Alright. I'll give you a ride over to your dad's house. We can pick up some dinner on the way."

"Perfect," Gracie said, and Forrest noticed that for the first time since he'd arrived, his sister had a genuine smile on her face.

CHAPTER 12

Lucy called them in a pizza before they left the hospital. It arrived a few minutes after they walked into Mr. Graham's home. While Forrest tipped the delivery person, Lucy walked around looking at pictures, bookshelves, and the small architectural details of the old home. The house was a mess, clearly having lacked an owner who could keep up with the demands of home-ownership. But beneath the disrepair, there was character that spoke to Lucy's old soul.

"I can't believe your dad had plaster crown molding. It's beautiful."

"Yes. He hasn't changed anything in this house since I was in college. When I came home for the summers, he and I would do a few projects here and there. But these last few years, he sort of let it go. I should've come down here more to help him out."

"Forrest." Lucy's voice held warning in it. "Don't go down the guilt-trip road. Everyone wants to when they see their parent sick, truly sick. But it isn't worth it. You love your father. That's enough."

"That sounds right, but I fear it's easier said than done."

"True. Let's get some food in us, though, and see if that helps."

They walked back to his father's kitchen, and Lucy began looking through the cabinets for plates. Forrest rummaged through the fridge assessing beverage options.

"Found it!"

"What did you find?" Lucy asked.

"Dad has never been a wino, preferring harder stuff. But he usually kept a bottle in the back of the fridge for when he ordered from Joe's Italian. And here it is."

"I thought you didn't drink wine? Just Dr. Hubert's bourbon?" Even that was rare. Lucy could count on her hands the number of times he'd accepted a glass as the crew gathered in Dr. Hubert's office to wind down after a particularly long day.

"Every once and a while, I like a glass with dinner. Today demands it."

"Well, I for one will not complain."

Lucy walked over to an antique hutch, hoping to find wine glasses. She opened the bottom cabinet. Instead of stemware, there was a foot-tall stack of academic journals.

"Oh, I found your dad's stash of your publications."

"What?" Forrest walked over, confusion marking his brow.

"It's everything you've gotten published since you started working at PSU. Your dad has me pick up an extra copy and mail it to him anytime you get something in a journal. You didn't know that?"

"No." Forrest squatted by the opened door and ran a thumb down the stack. Lucy saw raw emotion pass over his face. She turned around, granting privacy while resuming her hunt for wine glasses.

There were no wine glasses to be found, so Solo cups would have to do. Lucy and Forrest sat across from each other, each eating a slice of pizza with a roll of paper towels between them. Forrest removed his blazer and tie, draping them over the back of his chair. The first two buttons of his shirt were unbuttoned, giving him room to breathe and relax. Lucy tried to not notice the lines of his neck or the few chest hairs visible where his collar was open. She did not succeed, but she did try.

Suddenly, Forrest jumped up, "We forgot about Clark. We've got to get you home."

Lucy waved a dismissive hand. "I called Miriam while you were with your dad. Clark is having a sleep-over at her house. Both are thrilled at the arrangement."

Forrest sat back down, but Lucy could still feel energy pulsing off of him.

"This table looks well-used. Did you grow up eating on it? Are we having a typical Graham dinner here?"

"I have a lot of memories around this table, but they aren't Norman Rockwell family meals."

Lucy stayed silent, watching him take a deeper gulp of the wine.

Forrest said, "I came home late one night from a basketball game. My friend, Kevin, had been starting that night, and I stayed through two overtimes. We actually won. It was a great game. So, anyways, I came home, and my dad was sitting at this table." Forrest's hands firmly clutched the edge of the table. "Usually, he was passed out by that time of night, so it was strange seeing him sitting there. I noticed that he was holding one of my papers, an essay I'd written over the role of the Mississippi River in *Huckleberry Finn*."

"Dr. Forrest Graham's first paper on Mark Twain?"

A smile brushed his lips. "Yes. I was so damn proud of that paper. It was my first essay I'd ever written over 10 pages. It felt like I'd written a tome." The smile deepened, and a dimple flashed for just a moment at the memory.

"I sat down across the table and asked dad what he was doing with the paper. He said, 'Oh, I was just reading it, son.'" A vague Southern lilt snuck into Forrest's voice as he repeated his father's words.

"I asked him what he thought. He said, 'You're different son. You're not like me. You're so much better than me. I have no idea how you happened.'" Another laugh sputtered from Forrest, but the dimples didn't show. It was a laugh without mirth. "He said he didn't know if I was some weird glitch in the gene pool or if one of those," Forrest slipped back into an imitation of his father's drink-scratched, accented voice, "'damned pretentious teachers had worked some miracle.'"

Melancholy was gathering in Forrest's brown eyes as he relived the memory. Lucy said, "I suppose that is a compliment to you. Or the damned teachers?"

"I suppose so. He didn't stop there, though. It's funny, with all of the books I've read through the years and all of the great literature I've studied, no story is as cemented in my mind like the words he spoke that night. He told me, 'You are an absolute wonder.' A wonder. And he made me promise that I would never pickle my brain 'with this shit you see me drink every day.' I promised him. Which is why, despite really wanting to be numbed tonight, I will stop drinking after this one glass of wine."

"There's a lot that's beautiful in that story, Forrest."

"I guess. You know what I think, though, when I think back on that night?"

"What?"

"I wonder why, in all the countless nights I came home late from a game or studying at the library or studying at some friend's house, why was that the only night he wasn't passed out or so drunk he couldn't talk."

"Maybe, if you'd been given countless nights like that, nights where your father had been fully present to you, maybe you wouldn't have this one beautiful memory."

"Maybe. But I think that is a trade I would've been willing to make."

Lucy thought of Forrest's loyalty and dependability and sobriety. Not just sobriety from drink, but sobriety in how he lived. Always thoughtful of others, never beholden to vices that might hurt those he loved. She said, "Yes, but then you might not have become who you are, and that would've been a tragedy."

Forrest looked into her eyes for a long moment. *Honestly, Lucy*, she thought to herself, *You have to break the long-moments-of-eye-contact habit you have formed with Forrest.*

For the rest of the meal, Lucy talked about various campus gossip. Forrest seemed to welcome the banality of it all. As she was enumerating which English Department students had recently hooked up and the drama in the Psychology Department over who would be the next chair, it occurred to Lucy that she could easily tell Forrest about the job offer. He might even have insights that would help her make the decision. But each time she looked up into his eyes, she stopped herself. They looked so heavy with worry, the line on his forehead between his eyes creased deeper than usual. She reached for something that might distract him.

"So today in the office, I somehow ended up getting a makeover from Edith."

He barely kept from spitting wine across the table. "How did you end up in that situation?"

"I told her I was wanting to add more color to my wardrobe."

"What were you thinking?"

"She walked in on me browsing clothing websites. I didn't have a choice."

"So you basically volunteered."

Lucy groaned.

"The green does look wonderful on you. It's perfect with your eyes."

Lucy felt heat rise into her cheeks. "So I've heard. The way Dr. Hubert, Porter, and Edith were talking, it was like the invention of Technicolor."

"In their defense, it isn't often we see you in color. I've never thought about it before today, but you do mostly wear black."

"And gray and sometimes navy blue."

Forrest held up his hands. "Excuse me. I forgot those. Oh, and I believe I've seen you in beige."

"On several occasions, I'm sure."

He leaned back in his chair, his shoulders slumping forward. It was better than the tense statue he had been when they'd started the meal.

"So, I've shared one of my more personal memories..."

Lucy squinted her eyes. Where was he going with this?

"Tell me, Luce, why don't you wear color?"

***

Lucy gulped the last bit of wine and placed the red plastic cup down with intentionality. Forrest could see that the question made her uncomfortable, and if she chose to not answer it, he would not push her. After all, they weren't sixteen and this was not a sordid game of Truth or Dare.

However, he wanted to know more about her and what had shaped her into the person she was. He knew she preferred mustard to mayo, and that she and her best friend could do decent carpentry with a few tools and YouTube videos. He knew that she read romance novels with shirtless men on the cover, and that she blushed the deep rose color at the top of a peach when he saw those books. He knew she pushed her glasses up her nose about once every five minutes and that those glasses actually framed and drew attention to her green eyes instead of taking away from them.

But he did not know why a woman so remarkable dressed in a way so unremarkable. It didn't bother him. If she simply was not one to care about clothing and preferred to keep things neutral, he was fine with that. Her striking hair and eye color and porcelain complexion and height all made her beautiful in ways clothes couldn't. But he sensed there was more behind her choice than merely personal preference.

After looking at her cup for a smidgen too long, Lucy finally said, "You know I grew up in rural Tennessee?"

"Yes."

"And you met my mother a few times,..."

"Mhh-hum."

"...but you didn't really get to know her."

"I can't say I had the pleasure."

"Well, I don't know if pleasure is the word I would use. I know that sounds terrible, and I did love my mother. I really did. It's just that she could be blunt at times."

"Blunt about what?"

"About her disappointments with me."

"Disappointments?" Forrest couldn't imagine a single aspect of Lucy being deemed disappointing.

"My mother was very feminine. Being a Southern belle was in her bones. She believed in the ideology behind the whole concept." Lucy started talking with her hands, warming up to her subject. "She wanted to be seen as frail, in need of masculine rescue."

"And having an intelligent, self-efficient daughter didn't fit her ideal?"

"It wasn't even that. She was intelligent, and I think she was mostly fine with those parts of me. It wasn't who I was inside as much as it was my inability to project the image she wanted me to project. I was, unlike her, far, very far, from delicate. With my height, my build, my crazy, untamable hair, I made the frilly clothes she wanted me to wear look ridiculous. Thankfully, she had enough awareness to see that all the feminine clothes looked like a parody on me."

"So you started wearing the plainest clothes you could find?"

"Basically. When I would try something a little louder, she would always have something to say. 'Oh Lucy, that color brings attention to your hair. Can't you do something with it?' Or, 'Lucy, that pattern shouldn't be worn by anyone above a size 6.' And then she would pull out a magazine article on dieting she'd cut out for me."

Forrest was speechless, his jaw refusing to shut. Finally, he said, "But, wait, back-up here a second. Your height? Your, what did you call it? Your build? Your hair? She didn't approve of these things about you?"

"Not exactly."

"And you believed her?"

"She typically phrased it as if it were motherly, constructive criticism. They were all little things she encouraged me to work on. Well, not the height, of course. There was no strategy for that shortcoming." Lucy tucked a wave behind her ear, then added, "No pun intended."

"Lucy," Forrest didn't know what to say after breathing out her name. Lucy, I love that I can recognize you walking across campus from far away just by the strawberry-blond bun bouncing atop your head. Lucy, when you were pressed against me, each part lined up so perfectly, I wanted to thank Clark for knocking you over. Lucy, how can you not see how stunning you are? "Lucy, that wasn't constructive criticism. It was ignorance. Her ideal of femininity might appeal to Southern gentlemen with very small penises..."

Lucy's eyes swelled to twice their size and she placed a hand over her mouth, hiding her laughter. "I can't believe you said that."

"I mean, really, really small penises. But men who don't need to see women as weak to see beauty in them, men like that look at you and..."

Suddenly, the room got very quiet. Forrest heard the ticking of the kitchen clock seeming to mock how long his pause was.

"They look at you, and damn it, Lucy, you're just perfect."

The peachy blush returned, and Forrest wished desperately he could skim his lips across her cheek and feel the warmth she must be radiating to create such a color. Lucy bit one side of her bottom lip, the other side puckering out. Then, she said, "I'm hardly perfect. And I certainly don't have many men noticing if I am."

"You just don't look up enough, Luce. They notice. Trust me."

If his father weren't in the hospital and if he weren't a dozen insignificant relationships into adulthood and if he weren't a Graham, he would reach across the table and push up her glasses for her and feel the soft waves that had fallen out of her bun. He would tell her all he saw. The perfect coral shade of her lips. The smattering of freckles across her cheeks and nose that made her look like a model for one of those organic facial cleanser ads. The bright and attentive eyes that always charmed him within their perfectly-Lucy frames. He would point out each perfect detail until his voice replaced that of her mother's when she got dressed in the mornings. Afterward, she would wear red dresses and high heels. If she wanted to, that is.

But he would not be saying any of those things tonight. He had already butted up against the boundaries of prudence.

In almost a whisper, Lucy said, "It's getting late. I'd better go. I'll just drive home and come back tomorrow morning. If you want, that is. I don't want to intrude."

"It's too late. It's dark outside, and you've had wine, and I won't sleep if you're on the road. You can stay here in Gracie's room. Our rooms are perfect little archives from when we were home. You'll feel sixteen again. We'll see how things are tomorrow, and then we can figure out what to do."

"Are you sure?"

"Please, Lucy. I'd just worry, and I have enough to worry about."

Lucy yawned, conceding any argument she might have had that she was in a state to drive. "Okay. I'll stay."

"Good." Forrest was relieved she had chosen to not drive. Just as he was about to stand up, a question intruded his thoughts. "But before we tuck in for the night, I have one more question after this very informative evening."

"Shoot."

"Why, in all of these years of friendship with me sharing every nitty gritty detail of my relationship with my dad - why did you never tell me about your mother?"

"You knew I had a mom."

Forrest smirked. "You know what I mean. You never told me about how critical she was."

"Oh." Lucy feigned sudden understanding. "You mean I never shared the immense baggage my mother sent with me into adulthood."

"Yeah. That."

Lucy shifted seamlessly from teasing to earnest. "It felt wrong to complain about my mom when you grew up motherless. World's smallest violin and all."

Forrest shook his head. "No, Lucy. What your mother did wasn't the stuff of small violins. While they went about it in different ways, our mothers inflicted similar wounds on us. My mother wounded me with her absence and all the lies it told me about my self-worth. Your mother also stripped away at your sense of worth with a bunch of lies. She was just present to tell them."

Lucy's eyes were locked on him,the second-hand of the kitchen clock continuing its incessant ticking. Lucy said, "That makes us quite a pair, doesn't it? Thirty-somethings with mommy issues."

"At least we're in good company."

Lucy yawned again as she said, "That we are."

"And on that note," Forrest said while pushing back his chair, "let's get some sleep."

Now, he just had to keep the boundary they had built between each other stable through one night under the same roof.

CHAPTER 13

M r. Graham's home had two bathrooms: a full bathroom upstairs for the three bedrooms to share, and a small bathroom downstairs with a walk-in shower that looked as spacious as dorm room accommodations. Forrest had insisted Lucy take the nicer bathroom. After the conversation about her mother, Lucy felt too drained to mount a polite argument.

Lucy undressed, draping Edith's green shirt over a towel rack. She ran her hand over the satiny fabric, marveling at how different she'd felt throughout the day simply because of a green shirt. Every time she had passed a window in the hospital, she'd glanced at her reflection, secretly relishing the image. Lucy had never considered herself vain. In fact, she'd spent much of her life resisting vanity. Lucy had hated feeling like her mother's doll to be dressed up.

But this afternoon in the office, it had been fun being dressed up by a giddy Edith. There was something so counterintuitive about a fierce feminist jumping up and down clapping at the sight of Lucy walking out in a green blouse. It didn't feel like Lucy was being forced into some image she would never fit. Instead, it felt like a dear friend was revealing something Lucy had yet to ever recognize in herself.

Lucy wondered what it would mean to stop listening to her mother's voice, still so strong inside of her. Would it simply make dressing in the morning more entertaining, or would it mean more? And what did it say that someone who'd been dead so many years was still dictating her life? *Impressive, Mom.*

For the first time in her long acquaintance with Forrest, Lucy wondered if he heard a similar voice in his head. He'd said that his mother's absence had told him lies. Did he have to exert as much effort to quiet those lies as Lucy did? A part of Lucy regretted that it had taken them so many years to realize they shared a similar wound. What support had she missed giving or receiving?

Lucy stepped into the opening of the shower curtain that wrapped around a claw-foot bathtub into warm water. She wouldn't wash her hair tonight, but she needed to wash off the hospital air. It clung to her, drawing her back to memories on which she would rather not dwell. The generic bar soap was not like the scented, liquid soaps she usually indulged in, but that didn't dampen the cathartic effect.

Once she finished standing beneath the shower head for a few extra minutes, Lucy dried off and removed the scrunchie that had been holding her hair in place. She took the brush she always kept in her purse and ran it over her hair, but it did little to smooth her hair. The bun had misshaped it, creating large, unruly waves that cascaded down her back.

There was no choice but to put the same pants on from the day. Lucy pulled on the camisole she'd worn beneath her sweater that morning and that she had kept on all day under the green shirt. It was thin black fabric that clung tightly to her, never meant to be shown fully. She knew she should put her bra on underneath it, but it would be a hassle to take it off again when she got to her room. The odds of her running into Forrest on the short walk to Gracie's old room were fairly low.

Finally, it was time to walk to her room where she planned to collapse into bed and hope that her fatigue was sufficient to keep thoughts of Forrest being only one door down from intruding into her dreams. She wouldn't think about what degree of undress he might be sleeping in since they had left Paducah without packing pajamas. She would not. She really wouldn't. Soon, Lucy had an internal chant worthy of the little engine that could.

Forrest had called her perfect tonight. Not her editing abilities or her secretarial efficiencies. No, just Lucy herself. Lucy would try to not think about this, as well.

Lucy left the bathroom, the old brass door hinges creaking loudly. She headed towards Gracie's room, but her steps paused when she noticed the door cracked open on Forrest's room.

He had said it was perfectly preserved from his youth. What had sixteen-year-old Forrest been like? Lucy calculated the time-line. He would've been a teen in the 90s. Would there be a poster of Cindy Crawford pouting in a bikini? Or would Nirvana's naked baby be swimming across a wall? Lucy squeezed into the opening, not wanting this door's squeaky hinge to broadcast where she was going.

Lucy immediately noticed that the room didn't smell like Forrest. It didn't smell bad, just abandoned. The leather and pine scent that defined Forrest's office and, well, Forrest was absent. Lucy had always wondered if the leathery scent came from his book bindings or his briefcase or his elbow patches, or if it was simply him. If she were nuzzled into the space right below his ear, and if she were to inhale deeply, would she smell warm soft leather there?

Moonlight beams streaked across the room through a dormer window, providing enough light for Lucy to notice a lamp on a dresser. She walked over and turned it on, flinching at the sound of the switch, and wondering how many great American novels had been read deep into the night by its light. Sure enough, it illuminated a worn paperback of *A Connecticut Yankee in King Arthur's Court.* "There's a shocker, Forrest," she whispered.

Lucy's eyes scanned the room. The walls were a dark navy blue. There were no little league trophies or a basketball hoop hanging over a laundry basket. Nor was Cindy Crawford or rock band posters hanging on the wall. There were, though, bookshelves on every wall, far too many for the average teenage boy. The shelves were over-stuffed, books laying horizontal on top of the rows of vertical books.

On one shelf, a frame was lying face-down. Lucy picked it up and removed a layer of dust with her hand. The logo for a Kentucky water park was printed on the bottom. It must have been one of those souvenir photos for which families paid exorbitant prices to prove they had been on a proper family vacation. A family of four looked out at her, the children very young. Lucy saw hints of

Gracie and Forrest in the children. The boy, barely beyond walking, had the same dimples she'd seen beneath Forrest's beard for a decade. Mr. Graham was holding him and looking healthy and vibrant. Gracie was held by a woman who was tall and lean in the same fashion as Forrest. Her hair was a perfect match for his own light brown.

Lucy laid the photo face-down again. Other frames were standing up; pictures of him and Gracie, and several with people she didn't recognize, all young and beautiful and dressed in the denim jackets and plaid flannel clothes of 90s youth. Forrest always had an arm draped around someone and a smile. He'd been a bean-pole in high school, which wasn't shocking in the least.

On the walls, there was a collection of medals pinned with thumb tacks. Lucy read the medals, each for various debate and academic competitions. He had been consistent throughout his life, hadn't he? The only poster, shockingly, was a large illustrated poster of Gandalf from *Lord of the Rings*. A small huff of laughter escaped Lucy. She had never known him to read fantasy novels, but she was happy teenage Forrest had. He would have needed the escape, the good versus evil battles where the light always triumphed in the end.

In the corner to the side of the dormer window, there was a small desk buried under stacks of paper. Lucy walked around the foot of the bed to the desk, and shuffled through the corner of one stack. It was page after page of double-spaced typing in Times New Roman, 12-point font, likely essays he had saved. Would the study on the Mississippi River in *Huckleberry Finn* be there? Most boys hoarded baseball cards or comic books.

Lucy picked up the first essay on the stack and scanned the first paragraph. Immediately, she was lost to the familiar voice - less mature, but essentially the same - that occupied so much of her time.

***

Forrest was bent over, furiously drying his hair within his towel. Once again, Forrest had found himself turning down the temperature on his shower, trying to chill thoughts of Lucy. Lucy's hair. Lucy glowing in an emerald green shirt.

Lucy laughing at a joke he said. Lucy looking sad at old memories he wished he could somehow edit and improve.

His father was lying in a hospital in critical condition, and all Forrest could think about was that he and Lucy were under the same roof. And this time, it wasn't Hart Building. Forrest thought about the last time he had been in this house. Knowing his father, he'd be thrilled Forrest was thinking about Lucy instead of him.

The small closet-like shower had been inadequate for the mood Forrest was in. He had knocked elbows against the edge as he slammed down shampoo and splashed the cool water repeatedly over his head with cupped hands. He was at least a foot too tall for the shower head.

After he was dry enough, Forrest yanked on his khakis, not bothering with the belt. The buckle on it clanged as he left the room, bouncing with each step. Forrest headed to the stairs. He would go up the stairs and walk directly to his room while looking downward. Better to avoid even a passing glance at the shut door to Gracie's room. He would then collapse into the lumpy twin bed where he had once fantasized about Gwyneth Paltrow from *Shakespeare in Love* and a whole slew of other 90s beauties, all of whom seemed to pale in comparison to Lucy. And he would refuse, absolutely refuse, to let his mind wonder in the way it had at sixteen. He wasn't a horny teenager, after all. He was a man well in control of his baser impulses.

He walked up the stairs, straightening a few crooked picture frames along the way. Each school year, Gracie had framed Forrest's and her official school pictures, because having various stages of acne documented in yearbooks had not been enough. His dad, in a rare show of normalcy, had hung them along the stairway. The cute Forrest at the base of the stairs aged into his awkward junior-high years halfway up, only to end with a cap-and-gown photo at the top, his valedictory medal hung around his neck. With a flicker of pride, Forrest admitted to himself that he did like that picture, at least.

Sure enough, the door to Gracie's room was shut when Forrest walked past it to his own door. He turned into his room, and immediately froze in place. Lucy stood at his desk, reading one of the many essays he had saved from his high school years. Her hair, usually up in a bun or clipped in some kind of twist, hung loose. Had he ever seen her hair down? He couldn't remember, and surely if he had, he'd remember. Broad, thick waves imprinted from her bun went all the way to the middle of her back. The light from his reading lamp shone on it, bringing out all of the streaks of red that were, perhaps more than any other part of Lucy, so very recognizable as being her.

It also occurred to Forrest that Lucy was no longer wearing Edith's green shirt. Instead, there was just a thin, spaghetti-strapped shirt revealing shoulders he was absolutely certain he had never seen. Forrest realized that he had not taken a breath since walking into the room, and he forced himself to inhale.

At the sound, Lucy turned around and jumped. She clutched the green shirt to her chest, which had the uncomfortable effect of making Forrest acutely aware that he wasn't wearing a shirt, nor was he holding anything to cover any of the bare skin on display.

Lucy stepped back into his desk, catching herself on the edge. Clearly fumbling for words while her eyes seemed glued to his torso, Lucy finally managed to make eye contact while issuing an apology: "I'm so sorry, Forrest."

She looked nothing short of mortified. Unsure how to respond and supremely uncomfortable in his own skin, Forrest settled on imitation. "No, I'm sorry."

Lucy's fist clutched the green fabric harder, her knuckles whitening. "For what? Stepping into your own room in your own house?"

"No, just..." Forrest could hardly say he was sorry for not being more dressed. "I'm sorry I startled you."

"That's my fault, not yours. I'm the one being unforgivably nosy."

"I don't mind. Really." Forrest took a step further into the room. "Are you itching for a red pen reading that paper?"

Lucy returned the essay to the pile, a soft smile easing her stricken, embarrassed expression. She said, "No red pen. Although, it's incredible how an author's voice works. It's clearly your writing. I could've identified it in a line-up."

Forrest matched her expression with his own modest grin. "Besides looking for the early works of Forrest Graham, were you wanting to see anything else. Shall I give you the tour?"

Lucy waved off his suggestion, her eyes still diverting from his own with obvious embarrassment. "Nah, I was just curious. Curious what 17-year-old Forrest had been like."

"Yeah. And what did you find? That I was a giant nerd."

"Pretty much, yes."

He laughed softly.

Lucy said, "Who are all of these people in the pictures? Any girlfriends?"

"A few. Nothing serious. Unsurprisingly." Lucy knew his dating record. His habit of going from girlfriend to girlfriend before anything significant occurred started mid-high school.

"So...Gandalf?"

Forrest ran a hand through his hair grimacing. "Yes. I might have gone through a fantasy stage in high school."

"But no longer? Dr. Graham doesn't secretly read about orcs and fairies in between classes?"

"Is everything that is said in this room strictly confidential?"

An electric shock went through the air at the question. Forrest had not meant the question in *that* way. Or at least, he hadn't consciously meant it so.

Lucy licked her lips, their natural color glowing in the dim light. "Completely confidential."

"I re-read the *Lord of the Rings* series at least once every five years."

"I've never gotten around to reading them."

"You should. They're wonderful."

"Are there any dukes? Especially of the rakish variety."

"I'm afraid not," he said with a chuckle. "But there is love in it."

Forrest looked around the room, at the crowded bookshelves and medals and pictures, trying to imagine what it looked like through Lucy's eyes. But then his mind zeroed in on the astonishing presence of Lucy within the dark blue walls, and he wondered what his 17-year-old self would think if he saw the room right now. All the same surroundings, but with a tall, striking, perfectly-nerdy woman standing next to the bed. He'd never thought of it before, but she was basically his high-school-self's dream-girl.

He had been quiet too long. Lucy said, "What are you thinking?"

"I was thinking about time-travel."

She quirked her head in question.

"I was thinking how completely thrilled teenage Forrest would be to know a beautiful girl is standing in his room right now."

"Perfect earlier tonight? Now beautiful? Forrest, you have to stop saying words like that to me." She spoke softly, but there was pleading in her words.

"Why?"

"You know why." It was a whisper. He knew why.

Forrest walked around the end of the bed to her, never breaking eye contact. He had no plans for when he reached her, but the pull to go was overpowering. When he did stand in front of her, he stopped about a foot away and did something he had wanted to do for longer than he could remember: he brushed the hair framing her face away, running his hand down the length of that hair. It was as soft as he had always suspected it would be. Then, still moving methodically, he removed her glasses, folding them in, reaching around her, and laying them on the stack of papers she had been examining. Looking into her eyes, eyes glazed over in the haze that had settled over the room, Forrest wrapped a hand around the back of her neck. He'd spent years wondering how the curls at the base of her neck would feel to the touch. They tickled.

The other hand remained at his side. Perhaps, if he left it there, he wouldn't go too far. He wouldn't scare her away or cross that next line. Forrest knew he was approaching one line, a line he had firmly drawn and obeyed for a very long time. But he would try to not push it further. He just needed to know what it would be like to kiss Lucy O'Shields.

Slowly, giving her time to pull away or indicate in some way, any way, that she did not want this, Forrest leaned towards her. She angled her head, parting her lips slightly. Forrest inhaled. It was an invitation.

Finally, their lips met, at first as tentative as middle schoolers on their first kiss. It was so foreign, so other-worldly, to be standing so close to, to be breathing the same air as Lucy.

But then, Lucy dropped the green shirt she had been hugging between them. It landed on their bare feet. She placed her hands firmly on his bare abdomen, and then, in a movement more brazen and daring than he had ever dreamed, she ran her hands all the way up his bare chest, wrapping her arms around his neck, sending shivers down Forrest. Her breast, covered only with the thin jersey fabric of her camisole, pressed against his chest.

Forrest groaned, wrapping his other hand around her waist, pulling her into him. She would feel how much he wanted her. He could no longer hide the storm of desire that had been brewing in him for the past month and possibly even longer. He couldn't hide it from himself or from Lucy.

As the kiss deepened, there were no hospitals or painful pasts or invalidating mothers or English departments or risks. There was just Forrest wrapped around Lucy, finally living the fantasies he had only ever allowed to exist in the most secret corners of his mind.

Forrest finally broke the kiss only to begin a stream of kisses down her neck, to her collar bone and her shoulders. He noticed that on each shoulder, there was a dusting of freckles identical to the ones across her nose. In wonder, he said, "You have freckles here, too." He kissed them.

Turning her in his arms, Forrest guided her down onto the plaid comforter of his bed. She awed him by sitting down, guiding him in return with a hand behind his neck, bringing his lips back to her own. Forrest fell on top of her.

The bed was only a twin, but they didn't need more space than it provided. Their bodies were completely entwined from their lips to their centers to their feet. Forrest began exploring again with his lips. His hand pulled down a strap at her shoulder. It was so easy, offering no resistance. There was no bra to unclip or push away. Lucy's breast was immediately exposed to him.

Forrest took it into his mouth, and Lucy inhaled with shock and moaned, pressing against his erection with her pelvis. Forrest felt undone, knowing all of the lines had been lost. How could he cross a line when he no longer remembered lines existed? Tonight, he would explore all the parts of Lucy he had wondered about for so long.

Forrest wanted to see her, all of her. He pulled her shirt up, and she raised her arms in complete acquiescence. As soon as the shirt was off, she pulled Forrest back to her, kissing him with a passion he had never experienced from another woman.

Forrest reached for the clasp of her pants. "Lucy, can I..."

She unhooked a clasp or undid a button or unzipped a zipper. Forrest wasn't sure what contraption had been undone, but suddenly, he was pulling her pants down the length of her long legs, running his hands over the smooth, porcelain skin.

Finally, she was in front of him, completely bare, breathing deeply as if they had just run a marathon.

"Oh, Lucy. You're so...beautiful isn't enough. You are more than I ever imagined."

She propped herself on an elbow, and reached to the waistband of his pants. "Please."

"I need a condom."

"I'm on the pill. Please."

Forrest had never had sex without a condom, but he had never had sex with Lucy. He had never slept with anyone with whom he had told stories about his father on late nights after school. He had never had sex with someone who knew his father, who talked to him and checked up on him. He had never had conversations with a girlfriend about her own struggles with family.

There were a thousand layers he kept between himself and his past partners that did not exist between him and Lucy. And so, after he removed his pants, Forrest laid on top of Lucy, aligned himself with her, and entered with nothing between them. It was just him and Lucy being together in body, reflecting all that they already were to each other.

In perfect unison to a rhythm they both recognized in the other, Forrest and Lucy moved together until he felt her gasp and dig her fingertips into his back, pulsing around him.

Forrest jerked with each pulse, and then he shivered and released all of the
built-up desire and need and love into Lucy, his Lucy. She held him gently,
brushing her lips lightly across his ear and cheek and neck as he tried to recover.

Forrest could swear there was a lump building in his throat, a sensation
completely foreign to him. Forrest was not a person who cried. He had not cried
since childhood.

Gently, Forrest pulled out of Lucy, and positioned himself to her side. She
turned, allowing him to pull her back against his chest. His arms wrapped firmly
around her and his face buried in her vanilla-scented hair, Forrest waited for
sleep to come and silence the swell of emotion he felt completely unable to
address.

***

Lucy woke, wrapped in the warmth of Forrest's arms around her, his body
pressed all the way down her back and legs. Immediately, the image of Forrest
standing in the doorway of his room returned to Lucy. She had been completely
trapped by the sight of his shirtless chest. The lamp light had sparkled on his
shoulders - whether it was from water droplets left from his shower or whatever
spell had come over them that night, she did not know. His stomach was completely flat. Of course it was, Lucy thought, almost irritated at him for having the
audacity to be so perfect. He wasn't overly muscled. That wouldn't fit Forrest.
But Lucy could see subtle lines and grooves down his abdomen. She had been
right when she had seen the inch of skin in her apartment last week. Forrest was
beautiful.

Her neck and breast were pleasantly achy from the friction of Forrest's beard,
and she still felt the warm glow of satisfaction thrumming at her core. The radio
clock on top of the nearest bookshelf said three o'clock, and the darkness outside
confirmed the hour.

Lucy was shocked she'd fallen asleep. Although, that was perhaps the least
shocking thing that had occurred that evening.

As she recapped the evening, groggily processing all that had happened, Lucy blushed at her own brazenness. She had more than just gone with the flow. There had been multiple moments when she had led, initiated, pushed it further.

But how could she possibly have not done so? Of all the men in her life, no one had ever been to her what Forrest was. The (very few) ex-boyfriends had always paled in comparison to Forrest, each less tall, less intelligent, less funny, none quite so authentic and warm. In the dark of Forrest's adolescent bedroom, Lucy realized she had compared every potential match to Forrest. Yes, she had compared and found lacking every single one.

And it wasn't even just men with romantic potential. No man in her life had ever been as natural to talk with and easy to be around. Maybe, Lucy thought, that explained why it was with Forrest that she had run her hands along his body and pulled herself to him. She revealed more to him when talking than with anyone else. Of course, she would be more impulsive, more honest when she was with him physically.

Forrest nuzzled the back of her neck, his beard tickling. She didn't know if that meant he was waking up, as well, or if he moved like this in his sleep. She knew so much about Forrest, but she did not know this. She did not know how he slept or cuddled or held a woman. She was learning all in real time.

A dark foreboding threatened at the edge of Lucy's wonderment and contentment. Yes, she and Forrest had, much to her dismay, had sex. For goodness's sake, they were spooning. His pelvis was tucked firmly against her ass, and she could feel a hardening as Forrest once again stirred behind her.

But for all of this connection, Lucy knew that the talking had stopped the moment he'd walked around that bed to her. There had been so much conversation and sharing up to that moment, and then it had just been doing and being, silence except for pants and moans and whispered names. At some point, she and Forrest would have to talk about what had transpired, and Lucy feared how it might torpedo her entire existence.

But as Forrest's hand moved up her abdomen, cupping her breast and gently squeezing, Lucy knew that for now, she did not want to think about the future.

They had already done the unthinkable. Would it really hurt to do it again? To do it again in the dark of this single night before harsh daylight shone in and illuminated whatever consequences might be awaiting them.

Lucy, the highly proficient secretary of the PSU English Department, turned over in Forrest's arms, pushed him onto his back, and rolled on top of him.

CHAPTER 14

Forrest sat on the wooden desk chair next to his bed, and stared at the way Lucy's hair spread across the pillowcase, covering the entire surface. He wasn't sure why she always kept it confined, never letting it loose in all of its striking glory. Probably something stupid her mother had said years ago, something that if he heard, he would burn to erase.

The sky outside the window had a subtle, greenish tone. In the next half hour, the first rays would peek out. Forrest was in awe of the night that had just passed, unable to fully grasp the experience.

At almost forty, Forrest had come to assume that he knew most of what life had to offer. He had never, though, experienced anything that compared to this. He had not known he could feel passion so overwhelming. In his youth, he had feared the possibility, feared the loss of control that might come with such passion. But after two decades of convenience-based relationships, he had become complacent, quite certain he was incapable of overwhelming feelings, safe from the danger they would pose. Perhaps it was the motherless childhood or the constant presence of addiction in the periphery of his life, but Forrest had been certain he was damaged goods, too leery of human relationships to ever connect with another in the ways that made the dukes on Lucy's book covers give up their standing for the poor governess.

Last night made him question all of these assumptions. He was damaged goods, alright. But his ability to feel control-stripping, all-consuming passion was well intact. And Forrest feared it was terribly dangerous, especially for Lucy.

Lucy stirred, turning from her side to her back, the sheet stretching taught against her breasts. Forrest's hand knew how they felt to the touch. He clenched his fists.

Forrest had also assumed he knew Lucy, knew her nature, but last night she had proven she was so much more than his assumptions. And for that, Forrest regretted not seeing sooner how strong and assertive and powerful she was. He had confined her to her roles. She was intelligent, hard-working, resourceful Lucy, the best departmental secretary PSU had ever seen, the most promising student he'd ever taught, the best damn editor for over-ambitious academics. Somehow, he had missed that she was also a woman capable of great passion. After a lifetime of believing he could accurately label women, Forrest had somehow missed the one woman with whom he had been closest. In the face of such failure, Forrest rued his own arrogance.

Forrest picked up the pants that had been discarded at the foot of the bed, and with feather-light steps, left the room, sucking in as he squeezed through the doorway that had been squeaking since he was fourteen. He retrieved the phone from the pants pocket to check the time. Five thirty in the morning. He would go ahead and prepare to return to the hospital. Sleep was impossible now.

Just as he was tucking in his shirt, the phone rang. A picture popped up onto his screen, a picture of Grace with her children, Forrest's niece and nephew. Forrest's hands shook as he slid the answer bar across the screen.

***

The sun shone through the window directly onto Lucy's face, demanding she rise. She ached in all the best ways, the ways that told her she had lived sublimely in her body the night before. She stretched, enjoying the warmth of the sun.

As Lucy became more aware, though, she realized the house was too quiet, too still. Suddenly, she was no longer centered in her body with all of her morning-after glow. She was Lucy O'Shields, a person whose mother had regularly pointed out was overly cerebral. And cerebral-Lucy was reclaiming her turf.

Bullet-pointed facts ran through Lucy's thoughts, each one on the heels of the last. Lucy was the secretary of the PSU English Department, and she had just spent the most passionate night of her life with a professor of the PSU English Department. She had not come to the evening a virgin, but she had never been with anyone the way she had been last night, never experienced that level of passion and abandon. Forrest Graham, her co-worker, her friend, had been for a single evening her lover. And Mr. Graham was sick, so very sick.

Covers landed in a heap as Lucy threw them off and began dressing. She picked her pants up off the floor and pulled them on, jumping twice to pull them up. It did not make the process more efficient, but she was beyond logic. She just wanted to not be bare, not have her body be an artifact of what had transpired the night before.

Just as she was pulling the green blouse over her head, Lucy noticed that a handwritten note was sitting beneath her phone, both of which had been placed on the stack of essays on Forrest's desk. Lucy moved the phone to the side, finding her name written on the paper in handwriting as familiar as her own.

She unfolded the paper to find a short note: "Lucy, Gracie called, and my father has taken a turn for the worse. I didn't want to wake you so early, so I'm taking dad's truck to the hospital. Please know that I'll be okay. Don't worry. I'll see you later, Forrest."

Lucy wanted to stop and decipher each terse sentence. Don't worry? I'll see you later? Lucy was not sure what Forrest meant. Was she supposed to come? Was he planning on stoically facing the death of his father without the support of his friends? Should Lucy step back, go to Paducah, and let him be?

Lucy thought about calling Miriam and asking for a list of instructions that would take her through this day. It would be infinitely useful to possess a formula for how to console a friend slash co-worker with whom one had slept the previous evening. And if anyone could draft such a plan, it would be Miriam.

But in Lucy's gut, she already knew what she was going to do. She would drive to the hospital. She would sit next to Forrest and wait with him. She would be present as she had always been for him. And perhaps most importantly, she would not speak about whatever it was that had passed between them last night. It would wait.

As she walked out to the car, Lucy twisted her hair back into a bun at the top of her head. She opened the door, taking one last look at the home where Forrest's adolescent years were preserved. Shivering in the crisp morning air, she hopped into the car.

A little past seven, Lucy arrived at the hospital. As she walked into the waiting room, she immediately saw Gracie walking out of the ICU area. The look on her face told Lucy the grim reality.

Gracie noticed Lucy, turning her path to her, red eyes still moist.

"Oh Lucy, he didn't make it. Dad didn't make it through the night."

Lucy embraced Gracie. She thought of all the small, incidental phone calls she took weekly from Forrest's father. She thought of how the phone would never again ring with a call from Mr. Graham. She tried to digest the news, to see how it fit into all that had changed in her own life over the past evening. Then, she felt ashamed for thinking of herself, of how this impacted her. "I'm so sorry, Gracie. Was Forrest able to make it before he passed?"

"Yes, thank God. He was here for the last few minutes. But Dad never woke up. I don't know if he even knew we were there."

As Lucy stepped back, she said, "Yes, but it was important you two were here for yourselves. I was with my mom, and it helped."

Even as the embrace ended, Gracie held on to Lucy's hands. She looked directly into Lucy's eyes, the blatant grief disconcerting to see on a face so similar to Forrest's. Squeezing Lucy's hands, Gracie said, "Lucy, he's going to need you. He's hurting badly."

"I'm not sure what I can do, Gracie, but I'll try."

"That's all, Lucy. Just your presence will be enough."

A moment of silence passed between them.

"Lucy, I have to go fill out some paperwork. Can you go to Dad's old room and sit with Forrest? He's still in there, and I don't want him to be alone."

Lucy's stomach flipped. She desperately wanted to enter the room and alleviate in some way Forrest's grief. If she were in the office, she'd have supplies to meet the moment. But what if meeting this moment of profound grief required something different of her in the reality ushered forth by the previous evening? How did she meet this moment not only as his colleague or friend, but as - maybe - something more? Regardless, Lucy wouldn't allow her mind running amok prevent her from being the friend Forrest needed.

"Of course, Gracie. Whatever you need."

And with that, Lucy walked back to, once again, be with Forrest. When she arrived in the room, Lucy found Forrest facing the empty space where the hospital bed had been. She stood behind him, looking at the slump of his shoulders, willing herself not to remember the strong lines of his bare back. He was unaware of her presence, and Lucy left it that way for a moment as she tried to decide what to say. Why had she not just called Miriam?

With one timid step forward, Forrest became aware he was not alone. When their eyes met, Lucy gasped at the sight of his dark eyes, his signature smile lines engulfed by dark circles. He didn't look like Forrest. He didn't look like Lucy's Forrest.

"Forrest." The word escaped on a gasp, and tears rose to the surface. She had not known Mr. Graham well, not well enough to mourn his passing too deeply. But Forrest. Seeing Forrest in grief, someone who normally avoided big emotions, preferring to live them from the safe distance of literature, was more than Lucy could bear. "Forrest, I'm so sorry."

She wanted desperately to walk up to him and touch his face or sit on his lap and wrap her arms around his neck. But she did not yet know what the previous night meant. She didn't know if the intimacy of the evening could exist in the daylight. So she repeated, "I'm so sorry."

Finally, Forrest spoke, but it was in a voice she hardly recognized, one filled with hurt and grief. In a hard, harsh whisper, he said, "No, Lucy. I'm sorry."

"What do you mean?"

"I'm so sorry I pulled you into all of this. You shouldn't have to take care of me. This was mine to do."

"But I wanted to be with you. I want to be with you. I want to help. All of us, everyone at the office wanted you to have one of us with you."

"Yes, and what did I do? How did I handle this? I lived out some high school fantasy while my dad was dying. I took the one woman who I've ever really cared about, and I took advantage of you. I did what Graham men do. I numbed myself to all the shit that is around me. And don't you see, Lucy? I used you to do it. And I'm so wretchedly sorry." His voice broke on the last words, barely able to make it to the end of what he had to say.

A million words flew across Lucy's conscience for how she might respond, but in the end, she was too stunned for complete sentences or reasoned thoughts or conclusions that would clean up the mess she and Forrest had just made. Had she simply been a tool Forrest had used? Was all the passion of the night before merely a numbing agent for Forrest? Lucy had felt anything but numb.

"Forrest? I don't understand..."

Just as Lucy flailed, unable to finish the sentence she had begun, Gracie walked into the room.

"I have the papers, Forrest. They said we can take them home and fill them out there. Do you want to head over to Dad's, and we'll get this done and maybe make some decisions about the funeral and all?"

Forrest looked at Lucy while he said, "Sure, Gracie."

Gracie said, "Lucy, would you like to join us."

Lucy looked away from Forrest to Gracie, "No Gracie. I'm going to head back to campus. I'll get the paperwork done for Forrest's bereavement leave."

"Thank you, Luce."

Lucy really wished he had not used her nickname.

CHAPTER 15

The church was slowly clearing out. Miriam stood in the back within the light cast by a particularly brilliant stained-glass window. Her generous robes concealed all tattoos, making her look like an almost conventional priest. She shook hands and hugged the occasional old woman as people complimented her on her sermon and exchanged the regular Sunday-morning niceties.

One parishioner had not moved since the final benediction had been read over the congregation. Miriam looked at the messy, coppery bun with waves falling out from every direction. Within the black dress, shoulders slumped in a way that spoke clearly to Miriam. She did not know the details yet, but she did know that her friend was a little bit broken this morning.

Miriam looked down the aisle. Only a half-dozen parishioners to go.

"Good morning, Mother Miriam," a slender older woman said as she walked up to Miriam in a perfectly coordinated Sunday-best outfit. "Do you have plans for lunch? The altar committee is meeting for sandwiches and ice cream in the hall."

"I'm so sorry, Ms. Betty, but I believe my services are needed elsewhere today. Next time, though?"

"That's fine, dear. Have a good week."

It probably wasn't *completely* fine. She would need to do something to make up her absence to that particular committee.

Thankfully, as she was speaking to Ms. Betty, the last of the parishioners discreetly sneaked out. They were a group who Miriam was quite certain had not enjoyed her sermon this morning. Her commitment to preaching inclusion was not always appreciated by every member. But alas, she hadn't embarked on a career in ministry with the goal of maintaining a hundred percent approval rating. If she had, ministry would have quickly dispelled her of that notion.

Miriam walked over to her friend. Her stole had gone off-kilter in all of the handshaking and hugging. She straightened it, pulled at her collar to give herself some breathing room, lifted the hem of her robe an inch, and took a seat about a foot down the pew from Lucy.

The two friends sat for ten minutes in silence. The steep vaulted ceilings and stained-glass windows seemed to sanction the quiet. Who needs to fill a space with chatter when surrounded by such grandiosity?

From the months following Mrs. O'Shields passing, Miriam had learned that Lucy was stoic and quiet when she wrestled with grief. Miriam had never heard a silence so complete as existed in Lucy's apartment the evening after her mother's death. She'd rushed back to Paducah from seminary to be with her friend, and they had sat for hours in Lucy's apartment, the stillness being broken only occasionally by a brief reminiscence or Lucy asking Miriam if she needed something. Miriam had been amazed that Lucy had maintained some level of hostessing even in her grief.

Lucy broke the sacred silence first.

"Forrest's father died." There was a pause, and then, as if to try again, Lucy said, "Mr. Graham died."

"Yes. Forrest called me yesterday. I'll be doing the graveside service on Tuesday."

The silence returned.

Miriam had a feeling that while Lucy was likely quite sad at the passing of Mr. Graham, it did not entirely account for the bags under her eyes or the wadded-up tissue clutched with a white-knuckled grip in her hand.

Five more minutes passed.

Lucy said in a voice so quiet it almost escaped into the rafters, "I slept with Forrest the night before his father died."

"Oh."

Miriam let it sink in for a moment. The more it did, the more she felt a sense of rightness bubble within. But she could tell her friend was drowning. Drowning in... something. She knew she must tread carefully.

"Lucy, Forrest is wonderful. Except for me, he's been your closest friend for years. Why do you look like you've wilted, sweetie?"

At this question, Lucy did something Miriam had not thought possible. She wilted some more. Tears began flowing copiously down Lucy's freckled cheeks, and words finally broke loose.

"Oh, Miri. It was awful! I'm mean, not the sex. The sex wasn't awful. The sex was earth-shattering. But afterwards, when I walked into that hospital room..." A sob escaped. "He said he was sorry, *so sorry* it had happened. It was like he loathed himself. He said that he'd taken advantage of me, that he cared for me, but that he'd used me. Miriam, what am I going to do? I've ruined everything. I liked my life. I liked going to work and being with Edith and Porter and Dr. Hubert and, oh...and Forrest. I liked that they all needed me, that I could fix all of their problems. But now, now I've destroyed it. I've taken the one thing I've ever been good at, the one place where I've ever belonged, and I've ruined it. How will I ever look at him again? When he looks at me, all he will see is a mistake he made. And a mistake he made on the night his father was dying."

Miriam slid across the foot of pew that separated them, put her arms around her friend, and held her as she sobbed. Lucy's tissue was now hopelessly sodden, so Miriam did what any good priest would do: she handed Lucy the end of her stole and waited quietly as the tears slowed.

"Lucy, you are a lot of things. You are kind and funny and compulsively helpful. You are intelligent and patient and overly sentimental, especially about dogs and romance novels. You are many things, but a mistake you are not.

"I've known Forrest for a while now. I've seen the way he looks at you and the way he treats you, with respect and affection, and I'm certain that he doesn't think you're a mistake, either. Quick side-note, though, if he were the type to think that, I'd tell you he's a worthless piece of shit you should ignore for the rest of your life."

Lucy hiccupped. Miriam breathed deeply.

"But like I said, that isn't Forrest. It isn't who you know him to be. I don't know everything that happened or was said, but I do know that in the space that exists between you and him, there is an abundance of love."

Miriam thought about this love, and how at this very moment, it was pulsing between two hurting people, neither of whom realized they themselves were worthy of the other. She squeezed Lucy's shoulder a little tighter, and settled into the pew. They would be sitting together for a while.

CHAPTER 16

The service for Mr. Graham had been a perfect balance of celebration and mourning, all orchestrated and navigated by Miriam's deft touch. Lucy was, as ever, awed by her friend's aptitude for the very unexpected career path she had chosen. Lucy still remembered the day her tattooed friend had announced she would be starting seminary a few short months after their graduation from PSU. Lucy had been flabbergasted, unable to picture her friend in the role of a minister. But here she was, leading a grieving family through saying goodbye with grace and poise.

After the service, everyone gathered in Porter's home for a light lunch and conversation. At the service, Lucy had found it fairly easy to avoid Forrest. He was in the family rows while she stood in the back with non-family. Everything was formal, and there was no need for direct communication. Simply being present with Edith, Porter, and the Huberts had been sufficient. It was giving Forrest emotional support without costing herself too much pain.

She had spent the past three days drowning in her own sorrow, an entirely different variety than that expressed in a funeral. Laying on her couch, she'd eaten popcorn and chocolate while watching the least romantic movies she could find on Netflix, mostly of the apocalyptic variety. Clark rested his chin on the seat of the couch as asteroids struck and zombies took over, sensing Lucy's distress and offering what comfort he could. Seeing his devoted eyes raised in concern usually had the unintended effect of making Lucy cry all the more.

After driving back Friday and then all of Monday, Lucy had worked in the office. Thankfully, her frowns and slouches and sighs passed largely unnoticed with a cloud hanging over the whole office in solidarity with Forrest. Surely, no one suspected that she was spending her evenings crying because she might possibly be in love with a man with whom she'd just had the most passionate sex of her life, and he had deemed it all a giant screw-up. Oh, and that man worked in the same office as them.

As for Forrest, Lucy had received exactly two text messages from him: one on Saturday repeating how sorry he was, and one on Monday saying they should talk. Given the little he'd said at the hospital, Lucy had an uncomfortable feeling she would not want to hear what he had to say.

Despite everything, Lucy was incapable of being angry at him. He had looked so down-trodden sitting next to Gracie in front of his father's coffin, a hand raising every few minutes to wipe at an eye. And for the first time in a decade, Lucy found she couldn't fix whatever problem one of her professors was facing.

Now that they were all at Porter's house, Lucy was keeping her distance by helping. The caterers Porter and Charlotte had engaged were very efficient, but not so efficient Lucy couldn't find a few things to do in the kitchen. Forrest was on the front porch talking with family he hadn't seen in years, leaving the kitchen safe.

Just as Lucy was drying her second round of washed dishes, Edith swung around the corner into the kitchen with a determined scowl on her face. Lucy had no obvious reason to assume she was the object of Edith's brisk walk and searching eyes, but it was best to be cautious. Lucy bent over, opened a cabinet door, and pretended to be occupied with an urgent search for the perfect tea pitcher.

"Lucy O'Shields."

Damn it.

"We need to talk."

Double damn it.

Lucy crawled back from the cabinet and stood. Edith grabbed her hand and dragged her into the old butler's pantry tucked behind the kitchen. The tiny room was a relic with a small sink and cabinets still original to the house. But in the shelves were signs of a home with twenty-first century children: Jello cups,

Goldfish, and pretzels abounded. The two women were squished into the space with no room for Lucy to run from the interrogation coming from Dr. Edith Rose.

"Yes, Edith?"

"For the past few days, it's been obvious something is wrong. Our office has been musty because you haven't been doing all of those candle things..." Edith waved her hand, "you know, all the things you do to make it all nice and cozy. And Dr. Hubert snuck three brownies in Friday without you even noticing. I can only imagine his cholesterol right now. And worst of all, when I left for the faculty meeting on Monday, you forgot to tell me to be nice, which incidentally, I always thought was pointless, but it turns out, it actually makes me nicer. I made two accounting professors cry, Lucy. Two."

"I'm sorry?"

"And today, it is as clear as day, even to someone as emotionally stunted as myself, that something between you and Forrest has gone amiss, and that's not okay. I can't handle that. So you are going to tell me what the hell happened. And we're going to fix it."

Lucy spoke before thinking, her impulse to make things seem okay greater than an impulse for truth. "I don't know what you're talking about, Edith. Forrest and I are fine. He's just busy with family, and I'm helping around here. Everything is fine."

Edith squinted her eyes and pointed a finger within two inches of Lucy's nose as she said, "Everything. Is. Not. Fine. You two have a way about you, a way of looking at each other that is as familiar to me as Hart Building or the feminist section of the library. And something has screwed it up. Lucy, you help me every single day. Let me help you."

A lump formed in Lucy's throat at alarming speed, and the impulse to paint a rosy picture abandoned her.

"How uncomfortable are you going to be if I cry?"

"Very."

"Well, if I tell you everything, I might cry."

Edith closed her eyes, took a fortifying breath, and said, "Okay, I'm ready."

"Okay. Here it goes." Lucy took her own deep breath. "Forrest and I slept together."

"Where?"

"At his childhood home, in the twin bed of his room."

"When?"

"The night before his father died."

"And was it good?"

"Edith!"

"I'm sorry, Lucy, but it matters. You know it does."

Lucy fought back a tear of sadness or frustration or anger. She wasn't sure what. "It was unlike anything I've ever experienced. Not being hyperbolic here, either. It was soul-crushingly amazing. At least it was for me."

"We need chocolate." Edith grabbed a bag of chocolate chips from the section of the pantry reserved for baking ingredients, ripped the bag open, poured some into her own and Lucy's hands, and started popping the small chocolates while staring at Lucy with a level of scrutiny that was unsettling.

"You know I love Forrest like a brother, right?"

"Yes."

"Then, Lucy, don't be offended by what I'm about to say."

"Okay."

"When it comes to relationships, Forrest is a dumb-shit. I mean, he dated Dr. Bugs for six months. She once suggested at a faculty meeting that the university erect a statue of a beetle. A beetle. Lucy, I can't even make this stuff up."

"And your point is?"

"If it really was that mind-boggling, and given the chemistry you two have, I have no doubt it was, Forrest isn't going to have a clue what to do. Because, as I said, he's a dumb-shit."

"So, I can't believe I'm asking this, but Edith, what do you think I should do?"

Edith's eyes bulged. Was that a dampness at the corner? She whispered, "No girl has ever asked me what to do about a romantic problem."

"Huh." Lucy didn't trust herself to not be sarcastic, so she stuck with non-sensical sounds.

"I know, right? I think it's because people are terrified of me."

For the first time in days, Lucy felt a hint of laughter - not enough to escape, but it was there. Lucy cupped her hands.

"More chocolate chips, please?"

***

Sitting on the front porch of Porter's home, Forrest was surrounded by family he had almost forgotten existed. It had been years since he'd seen his father's siblings and the multitude of cousins whose names he hardly knew. Multiple conversations were going at once, and he was in the center, trying to follow each strain. Thankfully, Gracie juggled seamlessly all of the condolences and stories of his father from his youth, stories from before alcohol took over and distanced him from his family. She kept the conversations easy and flowing with no help from Forrest.

Dr. Hubert was also on the porch, talking about the most legendary horses of past Kentucky Derbies with one of Forrest's more distant relatives. Mrs. Hubert was perched next to him, making sure caterers were waved away who brought anything near her husband that wasn't strictly low-cholesterol. The small plate of raw vegetables sitting on Dr. Hubert's lap had been untouched for at least a half-hour.

Forrest felt overwhelmed with gratitude for the presence of each of his colleagues, each one engaging in conversations with his family members that helped everyone feel welcomed. He was wholly inadequate to the task. For the past few days, Forrest had sat next to Gracie in meetings with lawyers and the funeral home and Miriam, nodding his head at whatever she said but not contributing near as much as he should.

The truth was, though, that his world had been flipped upside-down, and not only because his father had died. Yes, his father's death was enough to send him reeling. He went from making bologna sandwiches to gone with so little warning. But in addition to this blow, the solid friendship and camaraderie he'd shared with Lucy for so many years was likely gone. That knowledge left him unable to sleep or eat or remember the name of the cousin who had just asked him what their plans were for his father's house.

"We haven't made plans yet."

In Forrest's mind, that house was now associated with Lucy. Visceral memories of her hair and lips and smooth skin outshone the sepia-toned remembrances of his youth.

She looked beautiful today. She was wearing a fitted black dress that hugged each curve perfectly. Lucy had never been one to wear frumpy clothes. Everything was always nicely fitted, precise in the way she was always precise. But before, Forrest hadn't known the feel of each curve, the perfect weight each one held in his hands.

At the service when he had dared to glance at her, evidence of tears had been clearly written across her face, deepening the ache in his own wounds. Miriam's words in the service had been perfect, evoking for a moment the feelings he had been too overwhelmed to process. The emotions tugged his eyes back to Lucy. She'd removed her glasses long enough to dab beneath each eye. If she were sitting with him, he would hold her glasses for her.

Forrest realized another question had been directed at him.

"I'm sorry. What was that, Uncle Stan?"

"I asked how many years you've been at PSU now?"

"Oh, yes. Let me see here. I think I'm on my tenth year."

"We were afraid you'd never come back after all those Ivy league schools in the Northeast. And now you've stayed for a decade. That's just wonderful."

"Yes, well, PSU has been a wonderful place for me. Wonderful people, really." Forrest felt a weight crushing in on his chest. "Excuse me. I need to check on something."

Forrest walked inside, looking every direction for Porter. He heard a crash and a deep voice yelling, "Boys, what have you done?" Following the path of Legos through the formal living room, Forrest found his friend in his small home-office, the walls lined with his collection of antique books. Forrest had always loved the space for the old-book smell. Porter was currently on his knees, not looking terribly professorial among his books. Although, he was at least delivering a lecture.

"Now, Billy and Luke, run along and play, but for goodness's sake, don't injure any funeral guests."

As the boys ran past Forrest to the door, Billy elbowed Forrest's thigh with a solid jab. "Hey Forrest, dude!" Luke copied the gesture and said, "Fowwest, dude."

As they left the room, Forrest looked to Porter and said, "Their acknowledgment of my grief is really touching." It was the first time Forrest had smiled since lying in bed with Lucy.

Porter groaned as he stood up from his knees. "I'm raising hooligans."

"Yes, but who wants boring, well-behaved children anyways?"

"Yes, that would just be awful."

Forrest stepped further into the room. "Porter, can we talk?"

"Of course. Is something wrong? I mean, other than the obvious?"

"Yes, something's wrong."

As Porter looked on expectantly, Forrest ran a hand roughly through his hair, and then thought of Lucy pointing out that he did that when he was stressed. Well, he was stressed. "Porter, I made an awful mistake, and I don't know how to fix it. I don't even know if it can be fixed."

"Okay?"

Forrest shut the door. When he made this confession, he would make it to himself, Porter, and a wall of books. Once cloaked in privacy, Forrest spit out the confession. "I slept with Lucy."

"Oh." Porter backed up to one of the two wing-back chairs in the room and fell heavily into the seat. "Oh."

Forrest sat down across from Porter, his elbows on his knees and his head resting in his hands.

"How did it happen?"

Forrest leaned back in the chair, gripping his knees. "It was the night we were in Mayfield. Gracie wanted to stay at the hospital with dad, but she insisted I stay at Dad's house and get some rest. Lucy and I went back to the house together. We ate and talked and drank wine..."

"You drank wine?"

"Rare, I know. But it had been a rough day. Anyways, when it was time to go to bed, I didn't want Lucy driving all the way back to Paducah that late, especially with the wine. So we decided she'd stay in Gracie's room."

"And?"

"And we went to our separate bathrooms and got ready for bed, but when I went upstairs and walked into my room..." The image of Lucy clutching the green shirt against her chest, apologizing, looking so soft and ethereal in the lamplight was lodged in his chest. He squirmed, repositioning in his chair. Hoarsely, he continued, "When I went to my room, she was there. The room perfectly preserved from my teenage years. She was curious, I think. She hadn't come there to seduce me or anything, Porter. What happened after that was all my fault."

"So you walked into your high-school room?"

"Yes."

"Among your posters of, I don't know, some hot 90s icons?"

"Gandalf, actually."

Porter's eyes registered his surprise. "We'll get back to that in a moment. So you walk in, and there is standing a gorgeous red-head who you've been pining over for years."

"Strawberry-blond, and no, I haven't."

"Close enough, and yes, you have. My point is, you didn't stand a chance. The most devout monk would have said, 'Screw celibacy,' in that situation."

"Pun intended?"

"Definitely."

"What do you mean I've been pining over her? I've had at least a dozen girlfriends while we've been working together."

"Dr. Bugs? Dr. Sweats-a-lot?"

"She liked working out."

"Dr. Laughy-Hacky?"

"Her laugh was legitimately awful."

"Like nails on a chalkboard. With a cough." Forrest cringed at the remembrance of that shorter-than-normal relationship. Porter continued, "Forrest, your never-ending capacity for going-nowhere relationships isn't because you're just having a good time. It's because you're hung up on Lucy, but you don't think you can have her. Dr. Sneezy and the rest were just place holders so you can pretend you and Lucy don't have ten layers of sexual tension coming off of you at all times."

"That is patently false," Forrest could feel that he was flushing beneath his beard. He jumped up from his chair, but quickly realized the room was too small to pace. Grabbing the back of his chair, he said, "Porter, my admittedly sketchy dating past is the result of good old-fashion mommy-issues. It has nothing to do with Lucy."

Forrest wondered exactly how long Porter had been holding in all of the thoughts he was sharing, because they were sure flowing freely now. "Oh, sure, that's what was going on at first when you were young, fresh out of your doctoral program and just wanted companionship without responsibility. Sure. But for the past five years, you've been straight-up running from your own infatuation. Yes, I mean infatuation. With Lucy."

"That is absolutely insane."

"Really? Because Dr. Hubert and I have a drinking game where we take a shot of his bourbon anytime one of us catches you staring at Lucy for more than twenty seconds. I've taught more classes than I care to admit tipsy over the past few years."

To this, Forrest could think of no reply. "A drinking game?"

"Yes. It was the old man's idea."

"Dr. Hubert thinks I'm lusting after our secretary?"

"Dr. Hubert *knows* you're lusting after our secretary."

"But I didn't know. Not until recently."

"Your lack of self-awareness is truly a wonder to behold."

"Ouch. My dad just died. You should be nicer to me."

"You didn't come in here for me to be nice to you. I happen to know you value honesty, even if you find it hard to be honest with yourself. Perhaps, *because* you find it so hard."

Forrest sat back down in the chair, closing his eyes and running both hands down his beard. Was five years of infatuation the answer to the questions that had been haunting him for the past few days? Any moment he had walked past his room at his dad's house while he and Gracie had been making arrangements or sat in silence in between meetings or tried and failed to sleep, the same questions had racked his conscience: Why, at almost 40 years old, had he just now experienced sex with the all-consuming passion and fire described in books and poetry? And why had it been with Lucy O'Shields?

***

As Lucy popped another chocolate chip into her mouth, Edith had the expression generally accompanied by a light bulb in cartoons. "I know what to do, Lucy. As I was saying, I'm terrifying. Why don't I just have a talk with Forrest, if you know what I mean?"

Oh dear. "Edith, I appreciate your willingness to help. I really do. But we can't force Forrest to be my boyfriend. It's mortifying even using that word in this context. Forrest is probably right. All of this was just a giant mistake made in the chaos of his dad being sick and us being in his childhood room. It was crazy. Normal Forrest and Lucy would never have done what we did that night."

Suddenly, the pantry door opened, and Miriam appeared, closing the door behind her. She jumped when she saw she wasn't alone. "What are you two doing in here?"

Edith held up the chocolate chip bag, and Lucy tilted her head towards it.

"Thank God. And when I say that, I actually mean it."

Edith poured a generous heap into Miriam's palms and said, "What are you doing here?"

"Some distant relative of Forrest's cornered me and asked if I thought our current president was the anti-Christ. I told him someone was calling me."

Edith looked mortified. "Do you get questions like that often?"

"Wearing this?" Miriam pointed to her tab collar. "Basically every day. But other than chocolate, why are you hiding? I clearly have a good excuse."

"I was telling Edith about my situation." Lucy wanted to kick herself. She was stuck in a very small closet with two of the boldest, most honest women she knew, and she was using euphemisms like *my situation*? Lucy inhaled deeply and said, "You know, how Forrest and I had the greatest sex of my life and he said it was a horrible mistake."

"Yes, I suspected that was the situation to which you were referring." Miriam smiled primly. She knew it had cost Lucy to be so blunt.

Edith reached out and grabbed Miriam's forearm. "Mother Miriam..."

"Please, call me Miri."

"Okay, Miri. Can't you talk to Forrest and help him see reason. Like guilt-trip him or something."

"I could, if it weren't a breach of every ethical code known to ministry."

"Oh, yes. You have those in your profession, huh?"

"Afraid so. Ooh, but maybe you could talk to Porter about talking to Forrest?"

Lucy decided now would be the time to interject herself into the conversation about how to fix her life. "Ladies, I adore you both, and I appreciate your desire to help me. But this is between me and Forrest. I need to figure this out on my own."

"You know, Luce," Miriam said, "doing things on your own can be overrated. Itss okay to get help from the people who love you."

"I know. But Forrest and I made this bed..."

Edith interjected, "In splendid fashion by all accounts."

Lucy growled. "And we have to figure out how to live with it. How to live with each other post-sex."

A silence settled over the somber trio. Finally, Edith said, "I think I ate too much chocolate."

On this, they all agreed.

***

"So what the hell do I do, Porter?" Clearly, Porter was more aware of whatever was going on between Forrest and Lucy. Perhaps he could fix this mess, or at the very least, tell Forrest how to fix it.

Porter looked at Forrest pensively while his mouth tilted to the side in thought. If Porter was approaching a problem with this level of contemplation, Forrest really was in an awful situation. Porter was generally quick to act, intuitive in his decision making. It was a skill Forrest had always admired in his friend.

Just as Porter was opening his mouth, about to reveal the wisdom that would surely rescue Forrest from this mess of his own making, the door to the office opened.

"There you are, Forrest. I've been looking for you."

"Gracie, what do you need?" Forrest rose again, hoping his guilt wasn't written too plainly on his face. Gracie could always read him like a Bletchley code breaker.

"Just a quick word. We're about to leave, and I wanted to talk to you for a minute before we do."

Porter stood up. "Excuse me. I'm going to step out and assess what damage my kids have done since the last lecture..." he checked his wrist watch, "fifteen minutes ago."

Gracie caught his arm as Porter walked by. "Thank you, Porter, for the use of your home. This has been lovely."

"Of course, Gracie. It was our honor. I always liked your dad."

"I'm glad Forrest has you."

"Well, he does keep things exciting around here." Porter punched Forrest's upper arm in a brotherly fashion as he walked out, closing the door behind him.

Forrest rubbed his arm as he looked at Gracie. She'd been calm and strong through the entire ordeal, just as she had been through their whole childhood. "You amaze me, Gracie. It is like you were born with the maturity of a 40-year-old and have maintained that throughout all of the dysfunction that has been thrown your way. Honestly, Gracie, I don't know what I would've done growing up..." His voice cracked. He was so tired of being perched on the edge of tears.

"Oh Forrest. It's because I had you to take care of. I loved you so much, for as long as I can remember. I could never understand how Mom could have walked out on you. I don't know that I ever even wondered why she walked out on me. It was just so offensive she would walk out on you."

"I would argue that what she really missed out on was seeing you become the woman you are." Forrest noticed a box of tissues and got one for each of them.

Gracie blew her nose. "Geez, Forrest. You're turning into a sap."

"Dad was getting a little sappy there at the end."

"Yes. He was a surprisingly good grandfather the last few years, given his track record as a father."

"Are you angry at him?"

"Oh, no. I let that go years ago. The therapist's name was Sandy."

"Not a very therapist-y name."

"Didn't make her cost any less, though." She snorted a laugh and wiped again at her eyes. "Forrest, are you taking care of yourself? Have you thought about a therapist or something to help you process, I don't know, everything?"

"I never really felt like I needed it. I had a more secure childhood than you. Because I had you. You were the one dealt with a sorry hand. I was useless."

"Forrest. Don't say that. Like I said, it was having you to love that made me turn out okay."

"So what you're telling me is that I'm the reason the world missed out on Gracie Graham's epic rebellious phase."

Gracie shrugged. "I could've made a pretty great Emo girl, I'm sure."

He reached out and squeezed Gracie's hand.

"George is putting the kids in the car. I'd better get out there."

"I'll come with you to send you off."

"Forrest, before we go, I just want to say one more thing. I don't know what is between you and Lucy, but I just want to say she seems like a pretty great person to lean on. She clearly cares about you. She wants to help. You should let her."

Gracie's concern for Forrest came from such a genuine place, he did not want to explain to her that what she was asking was impossible. Lucy was a pretty great person who did care for him, and for that reason exactly, he couldn't allow himself the luxury of leaning on her. He would only hurt her, burden her in the way he was quite sure he had burdened Gracie, even if Gracie was too good to see it.

"Let's go. I want to tell my magnificent niece and nephew goodbye."

She accepted his silence, and they headed out of the room.

***

Everyone was leaving, and Forrest was in the front yard telling them goodbye. Lucy dashed around the kitchen doing various chores before she would escape to her apartment and Clark, hopefully before Forrest came back inside.

Lucy was disgusted with herself for dodging Forrest instead of facing the situation head-on, but emotionally, she just wasn't there yet. And a few days after losing his father, she suspected Forrest wasn't there, either.

Better to keep her distance, lick her wounds, and start focusing on what she was going to do about the president's office job. Forrest would have a couple of weeks of bereavement. She'd already booked an adjunct professor to teach his classes in the interim. By the end of his leave, it was quite possible she would be working across campus for President Burke.

Lucy cringed at the possibility that she might accept a job offer because of man-problems. But perhaps, in one of life's serendipitous tricks, she was simply getting the nudge she needed to pursue something new and exciting. Somehow, though, the thought of not being in the midst of Porter and Edith and Dr. Hubert and, yes, Forrest was hard to force into a positive spin.

Porter came in and plopped onto one of the bar stools at the kitchen island. "Lucy, I'm so tired. My kids, I swear, were intent on making as many poor choices as possible before all was said and done."

"What did you expect? An English professor and a successful journalist pro-create? Clearly, you're going to have over-achievers."

"I just thought they'd overachieve at reading freakishly early or something like that. Not at being relentlessly mischievous."

"Yes, but they're yours."

Porter glared. "Thanks."

"You're welcome. Where does this spoon go?"

Porter stood up, walked around the island, and took the spoon. Then, he said, "Lucy, you're so busy worrying about everything and everyone around you. But, are you okay?"

The look on Porter's face might as well have been a flashing neon sign saying, "I know what happened! I know what happened!"

"Oh no." As mortification rose in a red blush from her neck to the roots of her hair, Lucy exhaled. "He told you."

"Did you tell Miriam?"

Obviously. "Fair enough."

"He's crazy about you, you know?"

"Perhaps, but not quite enough. Or at least, that is what I suspect. Other than a few words of abject apology, we haven't really talked since...well, you know."

"Lucy, dear," Dr. Hubert walked into the room. "Have you seen my glasses? Mrs. Hubert is waiting, rather impatiently I might add, in the car for me."

"Yes, sir. I found them earlier, and put them on the hutch for safe keeping."

"Oh, thank you. I don't know what I'd do without you, Lucy." Lucy tried and failed to ignore the voice insisting that she'd rather Dr. Hubert not have to find out what he'd do.

After retrieving his glasses, Dr. Hubert walked up to Lucy, his eyebrows crushed against the top of the glasses he had just put on. "Lucy, before I leave, I just want to say that Forrest will need all of us right now, but he'll need you the most."

Lucy blanched. Surely, *Dr. Hubert* didn't know, too. She looked over his shoulder to Porter who was shrugging and silently mouthing, "It wasn't me." The resemblance to Billy was uncanny.

"Yes, sir. I'll do my best."

"Well, on that note, I must not keep Mrs. Hubert waiting. I'll see you kids tomorrow at work." He shuffled towards the front. As he opened it, Lucy jumped at the sound of a horn and Mrs. Hubert calling out, "Come on, old man."

Lucy said to Porter, "It's a romance for the ages."

"The crazy thing is, it really is." It only took a few moments in the presence of the Huberts to see their devotion to each other.

Lucy wet and wrung out a washrag. "Do you have any idea what he meant by that, Porter? That Forrest would need me in particular?"

"I have an idea. But you probably don't want to hear it right now."

Lucy suspected he was right. She feared the whole office had invested in some sitcom-esque notion of what the future held for her and Forrest. First, they would fall in love with each other right under their noses, and that love would be enough to change Forrest's ways, reaching far beyond the usual six-month expiration date. He would bend down on one knee right at her desk and propose to her, confessing he'd stared at her from his office for years, yearning for her. At the wedding, each professor would give a toast filled with literary references and inside jokes, and all the guest would be in awe of their little tribe. They would spoil the curiously-articulate children Forrest and Lucy were sure to have just as they did Porter's, and it would further solidify the family unit they had formed in Hart Building over the past ten years. The plot played out in Lucy's mind, each twist more fantastical and beautiful and sentimental and desirable than the previous. Every bit stamped with the words, "Too good to be true."

Lucy finished scrubbing one last already-clean space of the counter and said, "I'm off, Porter. Clark is going to start howling for me soon."

"And you don't want to be here when Forrest walks in?"

She looked at Porter and shrugged. "Tell him I said goodbye, please?"

"If you say so."

Lucy walked out the door and across the yard to her apartment.

CHAPTER 17

F orrest placed a hand on the rail going up to Lucy's apartment and stood still, frozen at the base of the stairs.

When they had sat around his father's grave earlier that day, the sun had kept a chill at bay. Now, gray clouds were gathering as the sun dipped to the horizon, allowing the fall chill to creep in on Forrest. Lucy's apartment would be warm and inviting, the kind of place where cookies came out of the oven and each upholstered chair would have a throw draped across an arm. He stepped onto the first step.

The last of the guests had left an hour earlier. While Forrest thanked Porter and Charlotte profusely, they offered for him to stay and have dinner. He'd made his excuses saying he needed time alone. The truth was, Forrest was feeling a gravitational pull to the tiny apartment in their backyard.

Miriam's words and the presence of friends and family had both helped Forrest find some level of closure. He still had much mourning ahead of him, but he felt more peace about his father's passing than he had experienced since the moment he and Gracie had watched him pass.

Perhaps it was the emotional space cleared by this small measure of closure or the fact that he was simply tired from trying to avoid Lucy while simultaneously feeling desperate to be near her, but Forrest walked out of Porter's house and straight to Lucy's stairs, certain he would not go home yet. Without any fore-planning, he lifted the antique knocker on her front door and let it fall.

Clark answered with rabid barking, announcing that a guest had arrived. Lucy cracked open the door, still looking down at Clark, hushing him futilely. When she finally looked up, her eyes widened and she flushed.

She had changed out of her black dress into black leggings and a long-sleeve, white v-neck shirt. She clearly had not expected to see anyone. The dark lines of a black bra, most likely left behind from the dress, were written through the white t-shirt. Forrest forced his eyes to hers. She pushed up her glasses. "Forrest?"

She was nervous. *He* made her nervous. Damn.

"Hey." Hey? Really? "Hello, Lucy. I was wondering if we could talk."

She opened the door wider, and Clark darted forward, circling frantically around Forrest's knees. "Hey, boy. I've missed you." He petted Clark, feeling excitement vibrating through the dog. It granted a moment for them each to regroup.

The apartment was dim except for a lamp next to the sofa. The same book he'd seen her reading at the hospital lay open beneath the lamplight. He had interrupted her reading. He was a little surprised she was still on the same book. Was she having trouble concentrating like he was? He'.d picked up *Leaves of Grass* the night before, hoping its familiarity would help him calm down enough to sleep. Instead, the subtle, erotic undertones of Whitman's poems had kept him up until the sun was starting to rise. He probably looked like hell. Actually, Edith's exact greeting to him as they all stood talking after the service had been, "You look like hell, Forrest."

As Clark calmed down, an uncomfortable silence settled over the apartment. After years of easy conversations, it felt tragic. What else could Forrest lose in a week? "I just wanted to thank you for being there today."

"Of course. Why wouldn't I be?"

"I don't know. After everything, after what I did." He turned from her, pretending to look at a houseplant she kept near a window. The thing about services for the dead is that the grief of those closest to the deceased is on stark display for everyone to see. Forrest was so tired of being seen, of people's eyes pausing for a moment on the bags beneath his own.

At the same time, even as he hid from her, Forrest wanted comforting. He wanted to find comfort in Lucy's embrace and in the cocoon her hair created around his face when she was straddled over him whispering into his ear. He imagined that given how perfectly Lucy-like the rest of her apartment was, her bedroom would be an oasis of her. The door was a few steps away from him. If he walked in there, would she follow? Forrest shook away the thought. He would not use her again. She deserved infinitely more.

Without any physical touch, Forrest knew that Lucy had walked up behind him. The air heated the entire length of his back. Tentatively, Lucy said, "Not what you did. What we did. It was both of us, Forrest. It was you and me."

He should not turn around. He could walk a few steps, put distance between them. He could bend over and pet Clark, breaking the pull he felt, as if a rope tied around him was being yanked by Lucy.

He turned around, though.

Lucy reached up, and smoothed his hair, running her hands all the way down the length of his beard. He closed his eyes and tilted his forehead so that it rested on Lucy's. He felt more present to her caress than he had felt to anything during the past few days. It was as if a haze had lifted, and everything was in hyper-focus.

He opened his eyes again and lifted his head, wanting to see again without fog. The lamp was behind Lucy, illuminating her hair with back-lighting. She looked ethereal, the curls perpetually loose from her bun each glowing individually. Lucy must have washed off her makeup from the day. Each freckle was articulated perfectly across her nose. Forrest was a student of poetry, but he'd never written a lyrical verse. In a week filled with things over which to mourn, this felt particularly tragic. Was he too old to learn new tricks?

With her hands still cupping each side of Forrest's beard, Lucy closed the distance between them simply by shifting to her toes. Forrest marveled again at how perfectly their bodies matched. Had he only dated short women before? No one had ever fit like Lucy.

They each tilted their faces in silent agreement that neither would or could resist the pull between them. When Lucy's lips touched his own, Forrest lost a few more battles. His hands wrapped around her, running up and down the length of her back. Then, they lowered to her ass, pressing her into him.

Wearing leggings as pants was a phenomenon that had come into fashion when Forrest was young and perpetually looking for his next partner. Then, as he had matured, they had faded into the surroundings, no longer particularly exciting. But as Forrest felt how thin the fabric was, the access it afforded for him to explore, he thanked the fashion powers that be. Hoisting upward, Lucy read his movements perfectly. Her legs went around his mid-section, and he walked them to the sofa, knocking over the coat rack heavy with fall jackets along their way.

Lacking finesse or grace, driven only by hunger, Forrest fell into the sofa, reveling in the weight of Lucy as she, too, fell on top of him. His lips trailed down her neck, pausing at her collar bones to dip his tongue into each nook and cranny before he pulled the white shirt off of her and continued trailing his kisses further down.

The bedside lamp in his bedroom had been too dim. Forrest had not noticed just how porcelain and smooth her breasts were. But maybe it wasn't the lighting. Maybe it was the way she contrasted against the black silk that brought it into focus. Whatever the cause, Forrest paused and stared, the lines still visible when he blinked. Then, he leaned forward, leaving no area untouched or unnoticed.

As Forrest paused to take a breath, Lucy took over, kissing his neck and giving particular attention to the area just below his ear. She was, as always, brilliant. One night with him, and she had already learned how to undo him.

Forrest turned his head to grant her better access. But then, damn his hyper-focus, Forrest noticed something that stopped him in his tracks.

Beneath the romance novel on the end table, there was another book with a bookmark at about the half-way point. It was a copy of Mark Twain's *Eve's Diary*, the widowed Twain's posthumous love letter to his wife. Forrest remembered telling Lucy about the book when he'd seen her shelf of romance novels. It portrayed Eve as cleverer than her husband and the center of his universe. Eve was everything Lucy should be and would be to the man with whom she one day fell in love.

Forrest had recommended that book because Lucy was a romantic and it was his favorite romance. She was reading about the love of a man for his treasured wife. She deserved to be the heroine of a great romance. She was built for that role.

Forrest pulled back. Lucy must have sensed the shift. She pulled back, too.

"I'm so sorry, Lucy. I can't do this."

***

Lucy dug through her shirt drawer until she found something black, long-sleeved, and with a very high neck. Her white v-neck was lying somewhere in her living room floor, discarded clandestinely and now wrinkled and covered in dog hair. *Like a metaphor for my life*, a bitter voice Lucy hardly recognized muttered in her head.

When Forrest had backed away and apologized (Apologized? Had she not received enough apologies from him to preemptively cover this little snafu?) Lucy had unceremoniously stood up and rushed to her room, mumbling, "I'll just be a moment."

I'll just be a moment? Had she really said that?

Lucy took a moment to play "What would Edith do?" She would have tilted her eyes into her signature a-comma-doesn't-go-there glare and said something along the lines of, "Stop treating me like some fragile, wilting flower from one of your damned 19th-century novels. Clearly, we want to have sex, so let's have sex."

Lucy shook her head. She would need more lessons from Edith before she worked up the gumption for that. How about "What would Miriam do?"

This one was easy. After so long a friendship, Lucy knew Miriam like she knew the back of her hand. Miriam would've calmly dismounted, somehow making it look cool and, like, no-big-deal. She then would have taken Forrest's hands, looked deeply into his eyes until he was too disconcerted to mutter some asinine apology, and said, "Forrest, clearly we need to talk about your shit before we move forward." Then she would've cleared up decades of mommy-issues and self-doubts with the precision of a surgeon.

Yes, Miriam would have handled the whole situation sublimely, but alas, Lucy was the one hiding in her bedroom from the man with whom she was now quite certain she was in love. Hiding because he wouldn't stop apologizing for what was happening between them. Hiding because she did not want to cry in front of him. Her tears were for Clark's eyes only. Hiding because if she walked back in there, she feared he would say something or she would say something that they would not be able to un-say. They stood at a precipice.

Lucy grabbed a knee-length sweater and put it on over her shirt. Best to cover her behind as well as her breasts. They were all causing her problems here lately. Lucy wrapped the sweater tightly around herself. Armored, she opened the door.

Forrest was pacing back and forth across the short distance of her living room, his hair standing on end. He stopped pacing as her door creaked, staring at her.

"Gee, Forrest. You look like hell."

"You sound like Edith."

"Ha. I wish."

Forrest looked perplexed. Resentment was not a normal tone to hear coming from Lucy. Maybe she did have more Edith in her than she realized.

"What are you thinking, Luce?"

The sound of her nickname pulled at Lucy. The tug hurt. She thought of the fantasy from earlier, of a future where she and Forrest are together. In that future, he would say, "Goodnight, Luce," right before he kissed her goodnight. And then, of course, the innocent goodnight kiss would turn into yet another late night. They would both be sleep-deprived in that future.

Lucy dismissed the thoughts. She had built a life on being practical, admitting that most fantasies, whether they be her own or her mother's, were not attainable.

Suddenly, Lucy felt something roiling inside of her, something she had not expected. It felt suspiciously like anger. She was angry at Forrest. How absolutely foreign to associate anger with Forrest, almost as foreign as it had felt to acknowledge attraction to him over these past few weeks. During their ten years of almost constant proximity, where had all of these feelings been? Why now? Why, just as Forrest was losing his father and Lucy was considering moving on from Hart Building, were they erupting? Anger and attraction and passion joined the party now?

"Luce?"

"I'm thinking that we're about to have a let's-be-friends-talk. A let's-pretend-this-never-happened talk. I don't know if I want to hear it from you, Forrest."

He looked ashen, drained. "I don't know what else to say. I don't have another or a better talk to give to you right now. I wish. I wish with all of myself that I could have any other talk with you. I do Lucy."

"Then let's do that, Forrest. Let's have another talk, a different talk. Let's talk about how good it felt to be with each other. Let's talk about how right we are together. Please, Forrest, please tell me I'm not the only one who feels this way." Lucy hated the pleading in her voice. She was angry with him. She didn't want to beg. She didn't want to ask to be loved in return.

"You're not the only one, Lucy. I have never..." His words broke off. He swiped at an eye with the same jerky movement he used when he ran his hands through his hair. "I've never felt anything like this with anyone. But, Lucy, I've never wanted to feel this. I've spent my whole adult life making sure I never felt like this. I have no control around you. You consume me."

"If that's the case, then why was it so easy to call a stop to it tonight."

"Lucy, I know you don't believe me, but it was the hardest thing I've ever done in my life."

A tense quiet built in the room. Clark whimpered.

"I've seen you date a dozen different women without a modicum of hesitation. Why now? Why are you all of the sudden unable to be with someone, to be with me?"

"Because you're you. Because you're Lucy O'Shields. Because Porter can't give you some ridiculous nickname that we all laugh at, and I sure as hell can't walk out on you six months from now with a clear conscience, and Lucy, you know you can't be casual. It's not you. That's part of what I love about you. I wouldn't want you to be different. I just can't live up to everything being with you would mean."

Part of what he loved about her? The word reverberated through her. She did not feel loved.

"Forrest, there are a hundred little voices in my head right now telling me all of the reasons you're walking away from me right now. Incidentally, most of them are my mother's."

"Lucy, I never wanted to make you feel this way. I'm so..."

"Don't, Forrest. Don't apologize. Don't worry about me. I have developed strategies over the years. I've had a lot of practice for how to deal with these voices."

"Don't you see, Lucy? That's what happens. That is what being in a real relationship with me would mean. Relationships are messy. You mean the world to me, but I end up making you feel bad things. I make you hear a bunch of lying, messed-up voices in your head. And it's a shame. It's a crying shame. Because, Lucy, you're so beautiful and brilliant. You're absolutely perfect. Please, don't listen to those voices. I'm the problem here, Lucy."

As he finished speaking, his shoulders slumped. Normally, Lucy would see slumped shoulders and immediately jump into action. She would order a latte or bake a pan of brownies or send a perfectly-curated playlist, whatever suited the individual. And she would fix it. She would fix their hurt with a perfectly timed gesture.

But for the first time in a very long time, Lucy did not have the emotional energy to tend another's wounds. Her own were too raw.

Forrest had paced one more time across the room, but he must have caught a second wind because he turned back to Lucy and said, "You really are the most brilliant person I know, Lucy. And you've been a secretary, *a secretary*, for a decade? What if that is me, Lucy? What if this thing we have, this friendship or attraction or whatever the hell it is, what if that is what has held you back all of these years?"

Suddenly, all the anger that had been building since she'd hid in her bedroom burst to the forefront, the reigns slipping from her grasp. "Forrest, don't you dare belittle the past decade of my life. You may think that making sure Dr. Hubert gets his afternoon nap or building Legos with Porter's boys or reminding Edith that she has a heart and it's a damn good one, you may think that was all a waste. But it wasn't. I have loved every single moment.

"And as for you, the late nights editing your articles or talking about what we're reading or making sure your Dad was okay or just being with you, being in an adjacent office to yours? I wouldn't trade those moments for anything. Not even some fancy job with a high salary.

"I didn't come to this job with a lot of fond memories from my childhood." Tears threatened, but Lucy forced herself to finish. "I was a failure. A failure at every dream my mother ever had for me. But in Hart Building, I'm not a failure. There, I'm indispensable. And I have somehow gained a family who has loved me for who I am. Or at least, I thought that was what I had."

Forrest was completely still, paralyzed in the presence of her anger. Finally, he said, "I'll start looking for another position. I'll leave PSU so you can stay in your job."

After gliding over countless opportunities to tell him, Lucy knew the moment had arrived. "No, Forrest. I've been offered a job as Administrative Assistant to President Burke, and I will be accepting the position. I'll be gone by the time you return from your bereavement leave."

The muscles in his jaw twitched. Was he angry she hadn't told him? Disappointed she was moving to another secretarial position? Regardless, his opinion hardly mattered now.

Not betraying any specific emotion, Forrest said, "I'll head out."

Another long pause followed, during which they stared into each other's eyes across the room without saying a word. Just when she most could have used the strength it provided, Lucy's anger ran out. Within their little English Department family, Forrest was so warm and loving and dependable. He would be a magnificent husband and father. If only his mother had not walked out on him. If only his father had not been a shell of a man most of his life. If only he could trust himself. What a waste it all was.

But hadn't she known? Wasn't this why she had spent the past few days curled around a bowl of popcorn on her sofa.

"I knew the second you looked at me in the hospital that next day. I knew right away."

He didn't ask her what she had known. He didn't need to.

"Goodnight, Lucy." The door clicked behind him.

Lucy walked around the couch and picked up the white shirt from the floor. She passed it several times between each hand, feeling its weight in the palms of her hands. Then, she threw it across the room, where it limply hit the front door, and landed in a heap right where Forrest had walked out.

***

Lucy was back on the sofa, but this time, there was nothing on the TV. Why watch a fictional apocalypse when the real thing had just happened in her living room? She sat in the dark in a silence only occasionally punctuated by a moan from Clark or Lucy's own sniffles.

Lucy had been through a few minor break-ups over the years. One was even not-so-minor, ending a year-long relationship the year after she'd graduated. The boyfriend, a fellow English student at PSU, had declared he would go to LA to try and make it as a screenwriter. Lucy had felt little more than a twinge of regret. She'd known instantly that a small twinge was not enough on which to build a long-distance, serious relationship. She had cried a few tears over the wasted year with him, but it had only taken a week or two for her to move past the break-up blues.

Tonight was completely different, like she had a gaping wound that would take eons to heal. She had only slept with this guy one-and-a-half times (this was how she had decided to quantify her physical encounters with Forrest at around the two-hour mark of sitting in dark silence). Why was this one so much more painful?

But, of course, Lucy knew the answer to her own question. While the one-and-a-half sexual encounters had been divine (there are so few non-ironic opportunities to use that word, but really, it applied here), they had only served to clarify what already existed between her and Forrest, the loss of which she was now mourning. The two were connected, each compatible halves of a heretofore contented whole. They had spent years staying up late editing his writing, laughing about campus gossip, simply existing together in the little world of their Hart Building office. And somewhere along the way, this companionship had morphed for Lucy into a deep, abiding love.

It was the kind of love Lucy had hoped existed just enough to keep her up late reading paperback romances into the wee hours of the morning on more than one occasion. It was also the kind of love that she had felt certain was not for girls like her. She was not a damsel in distress (despite current appearances), nor did she want to be. She liked being the fixer, the one who rescued others. She was not frail or fragile as her mother had hoped she would be, and while she did not project strength and power in the manner of Edith and Miriam, she knew both were in her possession. It was just that her strength was a steady undercurrent, quiet but present and determinative. It had carried her through the countless invalidations through her youth and the loss of her mother before their relationship could be mended. It had carried her through into the person she was today, a person capable of loving herself and others deeply and truly.

And so here she was, loving Forrest with every fiber of her being and suspecting he loved her in return, but unable to make him love himself enough to trust that they could be together. And if she were going to get through this pain, through the loss of the man who was likely the great love of her life, Lucy would need to draw on all the reserves of strength in her possession.

Clark whimpered again. "I know, Clark. I know, buddy."

Looking down where Clark's eyes were shining in the dark of the room, Lucy knew that she would need her friends to help her navigate the coming months. She would not be better in a week. She was a person familiar enough with the mechanics of grief to know the timetable.

And perhaps the hardest part of it all would be that one of her allies and pillars of strength would now be off limits. There would be no mysterious flowers showing up on her desk or books with silly inscriptions or questioning looks through his open doorway when she looked depressed. During the months following her mother's passing, he had honed a quirk of the shoulder that clearly said, "Are you okay?" He could do it at any time. During a staff meeting, when they were alone in his office working on some article, if they saw each other across campus.

Had that time been when she'd fallen in love with him? Or was it watching him come over when Charlotte was out of town to lend Porter a hand with the kids? Was it the surprisingly sappy speech he'd delivered at the Huberts' 50th wedding anniversary party or all the times he had thanked her for talking with his dad because he was so worried he might be lonely?

As Lucy composed a list of moments in which Forrest Graham had become a little dearer to her, a little more ingrained in the fabric of her heart, a knock came at the door. Clark immediately abandoned mourning as he barked in jubilation that someone new had arrived.

"Well, that got you in a good mood. I wish it was that easy for me, Clark."

She opened the door to find Edith and Miriam, each clutching their coats tightly around them against the cool night air. Edith wore an expression Lucy had never seen on her face. Was that sheepishness?

"So, I know I really suck at being nice and, you know, caring. But I'd like to try."

Miriam added, "And I'm sort of an expert at caring, so here we are."

Lucy opened the door wider, making room for Clark's greeting ritual. They walked in, Edith mumbling under her breath, "Oh, dear. Let's get some lights on in this place."

As Edith moved around the apartment finding and turning on lamps, Lucy said, "How did you two know? I mean, we broke up, or whatever you call ending a relationship that never really began, a few hours ago."

"Porter was spying from the kitchen window," Edith said.

"And he conference called Edith and I. Since you're not technically a member of Trinity and, thereby, one of my parishioners, I'm allowed to gossip about you."

"Hashtag ethics?" Lucy quipped.

"Exactly. So anyways, Porter reported that Forrest came to your place after he left their house. He then left these premises looking, in Porter's words, 'like he'd just been rejected by every academic publisher this side of the Mississippi.' So it didn't take a genius to figure out what had happened."

Edith, who was now rummaging around the kitchen, said, "Although, for the record, if it had taken a genius..."

Lucy finished the thought, "You clearly would have been just fine."

"Clearly."

For the first time since Forrest had left, Lucy's eyes were dry.

Edith passed wine glasses to Miriam who had brought her own corkscrew and was prepared to pour. Edith said, "We wanted to do something for you, you know, like you do for the men I break up with."

"Yes?"

Miriam said, "So I brought chocolate and wine..."

"...and I brought a Ruth Bader Ginsburg documentary." Edith was beaming with pride.

Lucy's chin shook in a horribly undignified manner. So much for the dry eyes. "Oh, girls. This is the nicest thing anyone has ever done for me."

CHAPTER 18

I t was the end of the day on Friday, and the week in which Forrest had buried his father, and Lucy's relationship with Forrest had both begun and imploded was coming to an end. It had been a busy week.

After the past few evenings on her couch, Lucy feared her eyes would never return to a non-puffy state. She'd shed tears like Kentucky house tea sheds condensation. During the day, she was in the office, constantly reminded of Forrest every time she looked up but at least too busy to wallow. When she went home, her mind was free to focus on Forrest, trying to decipher where exactly she had gone wrong. Was it the glass of wine (or was it two) that she had consumed at his father's table? Was it when she had agreed to go to Mayfield with him in the first place? Or was it Edith's damned green shirt?

Emails to students graduating in December had just been sent with a multitude of attachments Lucy would have to badger them to complete and return. Unfortunately, no part of college came without paperwork, including getting out of it. To reward herself, Lucy was taking a moment to do absolutely nothing. She sat in her swivel chair, rhythmically rotating it ninety degrees to the right and then back to the left with equal rotation. Back and forth. Back and forth. Swivel chairs were one of the few things in life that didn't completely lose their childhood charm. When Lucy was little, her dad would spin her in his office chair as she giggled until her mother would come in and complain about the indignity of it all.

After one last swoosh, Lucy shook herself from her reverie. Students had cleared off campus ready to start their weekend, so now was her chance to do the thing she'd been putting off all day: turn in her official resignation. President Burke had been thrilled with her phone call Wednesday morning, the day after the funeral.

Glancing through the doorway into Dr. Hubert's office, Lucy saw Edith sitting across from him with her feet propped on his desk, a glass of Kentucky Bourbon sitting on the arm of her chair. Dr. Hubert was leaning back in his own chair, a glass of amber liquid propped on his ample stomach. He was laughing at whatever outrageous and boundary-pushing statement Edith had just made.

Lucy walked in and sat in the second chair he kept opposite his desk. Dr. Hubert immediately pulled a glass and flask from his bottom desk drawer. "Here, Lucy, dear. Let me get you a little something to start the weekend."

"That would be lovely. I could use it. I'm afraid I need to talk to you two."

In all reality, she was only obligated to tell Edith as the department chair. But since Forrest was out of the office on bereavement and Porter had headed home to start family movie night early, it seemed natural to tell the two who were in the office with her.

Edith quirked an eyebrow. "I don't know if I want to hear this. Would it be okay if I put my fingers in my ears and yelled 'Na-na-na-na'?"

Dr. Hubert swallowed a gulp. "I'm lucky. If I don't want to hear something, I just turn off my hearing aid."

Edith said, "Now might be a good time to do that."

"That won't be necessary," Lucy said. What she had to say would be sad in the way one gets sad the day after Christmas because something really good has passed. But Lucy was not naive. She knew the office would chug along without her. She took one fortifying sip of her drink and said through the burn, "I'm officially resigning my position as secretary. I've accepted the job as President Burke's assistant."

Edith and Dr. Hubert each took another sip of bourbon. "Damn it," Edith said.

"President Burke said I'm welcome to come here a couple hours a day while you transition and train someone new. I'm sorry. I really am. I just need a change of scenery. I need to try something new, see what I can do outside of this office."

"We understand, dear." Dr. Hubert's short proclamation reverberated through the room. His voice really was created by the gods of academia for lecture halls. Lucy fidgeted in her chair, as if repositioning would stop a tear from making an appearance.

"Thank you, Dr. Hubert."

Edith said, "And as for me, I understand, too. And I support you. I just think it is a shame you aren't leaving our office to, I don't know, run the UN or be Secretary of State or something. You're brilliant. And insanely competent. President Burke is lucky to get you."

"That's incredibly kind, Edith."

"I'm not trying to be kind."

Lucy held up her hands, the liquid swishing in her glass. "Of course not."

From her desk, Lucy heard a text message notification. "Let me go check on that."

When she got there, she saw the words, "Could you tell the old man I've arrived?"

Lucy returned to Dr. Hubert's doorway. "Time to put away the fun stuff and pop a mint. Mrs. Hubert is here to drive you home." She laid a tin of Altoids in front of him.

"Oh Lucy, there will never be another like you." He popped the mint, and then groaned at his knees as he stood up. Lucy could swear she heard joints popping across the room.

After he left and Lucy started cleaning up her desk, Edith came into her space with her arms crossed and questions in her eyes. "Lucy, is working in the President's office what you really want to do? Is this your top choice?"

"My top choice? What do you mean?"

"If you were dreaming, if you were at summer camp doing an ice-breaker activity and you had to say what you wanted to be when you grew up, would you say, 'I, Lucy O'Shields, want to be the administrative assistant to the president of a small liberal arts college?'"

"I mean, no? No, who wants to be that when they're fourteen and covered in bug spray next to some acne-riddled boy they have a crush on?"

"Wow, I really hit a chord with the summer camp analogy."

"But really, Edith. I wanted to be married to Colin Firth and have three daughters, all of whom would love to read Jane Austen and the Brontë sisters, and we would live in England, obviously, and have crumpets for whatever meal English people eat crumpets at. That was the level of my dreaming, and I'm pretty sure that ship has sailed."

"Okay, but 32-year-old Lucy. The one standing in front of me whose dreams of Colin Firth have clearly been crushed. What does that Lucy want?"

Lucy fell heavily into her chair. In reality, she'd spent so many years basking in being needed by the four people wreathing her office, she had not questioned her own lack of ambition. But now, she was beginning to wonder if she had just been biding her time, wondering if Colin Firth was actually the bearded guy in the office to the right, and he was just taking his time noticing that his perfect companion was answering the phone. Maybe she hadn't been content so much as she had simply been willing to wait for other people to fulfill her dreams.

"Edith, I'm so ashamed to admit this, but adult Lucy doesn't have dreams or goals. I forgot such things even existed."

Edith's voice softened, a rare phenomenon for her. "That's okay, Luce. Let's start with this question: What have you enjoyed doing the most, career-wise, during your time here with us?"

Lucy thought back to the conversation she'd had with Forrest a few weeks ago, when he had asked her why she edited for him. "Oh, well, that's easy. I love editing. I love finding all the mistakes you all make. I love the red ink, and I love being the one person who is really good at spotting typos or grammatical errors or gaps in lines of argument. I mean, that isn't part of my job as secretary. I've just done it on the side. But I've always loved it."

Edith nodded as Lucy talked. "Okay. That's good to know. We'll file that information away for now. But don't worry, we'll get back to it."

"Oh dear. Have you become my life coach? When did that happen?"

Edith tapped the edge of Lucy's desk. "Don't you worry about that. For now, I meant it when I said I understood why you had to take the other job."

"Good. Will you help me shop this weekend for clothes for my new gig?"

"Ooh, with color?"

"Yes."

"And prints?"

"Sure?"

"And accessories?"

"How can the world's biggest feminist be so girly?"

"I'll pick you up at nine o'clock tomorrow morning."

***

In the bleak gray and white landscape that was Forrest Graham's apartment, the lone occupant lay on the floor between the beige sofa and the television, his neck kinked so that his head wouldn't be on top of one of many greasy pizza boxes strewn across the area. He was wearing boxer briefs and an old Nirvana t-shirt he had found in the dresser of his childhood room. It smelled musty. He wasn't sure if the odor was a product of not having been worn for twenty years, or if it was from having now been worn three days by a man in desperate need of a shower. Either way, it was musty.

His beard, usually so smooth, looked as though he had slept on it from half a dozen different angles. He wasn't sure how he had achieved this effect seeing as how he had not slept on his face. Apparently, all those fancy oils Gracie supplied him with worked miracles. He had not walked into his bathroom for anything but the use of the toilet for days, leaving his facial landscape neglected to say the least.

Forrest had lowered himself into this position with much groaning, hoping it would ease the pain in his lower back, a gnawing ache that had started gathering about halfway through day two of sitting on his couch binging on war movies. Forrest stared at the circular ring of light cast onto the ceiling by the lamp. Once upon a time, Forrest would get sore from jogging too far or doing too many pull-ups in some college dorm competition. Now, he was sore because he had sat on the couch too long? Forrest cursed aging and couches and lower backs.

As he raised his arms over his head in an attempt to stretch his back, he cursed the need for showers while he was at it.

Forrest had seen a lot of blood and gore since walking out of Lucy's apartment Tuesday night. Somehow, crying during the motivational speeches that occurred before the climactic battle scenes seemed more acceptable than crying over the current wreck in which he found his life. So Forrest wept over basically the same words declared by similarly-muscled men in battles ranging from the Middle Ages to the Vietnam War. It didn't really matter the era. Apparently, generals have been giving the same speech for quite a while now, and the same short, doe-eyed sidekick has been dying for all of that time, as well. Despite the repetition, Forrest allowed the tears to flow each time. He had years of suppressed emotion to make up for. If he was stuck doing bereavement leave, he would bereave the hell out of it.

What Forrest did not think about when those tears were flowing was his father's weak whispers during that last day, how he had clearly wanted to have a normal conversation with the two kids he'd neglected so much when they had lived under the same roof as him during their youth. He did not think about the worry in Gracie's eyes when she had said goodbye, worry about him, Forrest. He banished thoughts of how damn tragic alcoholism was and what a good dad his father likely would have been had he not been sick with longing for the next glass.

And he sure as hell did not think about Lucy. About the hurt he had put in her eyes, or the pleading he had heard in her voice, or the way she felt when they were pressed together within the tight confines of a twin bed. Those thoughts were strictly off limits.

After determining that stretching had no beneficial effect on back pain, Forrest contemplated the possibility of bending a knee towards his chest. Just as he was groaning with the effort to do so, he heard a knock at the front door.

"Oh shit." He was going to have to stand up. And put pants on.

For the first time in half a week, Forrest moved quickly. Grimacing, he jumped up and ran to his bedroom, pulled on a pair of jeans that were crumpled on the floor. Running his hands down his legs, Forrest made a futile attempt to flatten the wrinkles. Apparently, wadding jeans within a pile of clothes was not the best storage option. Just as he reached the door, the bell rang for a third time.

Forrest opened the door to find Dr. Hubert and Porter standing side-by-side, and in front of them (and at least a foot shorter than either) was Mrs. Hubert, her finger still on the doorbell button. She was decked out in a purple tweed pantsuit and matching hat, and her other hand held the handle to a rectangular quilted case with "The Huberts" embroidered on the side. Dr. Hubert's eyes were inscrutable beneath the shadow of his eyebrows, Porter looked apologetic, and Mrs. Hubert simply looked determined.

"Forrest, boy," she declared as she held up the hand with the mystery container. "I've brought a casserole. When one is sad, one needs to eat. That is what I always say. So let's get you eating."

"How kind of you." Forrest stepped back, allowing Mrs. Hubert to step in.

She likely thought she was talking under her breath, but given her hearing loss, it was quite loud when she said, "Oh, dear. We've got some work to do." With that, Mrs. Hubert headed directly for his kitchen. Forrest flinched at the sound of her inhaling when she saw his kitchen, buried as it was under even more greasy pizza boxes.

"Hello, son," Dr. Hubert said as he walked in.

"Dr. Hubert, it's good to see you."

As Dr. Hubert headed for the couch and started moving some trash to clear a space to sit, Porter pulled Forrest onto the front porch. He frantically whispered, "Dr. Hubert said he wanted to come check on you. I had no idea Mrs. Hubert was coming, too, and she insisted on driving. Turns out, they're both too old to be driving, Forrest. Too damn old."

Forrest, lacking the emotional energy required to feel sorry for Porter's plight, said only, "Sorry, bud," while patting Porter's shoulder as he walked over the threshold into Forrest's den of slothfulness.

Porter paused mid-stride. "Whoa, Forrest. What happened here?"

"My dad just died." Forrest had not expected to play that card quite so soon.

"Forrest, dear?" Mrs. Hubert's voice rang from the kitchen.

"Yes, ma'am?"

"Where are your cleaning supplies?"

Forrest ran to the doorway of his kitchen. "Really, Mrs. Hubert, that isn't neces-"

"Oh, hush. Where are they?" Her tone left no room for argument.

"Under the sink."

"Good. Now you go keep the doctor company."

Although they were all technically doctors, Forrest didn't have to ask to whom she was referring. He returned to the living room, removed an empty soda can from the recliner next to the couch, and gingerly lowered himself into the seat.

Barely holding in a growl of pain, Forrest said, "Well, gentlemen, how are you today?"

"Actually, Forrest," Dr. Hubert said, "we have come to ask you that question."

Forrest pulled on the collar of his t-shirt the way he pulled on his tie when a student asked a question he didn't care to answer. Then he remembered he wasn't wearing a work shirt with a tie, but rather a Nirvana t-shirt with a hole in each armpit. He crossed his arms over Kirk Cobain's face.

"Oh, you know, all things considered, I'm doing fine."

"Really?" Porter said. "Is that why I had to move two empty bags of Extra Fiery Cheetos before I sat down. Because no man as close to forty as you are is okay after eating two bags of Extra Fiery Cheetos."

"I've been better, obviously." And, yes, those two bags had cost him dearly, but he would never admit it to Porter.

Dr. Hubert crossed his hands over his bulging mid-section and closed his eyes. Forrest braced himself for the truth-bombs Dr. Hubert was likely to drop. "Forrest, as you know, I am an avid reader of the great Sir Arthur Conan Doyle, and as such, have become more intuitive than I would be otherwise. So allow me to intuit a few things."

Shit. "Yes, sir."

"Since the time you first joined us, son, I have been impressed with your drive and fastidiousness and control. You were so young for a professor, and yet you immediately contributed immensely to the department. Looking around your apartment and seeing you today, I would say that our normal, self-controlled Forrest is in some dire straits. I'm sure that this is in large part due to the passing of your father, a man I'm convinced must have been wonderful to have raised a son like you despite struggling with the great onus of alcoholism."

An image of his father sitting at the table holding his essay after the basketball game flashed through Forrest's mind. With it came a flicker of gratitude, just enough to make him loosen his grip on his bitterness. "Yes, sir."

"However, I suspect that your father's passing does not account for all of your distress."

Forrest placed his right elbow on his left arm and propped his chin into his cupped hand. The position covered more of Cobain's face. "Hm-hmm?"

Dr. Hubert's eyebrows rose like an owl posturing as he looked directly at Forrest. "Our dear Lucy informed Dr. Rose and I yesterday afternoon that she has taken a position as the administrative assistant to President Burke. I suspect you know of this development."

"I'd heard." Forrest squirmed. Why wasn't Porter saying anything? Couldn't he have brought one of the boys for a little distraction?

"Furthermore..."

Of course there was more.

"Forrest, I suspect that losing Lucy's presence in our office just as you are dealing with another great loss must be quite devastating to you. Especially seeing as how you are so particularly fond of her."

Porter was checking a cuticle at very close range. Was he suppressing a smile? That bastard.

"Well, we are all fond of Lucy, aren't we?" Forrest said. Porter snorted. Forrest trudged on. "Admittedly, I have always found her to be charming and kind and an engaging conversationalist..."

"Forrest, son. Forgive me for interrupting your list making, as entertaining as it is, but I am no fool. It may have been many decades since I was in the first stages of love for my dear Mrs. Hubert, but I assure you, I remember each detail of how it felt and how it looked and how I acted. You, son, are smitten."

Just as Forrest was about to mount his counter-argument, Mrs. Hubert walked past them with a laundry basket that, good grief, had a pair of his boxers laying at the top. He jumped to his feet, "Mrs. Hubert, really, you don't have to do this. It's so kind..."

"Hush, boy. I will decide what I do or do not do. We all need help in our times of grief. So I'm here to help."

Forrest fell back into his seat, completely helpless. No wonder Lucy could always get Dr. Hubert to do whatever he was supposed to do simply by name-dropping Mrs. Hubert. "Yes, Mrs. Hubert."

After showing a remarkable ability to be completely silent, Porter said, "Good choice."

Forrest sent him a glare, and then in exasperation said, "Okay. Let's say you're right and I do have a thing for Lucy. I've already blown it."

"How's that?" Now Porter was going to join the conversation?

"I've never had a single disagreement with Lucy in the ten years I've worked by her side. At least not over anything more consequential than which is the best sandwich condiment. But we are together one time..." Oh no. That was definitely an admission in front of Dr. Hubert that he had slept with Lucy. "One time - well, really one-and-a-half - but anyways, now she hates me. You should have seen the look in her eyes the last time we spoke. It was hurt and anger and confusion. It was nothing good, and I put those feelings there."

"I would assume," Dr. Hubert said, "that you feel this anger and pain means you two did something wrong. Your conclusion after these events is that you and Lucy should not be together. Am I correct in interpreting what you are saying?"

"Of course that's what it means. People can't be together in a relationship if they are fighting all of the time."

"Says who?" Dr. Hubert sat up straighter, asking the question with the verve of a great orator. "After fifty years of marriage, I can assure you that arguing is an essential part of the package, and if done right, damn good foreplay."

Forrest's eyes swelled unblinkingly. Porter nodded his head once and said, "Quite right, sir. Quite right."

Dr. Hubert lifted his hands from his stomach, his palms facing outward as he said, "But perhaps I'm overstepping my bounds. Maybe you and Lucy just don't suit. Perhaps you tried and found you have no chemistry?"

Forrest immediately guffawed. He tried to articulate his denial, that no, indeed, a lack of chemistry was not their problem, but he couldn't seem to get past a bout of sputtering.

Porter looked to Dr. Hubert. "I had no idea a blush could be visible through such a bushy beard."

Dr. Hubert said nothing, but Forrest could swear he winked back at Porter.

Finally, Forrest managed to say, "A lack of chemistry is not the problem."

Just as the words left his mouth, Mrs. Hubert strode into the room with a feather duster. He didn't own a feather duster, did he? Had she brought her own feather duster? Who walks around with a feather duster in their purse? "We need some color in here, dear. Tomorrow, I'll bring over a few wall-hangings someone donated to the church's thrift store. We'll see what we can do."

Before he could come up with a way, anyway, to get out of redecorating, she was off to another room and another task. Forrest tried to decipher how he'd come to this moment in life. Was it only a month ago that he'd sat across from Dr. Wray bored out of his mind while listening to the latest research on some bug thing he couldn't remember? Now he was a disheveled wreck in the middle of a filthy apartment that Mrs. Hubert was cleaning while Dr. Hubert gave him relationship advice and Porter watched with a smirk.

Dr. Hubert continued, "So if chemistry isn't the problem, what is?"

Forrest didn't have to sputter or hesitate or even think. Because in between all the war movies and insides-torching food, he had been ruminating on this same question. "I'm the problem. When I was young, I saw what my mom leaving did to my dad. And Gracie told me what they had been like when they had been together. Crazy about each other one minute, fighting like cats and dogs the next. So I promised myself a long time ago that I wouldn't go down that road, I wouldn't fall madly in love and do all of that business. I don't want to ever hurt anyone that way, and I'd rather not be hurt either. And I haven't. I've been careful in all of my relationships. I've kept things neat and tidy, and no one has gotten hurt. And now, the one person, the *one* person I most don't want to hurt, I've hurt. Because for all of one night, I let my guard down."

"Oh Forrest," Porter was sighing and rubbing the bridge of his nose. "There is just so much misinterpretation going on there."

"There really is," Dr. Hubert confirmed with a nod.

"What? That's harsh." Forrest had been expecting consolation, support.

Porter said, "I don't really know where to start. I mean, I don't know where to start in explaining to you all of the different ways you're wrong about this. There are so many. You are the most brilliant scholar I've ever met. But this is just..." He sighed the sigh of the long-suffering.

"Porter?" He was suddenly chatty.

Porter continued, "Here's the thing, Forrest. I know I'm supposed to give you the you-are-not-your-dad talk right now, but really, it's more complex than that. To be fair, you are a little bit your dad. You are the part of your dad that calls his son's secretary at least once a week to check on him. The part that collects and reads the thousands on top of thousands of words his son writes over the most minuscule details of 19th-century American Literature."

"Your writing really is prolific, Forrest," Dr. Hubert said.

"Thank you?"

Porter continued, "That's the part of yourself that shows up at my house when Charlotte is out of town to play with my boys while I get Anna to bed. But the parts of your dad that missed school events and never made you dinner and didn't know how to talk with you about basic growing-up problems, those parts of your dad you clearly are not. In large part because he made sure you didn't become an alcoholic like him. He was just sick, Forrest. He didn't have some fundamental flaw passed through generations of Graham men that makes them unsuitable for relationships. It isn't that complicated. He was just sick.

"And as far as what happened between him and your mom, Forrest, there was stuff going on there that you don't understand nor are you likely to ever fully understand. They were both dealing with substance abuse and who knows what else. But the important thing to remember is that Lucy is not your mom. Clearly. I mean, is anyone more dependable than Lucy?"

Porter looked to Dr. Hubert who quickly added, "Decidedly not. At least, no one that I have ever had the pleasure of meeting."

"So while this avoid-love-like-the-plague strategy may have served you well for a long time, it is no longer working for you, friend. It's time to move on."

There was silence in the apartment except for the bustling of Mrs. Hubert in the kitchen. Finally, Forrest said, "Even if you're right, I'm afraid I've already blown it. I really hurt her."

Dr. Hubert's eyes shut again and he exhaled deeply. "Son, that is Lucy's decision to make. But you underestimate our Lucy severely if you think she would give up so flippantly on someone she cares about so deeply."

Forrest had thought several days ago that he'd reached the limits on how much pain he could feel. But Dr. Hubert's words tightened his chest with a flicker of hope that was in and of itself sweetly painful.

Mrs. Hubert poked her head out of the kitchen. "Gentlemen, go wash up. Dinner is ready."

His chest felt another squeeze, and he realized in horror that his eyes were watering. No one had ever cooked a meal for him in that bleak little gray kitchen during his entire ten years of occupancy.

All three men called out, "Yes, ma'am."

CHAPTER 19

Lucy had been President Burke's assistant for a week. Her last day in the English Department had also been Forrest's last day of bereavement leave, so they missed each other by the barest of margins. As she'd planned.

It wasn't that Lucy planned to spend the rest of her life dodging Forrest Graham. They worked at the same small university, so that was hardly possible. But she did intend to postpone until she could nonchalantly greet him while dressed in the perfect outfit, without a blush or a tear in sight. In this future, she'd also have a man hopelessly and conspicuously in love with her. A man with a British accent.

Each morning of her first week, Lucy woke up, chose an outfit from the line of new clothes she'd purchased on a particularly fun day trip to Memphis with Edith, and went to work hoping the new look and new job would make her feel like a better, more mature version of Lucy O'Shields. While she enjoyed catching glimpses of herself in non-beige clothing, the novelty of the new job had worn off in about three days. Soon, she realized she was doing the exact same tasks for Dr. Burke that she'd done in the English Department, only in this situation, it was without editing complicated academic pieces or laughing at the antics of Billy and Luke or sipping on bourbon with Dr. Hubert after a particularly busy week. What was the point of going to Broadway if you couldn't get tickets to a show?

This morning, Lucy was meeting Miriam for a coffee before heading to work. Occasionally, they met at the coffee kiosk in the center of campus for a cup of coffee so potent it could keep the most sleep-deprived of college students awake for their eight o'clock class. Sitting on a bench nearby, they would pretend for just a moment that they were carefree undergraduates watching their classmates rushing by, still wearing their plaid pajama pants.

Usually, they saved these walks down memory lane for special days, like birthdays or when one of them had a particular victory at work. Once, they met after a surprisingly controversial altar committee meeting in which the bane of Miriam's existence, a Mrs. Archibald Dunroe, finally resigned over the choice of peonies over lilies for an upcoming service. Miriam's relief had merited a second cup of coffee.

On this nippy fall morning with brightly colored fall foliage all around the campus, Lucy and Miriam weren't meeting for any particular reason. Rather, Miriam had set it up claiming she was in the mood for some extra-strong coffee. Lucy suspected, however, that Miriam was currently in full-tilt mother-hen mode. Since Mr. Graham's funeral, Miriam had thought of excuses to check on Lucy daily. She'd brought meals for them to share, a Frisbee to throw for Clark, or called to run by a line from an upcoming sermon; she liked to know Lucy's opinion on how likely she was to get in trouble. Lucy called it the Provacata-meter.

Lucy knew without doubt that Miriam's ministrations were in fact helping immensely. At times, she wanted to be left alone to stare at the copy of *Eve's Diary* that still lay on the table next to her couch. She'd wonder how Forrest, who loved the book, couldn't love her, too. She would ask herself how he could worship Mark Twain, but not want for himself the love Mark Twain had so eloquently memorialized.

Because if he wanted that kind of love, Lucy could provide it. She would love Forrest to distraction. She wouldn't be able to help herself.

But since she was in love with someone incapable of loving her back, Lucy was grateful the phone kept ringing, that it kept calling her away from *Eve's Diary* and gave her a moment of respite from memories of twin beds and Gandalf posters and the pleasant scratch of whiskers down her neck.

Lucy was standing in a line of groggy college students when Miriam joined her.

"Hey, you. How's it going?"

"Morning, Miri. I'm fine." I'm fine. I'm fine. How many times did one say those two words in life when they weren't exactly true? If you combined all of the *I'm-fine's* into a single setting, would it create a meditation in which a person was transformed until the words were true?

Miriam certainly heard how hollow they rang, but she graciously let it pass. "I desperately need a coffee. I was up until one o'clock last night working on my sermon for the Sunday before Thanksgiving."

"Are you stressed about it?"

"Not really, but it'll be a full house with people's families visiting, so I'd rather not sound like an ass."

Lucy shook her head as she chuckled. "Miriam, you've never sounded like an ass in your life."

"If that's true, which I sincerely doubt, it's because I've never walked into that pulpit unprepared. Can you imagine what would happen if I went off-script and did a stream-of-consciousness hour?"

"Ooh. Good point. You'd better lose some more sleep."

"Thanks, friend."

They moved up a few more steps in the line as a few more students headed to their eight-o'clocks with fuel clutched in their hands.

Miriam said, "So, what are your plans for Thanksgiving?"

Lucy thought about her conversation with her father earlier that week. He'd called a few times, eager to hear about her new job. It had been more hands-on parenting than she was used to, but she appreciated the effort. However, he'd let her know that he was heading South to his brother's Thanksgiving gathering. So unless she wanted a road-trip to Alabama, she was on her own.

"My dad is going out of town, so normally, I would join Porter and Charlotte. There is always an open invitation to their Thanksgiving, and Porter is always eager to take in all the pies I'm willing to bake."

"But?"

"But, I don't know what Forrest's plans are. Sometimes, he goes to his sister's, but sometimes he goes to Porter's. It depends on if Gracie is spending the holiday with her in-laws. Normally, I would be privy to all of this communication because I would be the one keeping up with everyone's plans in the office. But now..." Lucy's words ended on a sigh.

They moved up a step. Only two students to go.

"Are you missing them? Do you miss your old job?"

"Yep. Not very entrepreneurial of me, is it?"

"What do you mean?"

"I mean, I'm an intelligent, capable woman without a family of my own. My career should be my thing. I should be climbing to the top. But really, if I could rewind and spend a day as the Pam Beasley of the PSU English Department, I would. I still see Edith and Porter and Dr. Hubert around. Small campus and all. But it's not the same."

"The largest, most caffeinated beverage you have," Miriam said. Lucy hadn't realized they'd reached the front of the line. In all their time standing in line, she'd failed to actually decide on her order.

"Oh, um, I probably shouldn't have a latte. All the calories and such."

"She'll have a latte. Make it a large."

"Thanks, Miri."

The two took their warm drinks and sat down on a nearby bench. Miriam was clutching a scarf tightly around her neck. It concealed her tab collar, making it a little easier for Lucy to pretend for just a moment that they were their undergraduate selves. But then Lucy remembered the embarrassing crush she'd nursed on Forrest (or Dr. Graham) all those years ago, and she decided that reminiscing is overrated.

"So, you never answered my question. What are you doing for Thanksgiving?"

"Doing recognizance on Porter's Thanksgiving, and then I'll decide. Clark and I can always eat a frozen turkey dinner while watching *Planes, Trains, and Automobiles*."

"No, you are not going to have a lame-ass Thanksgiving for two with your dog and frozen dinners. I'll figure out something. For starters, Porter and Charlotte have invited me to their Thanksgiving, so I can call Charlotte and snoop around for you. If that is a no-go, we'll figure out something. But just for the record, you shouldn't let a guy determine whether you get to spend time with friends on Thanksgiving."

"You're right. And I want to be in that place, the place where I can be in the same room as Forrest without feeling like I'm drowning. But I'm not there yet. Not that I've tested the waters. I know his schedule well enough to be an expert at avoiding him."

They each took a sip of their coffee, soaking in the beauty of PSU in fall. Everywhere one turned, there were oranges and purples and hot, intense reddish-pinks.

Miriam broke the silence. "I'm sorry that bastard hurt you."

"He's not a bastard."

"I know."

"He's just a broken mess."

"Aren't we all?" On this point, Miriam was uniquely well-aware.

"I would have taken him all broken and messy." Lucy was surprised at the confession. She was surprised it had escaped so untethered and unbidden. By some miracle, though, her eyes remained dry.

Miriam reached over and squeezed Lucy's gloved hand. "I know, Luce. I know."

***

Forrest had been back at the office for a week. Being in the classroom had been a balm, soothing the more egregious aches from his father's passing. Lecturing and class discussions and speaking with inquiring students in the moments following class had all felt like he was right where he belonged, right where his father had been proud to have a son.

But then class would end, the last of the students would trickle out of the classroom, and Forrest was left still raw, still aching with another pain.

For the past ten years, the small suite of offices on the third floor of Hart Building had housed Forrest's family. Dr. Hubert with his depth of experience and wisdom that he never weaponized to make Forrest feel naive or less than. Dr. Rose with her fierce loyalty to the field they both loved, but also to the people in that suite. Dr. Finch with his warm and too-quirky-for-academia personality that denied any of them the opportunity to get too ensconced in their ivory tower.

And Lucy. Lucy who kept them fed when they were buried in grading or in good graces with the campus's political powers. Lucy who mothered their students and made their corner of campus feel warm on the coldest of Kentucky winter days. She'd been his proof-reader, his conversation companion on all topics ranging from campus gossip to the newest research idea he was pursuing, and here lately, she'd been his confidante as he had watched his father deteriorate. She was, ultimately, his friend.

But when Forrest was at his most honest, he knew that what he felt was not as simple as friendship. It was more powerful than any feeling he had ever had, even towards the dearest of friends. On that night in his childhood bedroom, all that he felt for Lucy had come bubbling over the surface. Slowly, Forrest was coming to admit that the night with Lucy had been so explosive not because of some cocktail of adolescent nostalgia and the presence of a tall, strawberry-blond beauty, but rather because he was, for the first time in his life, authentically and completely in love.

And while Forrest knew, although perhaps feared was a better word, that he was deeply in love, he didn't know how a person showed love or lived love when it was coupled with such mind-obliterating passion. Sure, he knew how to love Porter or Dr. Hubert or Edith. At the risk of being self-inflating, Forrest believed he had been a good friend to them during the past decade. But romantic love? All-consuming love?

So Forrest had decided this morning after yet another mostly-sleepless night in which he had tossed in bed with images of wisps of curls escaping a bun and glasses slipping down a freckled nose and, well, breasts (he was still in awe of how that particular asset had outpaced his most outrageous expectations), Forrest had decided that he would go to the one source that had never let him down: books. He would find books that would teach him how to love Lucy.

So in between his eight o'clock class and his eleven o'clock, Forrest used his short window of time to visit the campus library. For the first time in a while, he did not head directly to the fiction section or the biography section where he could find his favorite sources on the American authors who populated his studies and writings. Instead, he headed to the non-fiction section and, within that, the section on relationships. Because even Forrest Graham could admit that he was unlikely to find high-quality relationship advice in 19th-century literature.

As he stood running a finger over the spines of the top row, silently mouthing each title to himself, a crickety voice whispered from behind, "Dr. Graham, can I help you? This is not your normal section."

Forrest barely managed to not jump, turning quickly and, in the process, hitting his elbow on a shelf. Forrest grabbed the offended elbow, grimacing. Apparently, leather elbow patches did not protect one's funny bone.

"Mrs. Applebaum, yes, I'm venturing out of the 19th century today."

Mrs. Applebaum was a relic of the PSU library, a couple of decades past traditional retirement age. Her penciled-in eyebrows, shockingly black next to the tight, bluish curls of her hair, raised in shock as she looked over his shoulder. "Are you trying to work things out with Dr. Wray?"

Didn't they have policies against talking here? Apparently, campus gossip was as active in the library as it was in the PSU English Department, where he had recently learned from Dr. Hubert that the Dean of the Business College had been engaged in an affair with his secretary for the better part of the past two decades. To which Porter had replied, "Well, it is the Business College," and they had all nodded in agreement.

"No, I'm afraid that is a bit of a done deal. Just doing some research."

Her eyebrows raised even further, the wrinkles gathering like a topographical map of the Appalachians.

"I'm writing an article on Mark Twain and Olivia Clemens, his wife." Her quizzical expression was unmoved. "About their love story. I thought research on relationships might help me better understand what made theirs so special."

As Forrest said the words, he realized he wasn't lying. He really was going to write that article.

"Ooh, wonderful idea, Dr. Graham. I look forward to reading it. I've always been particularly fond of Mr. Twain."

Forrest smiled. "Aren't we all?"

"Indeed. I'll leave you to it."

Forrest turned back around, placed his finger on the spine of the first book in the second row, and continued scanning the titles.

CHAPTER 20

Paresident Burke's office suite made the PSU English Department's quaint corner of Hart Building look like a cheap studio apartment. Since her father was on the Board of Trustees, Lucy had often heard about the money woes that plagued all universities in the current economic climate. However, no expense had been spared on President Burke's quarters. According to her father, it was generally agreed that it was in the best interest of PSU to project an image of refinement and success in their highest levels of administration.

Since Lucy now served the highest levels, she sat beneath vaulted ceilings in a beam of light pouring from a towering window. Her desk was a massive oak piece that sat in front of the imposing double doors that led into President Burke's office. It was certainly grander than that from which she'd come. Here, she often needed a sweater.

Within this embodiment of strength and power, Lucy set chewing on the end of a pen. She knew it was a horrible habit, just a notch above smoking a pack a day. But really, what was she to do? Dr. Bugs was now aware of her heartache. Dr. Bugs?

An hour earlier, Lucy had been walking across campus, returning from the nearest Starbucks (a ten-minute drive from campus) where she'd been picking up a coffee with organic almond milk and two raw sugars for President Burke. In what she was now referring to as her former life, Lucy had never been asked to drive across town for organic almond milk and raw sugar in coffee. Dr. Hubert always raved over the kiosk coffee with hazelnut-flavored powdered creamer, the kind she had seen used on *MythBusters* to create bombs. Granted, combustible food products were probably not the smartest dietary choice, but when she'd surprised the professors with kiosk lattes instead of their normal coffee she made in the office, they'd all acted like she'd brought them David Sedaris for their own personal book-reading.

As she walked back to the Administration Building from her parking space with the six-dollar coffee and a grudge that her upward-career move was best encapsulated in slightly higher-class coffee runs, Lucy looked across campus towards Hart Building. She wouldn't say she was looking with longing. Her eyes definitely did not look like Clark's when he could hear Billy and Luke playing outside. They weren't near so sorrowful.

But she was gazing at the portico and the exceptionally heavy wooden door that she had always had to lean her entire body into to get it to open, and she was thinking about all the cheap-latte-loving people within when she saw Forrest walking towards those very doors, his chin resting on top of a Mt. Everest stack of books, his arms stretched to their limits in order to fit the volumes between his grip and his beard. Despite the fall wind blowing relentlessly and leaving Lucy's bun in shambles, Forrest looked perfectly put-together, each hair in place and his beard meticulously groomed. It had been two weeks since his father's funeral, two weeks since she had last kissed him and been kissed by him. Not that she was keeping count of that sort of thing. But he definitely seemed to be holding up well.

And just when she was finishing up her analysis on the condition of Forrest's hair, who should walk up to her but Dr. Bugs? Or, Dr. Wray, rather.

"Ms. O'Shields. How are you doing today?"

Lucy had jumped at the question, taking a moment to process that she'd just been caught staring (not lusting, *staring*) at Forrest by his most recent lover. Also, she had to process how innately cringe-worthy the word *lover* is and ask herself how she might be able to avoid thinking the word in the future. Lastly, she had to do a little mental gymnastics of Dr. Bu-Bu-Bu-Wray before she could make a somewhat coherent greeting. Belatedly, she said, "Dr. Wray, nice to see you. I'm doing fine today. Just enjoying the scenery for a second. Nothing beats PSU in the fall, right?"

"Oh, yes. This year the dry conditions later in the summer coupled with an earlier-than-usual fall created the perfect conditions for the carotenoids and anthocyanins to really shine. Magnificent showing."

Lucy blinked at least four times in rapid succession.

"Also, Dr. Graham makes for a good view, as well."

Lucy blinked considerably more than four times. Dr. Wray likely knew the exact biological mechanism that was causing Lucy to turn shades of red not even seen in the best Kentucky foliage.

Dr. Wray continued in her monotone, scientific drone, "Mrs. Applebaum told the library's acquisitions director, Mrs. Lourdes, who texted her husband, Dr. Lourdes, the chair of my department, who told our department secretary who just texted me that Dr. Graham was seen in the marriage and relationships section of the library perusing the books."

Lucy took a gulp of scalding coffee, coughing at the shock of heat. Then she remembered it was President Burke's coffee. Yes, powdered creamer, explosive or not, was better. Clearing her throat, she choked out, "His research often takes him into uncharted territory."

"That may be the case. But if one was to consider a scenario in which he was in fact researching that topic for very personal reasons as opposed to an academic endeavor, I would hypothesize that he was not doing that research with the possibility of rekindling our relationship on his mind, which was the supposition of our overly-romantic secretary. She was an art major in college."

Lucy harnessed all will-power she would normally use to not eat a second donut to instead resist rolling her eyes. She said, "And in this scenario in which For-, Dr. Graham is not doing academic research, what do you believe drew him to that section of the library?"

"Likely the person who he spent much of our relationship praising for her apparent secretarial super-powers. I am not prone to jealousy, but our six months together did at times remind me of the evolutionary reality of jealousy. You see, it developed within humanity because of our distant ancestors' need to maintain access to potential viable mates."

"Evolution?" Lucy was trying to follow, but, really, science had never been her forte.

"Yes, but seeing as how I do not personally see a need or have a desire to reproduce, my jealousy, while natural, was in fact unnecessary."

"Like an appendix?"

Dr. Wray's face suddenly lifted, breaking her usual inscrutable expression. "Exactly. Like an appendix."

"Dr. Wray, why are you telling me this?"

"Because, while I do not desire Forrest's services for procreation, I would like to see him happy."

Despite having whimpered over him into her dog's fur for the better part of two weeks, Lucy, too, wanted to see Forrest happy. Perhaps, that was a universal response to the brown eyes and deep dimples that still hinted at the boy who had endured a less-than-ideal childhood.

Dr. Wray continued, "And as for you, although I don't know you well and I've never been near as adept at reading people as I am at reading insects, I would say that the expression on your face moments ago was not one born of appreciating foliage. If there is a way to make one person happy that would also make a second person happy, well, those are good numbers."

After a brief pause, Dr. Wray straightened her already-straight shoulders, and said, "Well, I had best be off. I have a lab at ten o'clock, and my students, seeing as they are college students, are all quite eager to learn about the mating habits of beetles."

Lucy had wished Dr. Wray a good day, and then taken the immense mental and emotional load Dr. Wray had so concisely dropped in her lap to the presidential quarters. Having forced herself to put down the now thoroughly chewed pen, Lucy decided that since she was by all accounts a very good secretary, perhaps she should apply to her love-life (yet another distasteful term) the skills she brought to her occupation. So, Lucy pulled up an Excel sheet and started cataloging all that Dr. Wray had said under the headings of *Likely*, *Unlikely*, and *Confusing*. It was likely college students found mating habits of just about anything interesting. It was unlikely, surely, that she had been the reason Forrest checked out a stack of books on relationships. All else fell in the last category.

After exiting out of the document without saving its contents, the nine-foot tall solid wood door at the entrance to the office creaked opened, and none other than Edith Rose leaned her head through the crack, her straight bob falling like a stage curtain.

Lucy's eyes burned, although for reasons entirely different from the usual reason people cried around Edith. She was lonely and her new job was just her old job without any of the fun and she was still in love with Forrest and she had no idea what to do with all of the information Dr. Wray had given her this morning and even an Excel document had not fixed this mess. Before she could convey any of this, much less a hello, Edith whispered, "Meet me in the broom closet down the hall in five minutes. Also, that top is stunning on you."

Lucy was just about to say, "Well, you did pick it," when the door shut and Edith was gone. Lucy was wearing a boldly graphic black and white top with burgundy pants. It was one of the many pieces Edith had helped her pick on their shopping trip to Memphis. Lucy took out her "Be Back Soon" sign and propped it on her desk.

The broom closet was three doors down from President Burke's office. When she reached its door, Lucy checked each direction down the hallway before sliding inside. Immediately, Lucy felt overwhelmed by the smell of bleach and lemon. Sure enough, Edith was waiting in the dim, dusty interior.

Lucy said, "Edith, how do I keep ending up in closets with you?"

"Porter's pantry wasn't exactly a closet, but this," Edith moved the handle of a broom stick that had fallen onto her shoulder and rolled back a mop bucket to give Lucy a little more space, "This is definitely a closet."

"What are we doing in this closet?"

"Lucy, you have to tell me the absolute truth."

This sounded ominous. "Okay?"

"Do you like your new job? Is it something you want to do long-term?"

Lucy thought about the coffee run that morning, about the pristine office devoid of chaos, but also devoid of warmth. "No. I don't want to do this long-term."

"Good." Edith clapped her hands together, causing the broomstick to land again on her shoulder. Standing it back up, Edith said, "That's what I want to hear. So, you know how I've published a thing or two in my day?"

How many times in this single day was Lucy going to have to stop herself from rolling her eyes at a professor? Did Lucy know? No professor let a publication go unnoticed. Lucy had ordered a cake every time any of them had received word they were getting something else published. "I'm aware."

"Well, I was talking to a friend of mine in the publishing world about your particular talents..."

Lucy was intrigued despite herself. "Yes?"

"How you're the reason my work always looks so nice and shiny, and she has a friend at Dohlman Publishing..."

Now Lucy was more than intrigued. Dohlman Publishing was a titan in the industry, publishing books of all genres.

"And they are looking for editors to work remotely for their branch in Louisville. You would just have to go there a few times a month. But you would be an editor. If you're interested, they said they would like to have your application."

"I'm interested, Edith. Very interested."

Edith took Lucy's hands, squeezing a little too tightly. "You've been doing amazing work for me and Porter and Forrest for ages. It's time you share that talent with the world."

Coming from Edith, Lucy took the praise for the authentic expression of appreciation it was. Edith, after all, was not one for empty flattery.

"Thank you. So what do I do now? How do I apply?"

Edith gave Lucy the specifics. Then, as she wrestled the broomstick once again, she said, "Why don't you come by the office Monday after work and we'll go over some of the finer details? You know, in a place that doesn't smell of various antiseptics."

After bidding Edith goodbye, Lucy returned to her desk where the chewed pen remained in the center. She still had no answer on the Forrest front, but perhaps that was the hand she had been dealt. No one got everything they wanted, right? Lucy saw hope for a career that would be fulfilling and challenging, a career that would utilize her specific skill-set. Perhaps it was too much to ask for love, as well.

***

"She looked stunning - naturally, I had picked out her clothing. But she also looked miserable. Like a wilted flower. A sad, wilted, well-dressed little Lucy flower."

Dr. Hubert and Porter listened to Edith's assessment. They'd both been thrilled to hear her contact in publishing might have a job opportunity for Lucy. At one point in time, each of them had taught Lucy. They were more aware than most of her talents and eager for her to explore new ways to use those talents. However, that was not the only reason they were intrigued. They were also glad for the excuse for Edith to check up on their Lucy. After a week without her, it was time for a little reconnaissance to make sure President Burke's office was treating her right.

As the three stood around Lucy's desk, the area emptied of her decorations and scented candles and coffee mugs with Jane Austen quotes, Porter wanted clarification. "Sad about her job or sad about Forrest?"

"It's difficult to say for sure. A broom kept falling on me, so I had a hard time focusing and thinking of the right questions."

Dr. Hubert's eyebrows rose like a schnauzer who had just heard a rustling. "A broom?"

"We were in a broom closet."

The eyebrows inched further. "A broom closet?"

"It seemed like the best place at the time. I didn't want anyone overhearing us in the bathroom."

Porter pushed further. "So you told her about the job prospect and asked her if she was happy working with President Burke and she said..."

"She said she didn't care to do it for long."

"Did she say anything about Forrest?"

Edith crossed her arms and shot Porter her most disapproving glare. "You do realize two women can have a conversation that does not include talking about a man?"

Porter collapsed into Lucy's chair and laid his forehead on the desk. "You know I know that, Edith. I'm not a total douche. I just need them to fix the shit between them." He looked up at Edith. "I'm trying to make sure they don't collide at my place which requires all kinds of planning and forethought, and the kids are confused why Uncle Forrest and Aunt Lucy aren't around as much. And it just feels like we're in some messed-up shared-custody situation. Seriously, when we have incompetent students, we have to stop making jokes about them probably being from broken homes."

"Now this really is sucking the joy out of life."

Dr. Hubert patted Porter's shoulder. "I know this is hard for us all, but we might have to let Forrest and Lucy work this out on their own."

Both Porter and Edith scoffed. Loudly.

Edith said, "Boys, it's time we stop complaining and take charge. I've already fixed our first problem."

Dr. Hubert and Porter both looked at her in confusion. "Which was?"

"The problem that is this: if Lucy O'Shields isn't working for us, she had damn well better be doing a job worthy of her, not some slightly more hoity-toity secretarial gig."

Dr. Hubert said, "I've always wondered what hoity-toity means. What are the origins of that particular phrase? Do either of you know?"

Edith paused for a short breath and then plowed ahead. "Now we need to deal with the fact that two people we all care deeply about are clearly in love and need to be together."

Porter's forehead returned to the desk. Then, in his best impression of Luke after trying and failing to tie his shoes, Porter said, "We tried, Edith. Dr. Hubert and Mrs. Hubert and I gave it our best shot."

Dr. Hubert said, "It is true, Edith. I'm not sure what else we can do."

Just as Edith was about to demand greater effort on all of their parts, Forrest walked in carrying a small library in his arms.

***

Forrest walked into the office with his arms outstretched, barely able to hold the fifteen or so books he'd checked out from the library. This was his second library haul for the day. He wasn't able to carry everything after his morning visit, so he'd picked up the rest after his afternoon class.

It had been difficult to navigate the doors into the building and into the English Department suite, but each time, a student had walked up at just the right moment and offered to help. Tom, an English major who'd taken several classes from Forrest, had apparently read some of the titles. With a smirk, he'd said, "Can't wait to take the next course you offer, Dr. Graham."

"Thanks, Tom." Undergraduates could be real schmucks at times.

When he walked into the office, Dr. Hubert, Porter, and Edith were all gathered around Lucy's desk. They'd yet to find a new secretary, so it was still Lucy's desk. Heck, it would always be Lucy's desk. Perhaps, creating a plaque that said "Lucy's Desk" and hanging it on the front would be the kind of grand gesture that would show Lucy how much he loved her. Surely there was a chapter in one of these books on grand gestures. He'd check the indexes just as soon as he got to his office.

Forrest paused for a moment as the three looked at him, taking in the books he was carrying. They were suspiciously silent.

The spines to each book Forrest was holding were facing outward for all to see. Suddenly, Forrest felt very vulnerable. After all, there wasn't a person in this room who was unaware that he'd recently slept with their secretary and that it had led to them losing the greatest secretary in the history of university departments. Forrest had no hard evidence to support that ranking, but it felt sound enough. He finally decided to break the silence. "Hey everyone. What're you doing?"

They all remained silent, staring. Finally, Dr. Hubert said, "We were just discussing...," he cleared his throat, "things."

"Alright, then. I'm going to head into my office. I have some reading to do this weekend, and there's no time like four o'clock on a Friday to get started. Am I right?"

Crickets.

Forrest walked into his office and shut the door. Immediately, he heard the buzz of frantic whispering. It was as if the department had a ticking time-bomb, and it was up to Dr. Hubert, Porter, and Edith to stop detonation. Forrest decided that whatever was going on with them was less important than the task at hand. He took off his sports jacket, hung it on the back of his leather chair, and sat down. Leaning back comfortably, Forrest took the first book on the stack, *Building Lasting Romance in a Chaotic World*, and opened to the index.

Halfway through his first paragraph of reading, the door to Forrest's office burst open as all three of his esteemed colleagues stormed into the very small amount of floor space leftover after accounting for his bookshelves and whiteboards. Porter, usually smiling even when his kids were dismantling the world around him, looked as though he'd passed through Dante's inferno before arriving in Forrest's office. He was the first to speak. "Forrest, you have to do something. Everyone is miserable."

Dr. Hubert echoed, "Quite right. Completely miserable."

Porter continued, "We can't go on with you and Lucy being at odds. That is not how this department works. Or family works, for that matter. There is no part of my life, Forrest, that is not more stressful because of you and Lucy right now."

While he was talking, Edith walked over to one of the whiteboards and erased the notes Forrest had been taking on one of his more obscure research ideas. "Wait a second. What are you doing?"

Without speaking, Edith put down the eraser and picked up a marker. Then, at the top of the board, she wrote "Get Lucy Back." Turning to him, she said, "Alright Forrest. It's time to turn that brilliant mind of yours to this task and this task alone. You must get Lucy back. Not for the office. We want more for her than to be a secretary for the next thirty years. But we want her to be in our office, stopping by, still being part of this circle. And we want the two of you to have the damned love story you both deserve. While I might have written thousands of words against the patriarchy and romance and sentimentality, it doesn't mean I don't have a heart, Forrest. Have you considered my feelings?"

Forrest could honestly say the words *Edith* and *feelings* had never entered his mind in the same thought. Porter and Edith were both breathing hard from their individual meltdowns. Forrest turned his gaze to Dr. Hubert. "Has my love life inconvenienced you, Dr. Hubert?"

"Actually, Forrest," Dr. Hubert stood taller to deliver his verdict. "I have not truly enjoyed a glass of bourbon in over a week. It is not the same without Lucy here to promise she won't tell Mrs. Hubert. It tasted better when it was our little secret."

"Okay," Forrest said. "So everyone's miserable."

They all said in unison, "Yes."

"Well, imagine if you were the one in love with her." His hands flung up and landed hard on his desk. "And what do you think I'm doing with twenty books on relationships. I'm trying, people. I'm trying. I'm just working with a very low level of emotional competency here."

Everyone was quiet. Everyone studied their own shoes for a bit. Then Edith said, "I could take one or two of those books and make a list of bullet points, a cliff-notes of sorts. Let's face it: I could probably use the education myself."

Dr. Hubert and Porter each took a few books off the stack as well. Dr. Hubert said, "We might need to use more than one of your whiteboards, son."

"Yes, sir." Forrest swallowed hard. "Thank you."

***

The sun had set several hours ago. Extra chairs had been brought in, and the professors were positioned in a semi-circle reading around Forrest's desk. Occasionally, one would stand up and jot a note onto a board, the marker squeaking in the silence.

After laying down *Commitment Is for Lovers*, Forrest said, "What if it doesn't work? What if I do all of the studying, but I don't ace the exam?"

Porter smirked over the edge of *Saying I Do to Love*. "Seriously, Forrest. Has that ever happened to you before?"

"No, but Lucy isn't exactly an essay question, and she doesn't come with multiple choice answers built-in, either."

Without raising her eyes from *Magical Ingredients for a Marvelous Marriage*, Edith said, "If Lucy were a test, she definitely would *not* be multiple choice. Those are for ninnies."

Everyone nodded their heads in agreement. Clearly, Lucy would be essay questions. Long and involved essay questions.

Dr. Hubert set *Lifelong Partnerships are Possible!* onto his knee and cleared his throat. "Forrest, you and Lucy are people with much love to give. I, personally, have benefited much from my proximity to you both. To continue your metaphor, we will help you study for this exam of sorts because it will boost your confidence in your own ability moving forward. But if Lucy accepts your love, it will not be because you earned it, son. It will be because her heart is big and generous, and you are the one on whom she has chosen to bestow it. You will be worthy not because of something you did, but because of who you are, a person with a heart as big and generous as her own. You are each magnificent exactly as you are."

He picked up the book from his knee, likely the first book Dr. Hubert had ever read with an exclamation mark in the title, and resumed reading.

Forrest grabbed the next book on the stack, *Tango Partners in the Dance of Life*, and lifted it until his eyes were adequately hidden behind its cover.

CHAPTER 21

M onday afternoon, Lucy finished her work at precisely 4:59, shut down her computer, and headed across campus. She was eager to sit with Edith and learn more about the new job prospect. She'd spent the weekend working on her resume and cover letter, both tasks she had not done since applying for the English Department position ten years before.

The campus was buzzing with energy, everyone anticipating the upcoming Thanksgiving break. While playing in the yard with Billy, Luke, and Clark Sunday afternoon, Porter asked Lucy her Thanksgiving plans. She'd conveyed that as of yet, she had none. He told her to plan on spending lunch with them. Or dinner. Then he said he would talk to Charlotte about whether lunch or dinner would be best, which Lucy assumed was code for I'll-see-which-Forrest-is-coming-to-and-you-can-do-the-other. He had then broken into a sweat. It was forty-five degrees outside.

Lucy was wearing a green shirt-dress that cinched at the waist with black tights and knee-high boots for warmth. She was not wearing the green dress because she was going to Hart Building and possibly going to run into Forrest for the first time in two weeks. She was not wearing the green dress because he had once mentioned how a certain green shirt complemented her green eyes. The green dress had absolutely nothing to do with green eyes or some guy noticing green eyes.

Lucy jogged the last few steps to the portico at the entrance of Hart Building. Sure enough, the door was still monstrously heavy, requiring she lean completely into its bulk. As it gave way, the heat immediately hugged her, fogging up her glasses. She had not been so warm in days.

The old, worn handrail leading up the stairs felt smooth as Lucy's hand glided over the surface. The edge of each granite stair was rounded, eroded away by a century of college students rushing to class after over-sleeping. Lucy passed students and professors leaving for the day, all of whom she knew and was happy to see. Apparently, university presidents were not unlike grade-school principals; people generally avoided their office.

Finally, she made it to the door for office suite 3A. Her door. Even the metal of the doorknob was smoothed from decades of hands turning it. Lucy rested her forehead on the frosted-glass window pane on the upper half of the door, letting the light of the office illuminate her shut eyes for just a moment.

Turning the knob, Lucy opened the door slowly, and there, standing in her spot looking down at the empty landscape of her old desk and with a hand resting on the corner, was Forrest. For the brief second she saw him before he looked up to her, she was struck by how peaceful he seemed, so different from their last encounter.

At the telltale creak of the door, Forrest's eyes rose to her. As his gaze met her own, their eyes locked on one another, linking them in an iron grip. Lucy froze, mesmerized that she had managed to block out just how beautiful his eyes were, how their dark, chocolate brown was complemented by the light brown of his hair and beard. It was as if God had decided to give this one a perfect, fall-inspired color theme. The ache that followed this thought reminded her why she had likely banned such thoughts. Thankfully for her dignity's sake, he seemed frozen, too.

Then, breaking the stillness, a vague, sad smile touched Forrest's mouth, his dimples only hinting at their existence. Lucy pushed her glasses up the bridge of her nose.

Like the sound of gravel paving a road leading home, Lucy heard Dr. Hubert say, "Lucy O'Shields is among us again. That is the best thing I've seen this week."

His words broke the spell, allowing Lucy to turn her eyes elsewhere. Looking to his familiar, towering presence, Lucy said, "Hello, Dr. Hubert. To say it's good to see you would be a grievous understatement."

All of the doors around her desk were ajar, and one by one the professors appeared. Their greetings brought normalcy into the space, releasing a tension valve between Forrest and Lucy.

Forrest backed up several steps towards his office, placing Porter between himself and Lucy.

Porter said, "Lucy, it's dangerous you coming here. We might hold you hostage."

Lucy laughed. "I might let you. I sure miss all of you."

"Perhaps," Edith said, "if you get the editing job, we could work out something where you work from here, at least some of the time. It's remote. You just need a computer, right?"

Porter placed a hand over his chest, "As English educators, we want to do all we can to support the editors of America."

"Naturally," Lucy said, winking at him. "I'll definitely think about it." As the words were spoken, her gaze roamed involuntarily to Forrest. Could they be together under the same roof again? Could they go back to before?

Forrest cleared his throat. Then, as if answering in the negative, he said, "I guess I'd better head on out."

Immediately, Edith and Porter walked over to Forrest, Porter not-too-subtly pushing Forrest through the doorway into his office. Edith said, "Excuse me, Lucy. We have to talk to Forrest really quickly about a little student-issue we're having. I'll be right with you. Okay? Okay."

Forrest's door slammed behind Edith.

Lucy looked to Dr. Hubert. He did not need to shake his head and say, "Kids these days," for his message to be clearly conveyed by the pattern of wrinkles gathering on one side of his mouth. She smiled in return.

"Lucy, shall we have a sip of Kentucky's finest?"

"Can you make it a double, Dr. Hubert?"

"Absolutely, dear."

***

As the door slammed behind Edith, Forrest backed up until he was sitting on the edge of his desk. "What are you two doing?" he whispered in exasperation.

"What are we doing?" Porter said, taking Forrest's exasperation, and raising him several more exasperations.

"What are *we* doing?" Edith echoed, reaching a fever pitch.

"Yes, what are you two doing?" Forrest barely managed to maintain a whisper.

"Forrest Graham," Edith began, articulating each word with a clarity that would make any student pick up a pencil and prepare for serious note-taking. "The two of us and Dr. Hubert spent the entire weekend in this office reading books about relationships, Forrest. Relationships."

"Yes?"

"And now she's here, and you're going to, and I quote, 'head on out'?" On each of the last three words, Edith stepped forward until she was a foot in front of him and jabbing a finger into his chest.

"I'm not ready yet. I've only had a few days to prepare."

Porter gingerly placed a hand between Edith and Forrest, getting her to back up a few steps so that he could take on the fight for a round. "Forrest, you aren't preparing to defend your dissertation here. You've already done that. Ten years ago. You just need to tell her how you feel. Everything else, all the stuff you researched, the stuff we all researched, over the past few days, that will all fall into place later. But it's time to tell her how you feel. It's time to give her a chance to decide if she wants to read a few relationship books, too."

Looking at them, Forrest paused on each of their faces. They'd spent hours around his desk reading, writing notes, and only occasionally mocking the titles of the books. Since his father's death, Forrest had felt as though his life was burning around him. This weekend with Edith, Porter, and Dr. Hubert by his side, Forrest had laid a new and solid foundation.

Forrest tilted a nod of his head to Edith and Porter.

Edith, looking to Porter, said, "Let's do this."

She opened the door, and the three headed out single-file with Forrest the last to walk into their central office. Dr. Hubert and Lucy were sitting at the chairs in front of the secretary's desk, each nursing a glass of amber liquid.

"Lucy," Edith said as she walked straight through Lucy's area to her own office, grabbing her coat and briefcase as she spoke. "I am so sorry, but I just got a text message from the chair of the faculty union, and they have called an emergency meeting. Let's do lunch tomorrow. Sound good? See you then."

"Okay?" Lucy's forehead creased in confusion as she watched Edith button her trench coat and tie a belt around the waist, cinching tightly. Forrest had seen this exact expression on her face many times, usually as she was contemplating how to fix some problem one of the four of them had created.

"Yes, me too," Porter said, also going into his office to gather his things to leave. "If I'm not home in the next half-hour, Charlotte is going to kill me. She has a deadline tonight. Dr. Hubert, would you like a ride?"

"Uh, yes, just as soon as I finish this glass."

"Dr. Hubert." Edith reverted to her note-taking voice. Forrest smirked. She was terrifying when she was executing a plan.

"Actually, come to think of it, Mrs. Hubert was expecting me rather early tonight." He turned to Lucy and patted her hand. "It was lovely having you back, dear."

Within a short whirlwind of activity in which Forrest's view of Lucy was intermittently blocked by one of the professors running back or forth to grab something they had forgotten (they were all leaving in a rush after all), the door finally slammed, catching the arm of the coat Porter was carrying out with him. He opened the door again, mumbled a sheepish, "Sorry about that," and was gone.

Lucy's torso was twisted towards the door, looking as though she was processing a show that had clearly been canceled before the plot was finished developing. Forrest, on the other hand, did not stare at the door. He was staring at the reddish curls that he knew had slowly worked their way out of her bun throughout the work day and now lay against the rich green dress she was wearing. Green was now Forrest's favorite color. He hadn't had a favorite color since he was ten.

She slowly turned to Forrest, her freckles faded against the deep flush of her cheeks. Forrest said, "Well, that could've gone smoother."

***

Lucy rewound in her head the past few minutes, trying to decipher how a meeting with Edith had turned into her and Forrest together, alone, in 3a of Hart Building. It wasn't computing.

"Forrest, why am I here?"

Awareness suddenly dawned on Forrest's face. "Oh no. Did you think I engineered this? I promise I wouldn't force you to talk with me, Lucy. This was all them." He waved his hand toward the shut door and the silence left behind by their colleagues.

Lucy's eyebrows rose. "We've been parent-trapped."

Suddenly, the urgency to vacate the premises by three people who she knew good and well were typically just fine staying a few minutes late to talk with one another, suddenly it all made sense. Lucy stood up, grabbing the purse she had slid under her chair.

"Forrest, I'm going to head on out. Neither of us asked for this. Don't worry, I'm not angry at you. At least not for this. If I'm being completely honest, I'm probably angry at you for a few other things, but really, that's beside the..."

"Lucy?"

The stream of words that had been gushing from her instantly stopped at her name. Part of her wanted to thank him for halting her ramblings. There was no telling where it would've gone from there. But instead, sighing tiredly, she said, "Yes?"

"Can I show you something?"

Lucy thought of the pain she had felt on an almost constant basis for the past two weeks. If she stayed in his presence, even just long enough for him to show her one thing, was she putting herself in danger of even greater heartache?

Would the pain be worth it for just a few more minutes with him in this, their place?

"Okay. Show me."

Forrest walked back to his office door, opened it wide with one arm leaving his hand on the door knob, as if opening the curtain on a play he hoped would impress. "It's in here."

Lucy walked by him. The narrow doorway meant there was only an inch of space between them as she passed. She ached to lean into his chest, but kept walking.

As she entered, she looked around for what he might be showing her. Nothing had changed. The space still smelled like leather and book dust and the mild pine-y scent of his beard oil. Over the years, it had become in her mind simply his scent, as if his love of puns had led him to ensure that with a name like Forrest, he would smell of pine. There was an extra chair in the space, bringing the total to four, which was unusual but not shockingly so. The whiteboards still encircled the space, each filled to capacity with notes, likely on some 19th-century poet or essayist or a writing by Twain or Whitman so obscure only a handful of scholars would know of its existence.

Lucy looked back over her shoulder. Forrest's eyes were focused strictly on her, as if he'd been watching her for years.

"What did you want to show me?"

Forrest tilted his head towards the direction of the whiteboards. Lucy turned, taking a closer look at their contents.

On each board, there was a menagerie of handwritings. On closer inspection, she realized they were the exact handwritings that had left countless sticky notes of "Be back soon" or "Save me a donut" or "I've lost my phone. Ideas?" on her desk over the years. Each was achingly familiar.

On the first board, the one to her left, Lucy saw in Edith's bold, jagged cursive the words, "Get Lucy Back." Beneath it was a bullet-point list, each with a precise MLA citation.

Lucy read one of the bulleted items: "Dealing with anxiety and commitment (Dale 142)."

"Oh, yes. That was from *Commitment Is for Lovers*. I thought it was one of the stronger source materials we used. Fuller notes are in a document on my computer. Obviously."

On the next board, she saw Dr. Hubert's handwriting with the quote, "Honest communication is the cornerstone to a successful relationship (Frederick 252)." Next to the quote, Porter had written "Really???," and Edith had jotted, "Shut-up, Porter." Laughter bubbled up within Lucy, surprising her. What were these people doing without her?

Shaking her head, Lucy turned to Forrest. "What is this? When did you all do this? And most importantly, what the hell does it mean?"

"It means, Luce, that I want to try. I want to stop being afraid of living in my parents' shadow, and I want to build a life with you."

"So you did research?"

Forrest looked down, a hand coming up to rub the back of his neck. Shocked, Lucy realized he was embarrassed. He was vulnerable. He wanted to stop being afraid, but at this particular moment, he was afraid.

"Lucy, I did the only thing I know how to do well. I checked out a bunch of books on relationships..."

"So I heard."

"Huh?"

"It's PSU, Forrest. You venturing outside of 19th-century literature in the library was all the rage."

"Yes, well, even I had to admit 19th-century views on relationships weren't going to serve me well."

"So you checked out some 21st-century self-help books?"

He unbuttoned the cuffs on his sleeves and started rolling them up. It was getting a little warm, come to think of it.

"Exactly. And Dr. Hubert and Porter and Edith all agreed to help me. So we spent the weekend here at the office reading, and they let me know when there was something I should check out in one of their books. Dr. Hubert and Porter, being successfully married and all, were actually pretty good resources."

"And Edith?"

Forrest grinned. "She's hoping the endeavor might make her nicer."

Lucy shrugged. "That would sort of be a shame."

"That's exactly what we all said."

Lucy strolled to the last of the four boards. It had only Forrest's handwriting, and it was limited to a single quote. Lucy whispered the words as she read: "Wheresoever she was, there was Eden (Twain 104)." It was the final line from *Eve's Diary*. Lucy had underlined it in her own copy she'd read at home before...well, before.

Forrest walked up behind her, looking over her shoulders at the words. "To be completely honest, I didn't totally abandon the 19th century."

Lucy turned around, raising her eyes to his.

He lowered his gaze again, running a hand through his hair, unsettling the ends. Lucy reached out and smoothed them back into place, bringing his eyes back to hers.

"Lucy, you've never been to my apartment, but if you were to walk into it, you would come away with one word: gray. Or whatever that word is that means both gray and beige?"

"Greige?"

"Exactly. It's nothing. It's bland and cold and just a place I go to when I need to sleep. And that has worked just fine for me. For ten years, I've been fine living in a gray box because I knew that when I walked into this office, I was home. I had a home. And it was warm and inviting and clean and there's always someone to talk to and it always smelled nice."

"Does your place even smell gray?"

He smiled, "Yes, actually. It does.

"But, Lucy, what I'm trying to say in, admittedly, a less than concise way is that I thought this office was my home, but now I'm realizing that it's not the office. It's you. You are home. Where you are is home."

Lucy did not want to cry. Fair-skinned almost-red-heads get very blotchy when they cry. She bit the inside of her cheek. "Self-help books must be getting better since the last time I tried them out if you learned all of that."

"Actually, that was the part I figured out all by myself." He was no longer looking to his feet, but instead, raising his gaze directly at her.

"Oh yeah? Well, what did you learn from the books?"

"I learned that they should probably work on coming up with titles that are less cringe-worthy."

"And?"

"And I learned that all the things that lead to long-term, strong marriages, all those things, we already have. We've spent ten years cultivating trust and honesty and friendship and similar interests and..."

Lucy cut in, "As you're making this list, the works cited list is running through your head, isn't it?"

He squinted his eyes as he sheepishly said, "Maybe."

"How about attraction? Sexual compatibility? I didn't hear those on the list. Did the books mention those?"

"Yes."

"And do you think we have them?"

He pulled on his tie until it was loose enough to remove over his head. "I have zero doubt that we are well-equipped in those areas."

Lucy wanted to fall into him, let the past two weeks float into distant memories, and begin a life-time with Forrest right then and there. But the last two weeks had happened.

"Forrest, after we slept together, you just let me go. You acted as though we had made a mistake. It hurt so bad, Forrest. I've never been hurt like that before."

He reached up to her, cupping her cheek in the palm of his hand, brushing away moisture before his hand fell again.

"Lucy, I don't know words that can convey just how sorry I am about the days that followed that night in my room. It was so much, so much to process. And I completely failed you."

"Forrest, you'd just lost your dad. This isn't a matter of some failure."

"Perhaps, but I still wish I could rewind. I wish we could have a do-over." He clenched his jaw, frustration tensing his muscles. "Lucy, if you'll indulge me for just a moment, can I tell you what I'd do if I could rewind?"

Forrest had never been one to speak in romantic terms about anything, especially not his previous relationships. Lucy was mesmerized, both by his sudden effusiveness and by the fact that she was the subject. "Go on."

"If I could rewind, I would go back to that night after the basketball game, the one where you painted a paw print on Dr. Hubert's bald head and we read to Billy."

A whisper of laughter escaped. "Yes, I remember that night."

"I would go to that night and we would go back to your apartment because I love it so much. It is you through and through. It feels like you're surrounding me when I'm there. It's nothing like my place. So we'd go back there, to the exact moment when Clark knocked you into me. Do you remember that moment?"

She nodded.

"Except, in this alternative reality, I wouldn't let you go."

He stepped even closer, leaning towards her ear, whispering so close his beard grazed against her cheek.

"I would've kept you pressed against me, reveling in the way your body feels against mine, and I would've kissed you. And you would've led us back to your room. I bet your room is cozy and beautiful."

"It is."

"And I would've made love to you there. And this is the one part of the story that wouldn't change. The sex would've been exactly how it was in my old room..."

"But without the Gandalf poster?"

She couldn't see him smile with his face so close, but she could feel it.

"It would be the same, because, I swear to you, Lucy, there is not a single thing I would change about that night. It was perfect. You are perfect. But, the next morning would be different. We would wake up and spend the whole day barely dressed on your sofa, binging on Netflix..."

"Ken Burn's *Civil War*?"

"Naturally, but with intermittent breaks so that I could make love to you again and again. And we wouldn't leave the apartment for days because I would need to make up for years, and I mean years, Lucy, of suppressing feelings and attractions and desire when it comes to you."

"I like that version of our story."

Forrest leaned back just enough to look into her eyes. "It has taken me an interminably long time to figure out I'm in love with you, but I'm going to try so hard Lucy. You have no idea how hard I'm going to try to make it up to you. I..."

Lucy placed a finger gently over his lips, and they stilled beneath the pressure. "That's enough, Forrest. That is everything. I don't need a list of promises. Your love is enough. Our love is enough. I love you, too."

Apparently, it was all that Forrest needed to hear. Their lips collided with a hunger and a need built over two weeks of knowing exactly what they were missing and years of suspecting. Lucy's body immediately reacted to his touch, yearning striking every place he had touched before, every inch that still held memories of how he felt.

Once again, a forwardness erupted within her that she'd never experienced with anyone else. She became the curious teenager she had never been, the young woman new to her own sexuality she'd never been, the seductress she'd never been. Only with Forrest.

As she pulled Forrest towards his desk, he continued running kisses down her neck while huskily whispering *Luce* and *I love you* and *I want you*. She responded with "Forrest" over and over and over again. It was so much better than Dr. Graham. Maybe she hadn't said it all those years because she'd sensed that she was meant to whisper it in moments of passion and yearning.

Lucy sat on the edge of his desk and untied the belt around the waist of her dress, all while being ravished. Her neck would be red from his whiskers tomorrow. There were worse reasons to wear a turtleneck. She unbuttoned the buttons from her neck to her waist and allowed the silky fabric to pool around her waist.

As her breasts came into view, barely concealed within the black, lacy bra she wore (she may have bought a few undergarments on that trip to Memphis), Forrest stopped. She wondered if he was second-guessing what they were doing, and she knew that if that was the case, she would be bereft. Backing away a few inches, he stared at her chest, running a finger down the edge of the bra and hooking it where the cups met. Smiling, he raised his eyes to her and said, "First, in my teenage bedroom and now on the desk over which I've spent years staring at and lusting for you. It's like you're seeing how many of my sexual bucket-list items you can knock out in a month."

"You can give me the complete list later."

CHAPTER 22

T he kitchen at the Finches home was buzzing with activity. Outside, it was particularly cold for late November, a steady breeze keeping the air full of swirling leaves.

The Finches, Huberts, Edith, Lucy, Forrest, and Miriam were all there preparing for the Thanksgiving feast. Everyone was chopping or dicing or sautéing or stirring. Everyone except for Dr. Hubert, who was happily propped on one of the island's stools sampling bites of this and that whenever Mrs. Hubert turned her back, but still finding his hand regularly batted away when she inevitably caught him. Even Clark was weaving between their feet, cleaning any bits of food that were dropped.

Billy and Luke came zooming through the kitchen, one with a white-paper collar and the other with paper feathers on a headband, all leftovers from a preschool craft from earlier that week. Luke had a decorative corn cob in one hand he was using to jab at Billy, and Billy was swinging a (thankfully) hollow gourd back and forth like a club.

Porter looked to Forrest who was dicing onions for three different people's recipes, occasionally wiping tears on the cuff of his sleeve. He said, "Children are amazing. They really get the spirit of Thanksgiving."

Forrest finished the last slice of his knife, and stepped away from the potent pile of onions, his hands in the air. "Okay, ladies. The onions are chopped. I have made my contribution to this meal."

Porter put a hand on Forrest's shoulder and declared, "And now, Forrest and I will be off to make sure the boys don't weaponize the decorative pumpkins. After all, cooking is women's work."

He received several middle fingers and a hot-roll to the head as he bowed out of the room, dragging Forrest with him.

As they turned the corner into the living room, sure enough, a small pumpkin was hurtling through the air. Forrest caught it within inches of it colliding into a lamp.

"Alright, boys," Porter said in his best impression of a drill sergeant. "Outside. Now."

"Can we take the walnuts?" Billy asked.

"For ammu-tion?" Luke added.

"Where in the world did you learn about ammunition?" Porter said, his face contorted in shock. "And no on the walnuts. Even though I'm sort of impressed with your ingenuity."

Forrest and Porter grabbed their coats and followed the boys out. They each sat down in a rocking chair, watching the boys as they tried to catch leaves falling from trees.

As they each found a rhythm rocking, Porter said, "So exactly how many surfaces in our office have you now had sex on?"

Forrest laughed. "A gentleman doesn't tell. But don't worry, your room was safe."

"Why do you think I ran back in to lock it?"

They rocked some more in comfortable silence, then Forrest said, "I'm going to marry her, you know."

"Yes, you are. And I'm pretty sure nothing would have made your father happier than seeing you marry Lucy."

"That is one thing we definitely had in common."

***

Lucy stood at the island, carefully weaving pie-crust into a lattice top over a cinnamony apple filling. Across from her, Dr. Hubert intently watched her work.

"That is a work of art, Lucy."

She smiled. Clearly, Dr. Hubert did not get Martha Stewart's magazine. Lucy's crust work was decidedly amateurish. However, she would take the compliment.

"Thank you, sir."

"When will you start the new job?"

"In January. I'm going to finish out the year with President Burke, train a replacement. And then, I'll officially be an editor."

"That is just spectacular," Dr. Hubert said as he picked a piece of sugar-crusted apple out of Lucy's pie and popped it into his mouth.

"Dr. Hubert!" Mrs. Hubert was bent over digging in a cabinet for a salad bowl.

Lucy looked to Dr. Hubert, trying to mime with her confused expression and hands the question of how Mrs. Hubert knew he was snacking. He raised his hands and shook his head, miming back his own befuddlement.

Still bent over and with her head deep in the cabinet, Mrs. Hubert said, "You'll understand when you and Forrest have been together forty years, dear."

Lucy seriously doubted she would ever be as astute as Mrs. Hubert, but before she could say so, Edith walked into the room and declared that Anna was asleep for her afternoon nap.

Charlotte, who was sprinkling the fried onions onto the top of the green bean casserole said, "How did you do it so quickly? She's been fighting me like crazy on her afternoon naps."

"I recited the first ten minutes of *The Vagina Monologues* to her. Having it memorized has never come in so handy."

Edith either did not see or chose to ignore Charlotte's mystified reaction. Regardless, she took the stool next to Dr. Hubert, her cooking tasks done for the day.

Dr. Hubert said, "We were just discussing Lucy's new job."

Edith said, "Yes, and the best part is we're going to clean out the tiny room where we've always stored textbooks so that Lucy can work with us a few days a week."

"Yes," Lucy said. "I think I'd go crazy working by myself at home every day. I'll just bring in my laptop, and do my work in Hart. The joys of remote working." Lucy crimped the edges of her pie after finishing the last row on her lattice.

"Ah, yes," Dr. Hubert said, "I will have to make sure I schedule my doctor's appointments for the days you're in. I've missed two since you went over to President Burke's."

Lucy shook her head and smiled, "I'll give Mrs. Hubert my schedule so that she can coordinate things."

"Thank you, dear," Mrs. Hubert yelled from the butler's pantry.

"And I probably should schedule all of my appointments with students for your days in the office, as well."

Lucy leaned her head back, her eyes shut. She sighed deeply and long-sufferingly. But really, she could pass out chocolates while she edited. She was an amazing multi-tasker. She looked back down at her pie, fixing a part of the crust that was a little misshapen. "Okay, Edith. That'll be fine. But you're going to have to hire another secretary. You do realize that, right?"

Edith waved a dismissive hand. "Oh, I don't know. I was thinking we'd just hire a few of our students to cover all of the secretary duties, give them a work-study position."

Just then, Forrest's voice came from the doorway. "I've heard it said English majors need secretarial experience."

***

Forrest was heading back into the house after deciding the wind-chill was a little too biting when he ran into Miriam coming out of the downstairs bathroom. For the first time in a long time, she was not wearing her tab collar. Instead, she had on an oversized sweater in a chestnut color and jeans. Forrest assumed that this meant she didn't see the Finches merely as church members, but as friends.

"Oh, hey. I've been meaning to talk to you."

Forrest looked around. There was no one else in the room, so she was definitely talking to him. Thinking back to the very few rom-coms he had watched over the years, Forrest said, "Is this when you do one of those best-friend-of-your-girlfriend speeches? You know, where you threaten to kill me or something if Lucy ever gets hurt. Because, for the record, I'm not ever going to let that happen to Lucy."

Miriam just smiled and shook her head, her shortly-cropped curls bouncing. "No, I wasn't going to threaten to kill you. I'm not a mob boss, believe it or not. And I do trust you. I trust that the time you did hurt Lucy was just a dick-head-blip on an otherwise stellar record, caused by a bout of grief and confusion."

"Dick-head-blip? Yeah, that's pretty accurate, actually."

"And, just for the record, a member of the clergy would never threaten to kill someone. It's not really our thing."

"So, out of curiosity, what would you threaten to do to your best-friend's boyfriend if he weren't such a stand-up guy like I am."

Miriam thought for a moment. "Oh, I don't know. Damn your soul to eternal fires? Rain curses upon your house? Send locusts? Something like that."

"You have a really cool job, you know that?"

"Yes, I do."

They were about to head back into the kitchen when Forrest remembered why they'd started this conversation. "Wait a second. What were you going to tell me?"

Miriam shook her head as if clearing some cobwebs. "Oh yeah. I got distracted by the fun of brainstorming curses. I was just going to say that I'm really happy for you and Lucy, and just know I'm always here for you. That's how I do friendship. Now that you are Lucy's guy, well, you're in my circle now."

"Thank you, Miriam." They started walking back to the kitchen.

"Also, how are you doing processing your father's passing?"

The question was so blunt, it shocked Forrest for a moment. Most people other than Lucy tip-toed around his grief.

"I wish he could see me and Lucy together. It would've brought him a lot of joy."

"Well, I didn't know him personally. But I'd be willing to bet that he saw this coming. You two were obvious to everyone but yourselves."

As they walked into the kitchen, Miriam headed to a bowl and started working while Forrest leaned on the doorway, taking a moment to look at Lucy. She was standing over a pie, fiddling with the crust, while she talked with Dr. Hubert and Edith. Her cheeks were flushed from the heat of the cooking. She was wearing a wine-red sweater, jeans, and high-heeled boots that brought her to his eye-level. Her hair was worn down, allowing her waves to escape her signature bun for a day. It made him want to bury his face into the crook of her neck.

She was saying something that Forrest didn't catch, and then she pushed up her glasses as she looked at Edith for her response. He heard Edith say something about their students doing secretarial work for the department. Grinning, he said, "I've heard it said English majors need secretarial experience."

***

Lucy laughed, thinking back to her and Miriam gossiping before class and flippantly planning futures they could never have really understood. "It did work out well for me."

Forrest smiled at her, his expression making her wonder what he was thinking. It looked suspiciously like the expression she saw on his face right before he put his hands around her waist and started inching up her sweater. In the vast history of their relationship, it was a relatively new expression.

"Time to put the food on the table," Charlotte called out, immediately creating a hustle of people walking back and forth from the kitchen to the dining table with dishes and utensils and drinks.

Lucy put the pie in the oven. It would be ready just as people finished eating. As she was closing the door, Forrest's hand grabbed one of the belt loops on her jeans, and he walked her into the butler's pantry. He shut the door behind them, and immediately started kissing her hungrily. She wrapped her arms around his neck and pressed against him.

He was the one to break the kiss, his hands cupping her face as he pulled back to look at her. "I'm so glad I'm here with you."

"Not as glad as Porter is. I think he was really stressed about pulling off more than one meal to accommodate us in shifts."

She raised onto her toes, reengaging the kiss, still amazed that she was stealing secret kisses with Forrest Graham. This time, she pulled away. "This is so much better than the last time I hid in this pantry."

Forrest quirked his eyebrow.

"Long story for another day."

His hands started roaming, squeezing and probing and making Lucy forget that there was a house full of people on the other side of the door and mounds of food they were to eat and, well, Thanksgiving.

Suddenly, there was a banging on the door, causing Lucy to jump, knocking over a bear-shaped canister of animal crackers.

Porter's voice came through loud and clear. "Time to stop making out. The Thanksgiving feast is ready." A chorus of voices called out affirmations and jeers and laughter.

Lucy groaned.

Forrest smiled, lifting her chin to look into her eyes.

"You really are Eden."

He took her hand, opened the door, and they headed to the table.

EPILOGUE

ONE YEAR LATER

T he gel was uncomfortably slimy, but oddly enough, it was pleasantly warm.

Lucy glanced at the contraption the sonographer had pulled the bottle of lubricant from.

"Is that a warmer?"

"Yes," the older woman replied as she positioned the wand on Lucy's abdomen. "Things have come a long way since I had babies in the eighties. You girls have it easy now days."

Lucy wasn't convinced that anything about pregnancy was going to be easy, but she was committed to enjoying the ride as much as possible.

While she waited for the show to begin on the little screen mounted at the foot of the exam table, Lucy looked at her hand, marveling once more at the gold band with the emerald stone cocooned by a small diamond on each side. A 19th-century American antique ring, of course. Despite having worn it since her wedding day eight months ago, she still felt a little bewildered to find a wedding band each time she looked at her own hand.

Within her grasp were both of Forrest's tanned, smooth hands (academics have very little cause for calluses, after all), and she moved her eyes up to the face that had become such an indispensable part of her life.

Behind the perfectly groomed beard, Forrest's cheeks looked pale. Baby-powder pale. Lucy lifted her head from the exam table's pillow.

"You okay, Forrest?"

Jumping, the word "Yes," slipped from his mouth with a pre-pubescent squeak. He cleared his throat, readjusted, and tried again.

"Yes, I'm fine," this time, much, much lower.

"He'll be fine," the sonographer declared with a slight impatience in her voice. "Men have no stomach for such things. I've seen quite a few faint."

Lucy's eyebrows shot up. That didn't sound fine.

"But they generally make it through unscathed. In my day, men never came into the exam room during a pregnancy, but you kids have your own ways, I suppose."

Lucy glanced back at Forrest. Maybe people were onto something in the olden days. But just as she was beginning to formulate a birth plan in which Forrest would pace in a waiting room while puffing one cigar after another, his face transformed. A heaviness that had been weighing down his eyebrows lifted, and color crept back into his ashen cheeks. Lucy followed his eyes up to the screen.

And there it was. Or he was? Maybe she? Whatever he or she was, he or she was hers and Forrest's. They had made a baby. A baby that was up on a screen kicking and wiggling and squirming.

And then, as if an other-worldly being was echoing Lucy's thoughts from just a moment ago, a scratchy, aged voice said, "Well, is it a boy or a girl?"

Lucy jerked her eyes towards Forrest from where the sound had come. There, lying on his knee was his...cell phone?

Lucy began "Was that..."

"Dr. Hubert," Edith's voice interrupted, "We were supposed to be quiet. This is *their* moment."

Lucy's eyebrows knit together. "Edith?"

"Hey Lucy," came Porter's voice, carrying with it a smile in a way only he could.

Lucy smiled back. "Hey, everyone."

"You are only supposed to have one visitor in the sonogram exam room at a time per hospital policy," the woman snapped, clearly perturbed that once again, the ways of modernity were providing a wealth of irritation.

Using his stern-professor voice, Forrest said, "There's just one person. Me. Please proceed." It was a tone he reserved for plagiarism and severely missed due dates, and it brooked no argument. The sonographer's eyes returned to her screen, and she continued punching in numbers and readjusting the onscreen image in ways that were completely mysterious to her audience.

Looking back at Lucy, Forrest's stone-cold sheen melted, and a dimple slowly peeked over his beard on one side. Then, the little laugh lines around his eyes decided to join the party: "I figured this would be easier than one of them trying to throw a gender-reveal party without your help."

"And that, my dear, is why you have a Ph.D."

"We heard that," Edith said.

"I know," Lucy giggled, "and it is good to have you here."

Let the rules be damned. She wanted her whole family in the room.

"Well," the sonographer said, suddenly less stern and with a little (could it be?) warmth in her demeanor, "All measurements are right on track. Your baby is a fine specimen."

Forrest and Lucy both released huge sighs. Who knew they had been holding their breaths?

"Would you like to know the gender?"

Three voices clearly called out from Forrest's phone, "Yes!"

Lucy looked to Forrest. "Yes," he said with a nod.

She turned to the sonographer. "I believe that is a yes all around."

"Congratulations. You're having a boy."

Cheering came from the phone, and Forrest squeezed her hand even tighter, looking into her eyes.

Lucy returned his gaze, blinking away tears. "Well, Forrest, now we just have to decide which Mark Twain character we're naming this kid after."

<<<<>>>>

ABOUT THE AUTHOR

Librarian by day and crafter of cozy rom-coms by night, author Kalyn Gensic lives surrounded by stories. She resides in Texas with her charmingly grumpy husband, four precocious children, and two dogs who shed quite a lot of fur.

Connect Online

On Instagram @
KalynGensicWrites
&
kalyngensic.com

Made in the USA
Middletown, DE
27 July 2024

57902172R00156